D0859896

DISCARD

LIEBESTOD

OPERA BUFFA
with LEIB GOLDKORN

LIEBESTOD

OPERA BUFFA
with LEIB GOLDKORN

LESLIE EPSTEIN

W. W. NORTON & COMPANY

NEW YORK • LONDON

Parts of this novel were previously published in
Superstition Review and *The Seattle Review.*

The original manuscript of Gustav Mahler's
libretto for *Rübezahl* is in the Osborn Collection of the
Beinecke Rare Book and Manuscript Library, Yale University.

Some of the characters in this novel are based on those who have lived in the past or are living now;
but they have been so altered by the action of the author's imagination that it would be a mistake
to think that any resemblance between an incident or character in this book and an event or person
in real life is anything other than coincidental.

"On a Slow Boat to China" by Frank Loesser, copyright ©1948 (renewed) by Frank Music Corp. All
rights reserved. Reprinted by permission of Hal Leonard Corporation. "Pagan Love Song," words and
music by Arthur Freed and Nacio Herb Brown, copyright © 1929 (renewed 1957) by Metro-Goldwyn-
Mayer Inc. All rights administered by EMI Robbins Catalog Inc. (publishing) and Alfred Publishing
Co., Inc. (print). All rights reserved. Used by permission of Alfred Publishing Co., Inc. "I, Yi, Yi, Yi,
Yi (I Like You Very Much)," lyrics by Mack Gordon and music by Harry Warren, copyright © 1941
(renewed) by Twentieth Century Music Corporation. All rights controlled and administered by EMI
Miller Catalog Inc. (publishing) and Alfred Publishing Co., Inc. (print). All rights reserved. Used by
permission of Alfred Publishing Co., Inc. "The Continental," words by Herb Magidson and music by
Con Conrad, copyright © 1934 (renewed) by WB Music Corp. and Bernhardt Music. All rights administered by WB Music Corp. All rights reserved. Used by permission.

For information about permission to reproduce selections from this book,
write to Permissions, W. W. Norton & Company, Inc.,
500 Fifth Avenue, New York, NY 10110

For information about special discounts for bulk purchases, please contact
W. W. Norton Special Sales at specialsales@wwnorton.com or 800-233-4830

Manufacturing by Courier Westford
Book design by JAMdesign
Production manager: Julia Druskin

Library of Congress Cataloging-in-Publication Data

Epstein, Leslie.
Liebestod : opera buffa with Leib Goldkorn / Leslie Epstein. — 1st ed.
p. cm.
ISBN 978-0-393-08131-2
1. Goldkorn, Leib (Fictitious character)—Fiction. 2. Jews—New York (State)—
New York—Fiction. 3. Holocaust survivors—Fiction. 4. Jewish musicians—Fiction.
5. Mahler, Gustav, 1860–1911—Fiction. 6. Opera—Fiction. 7. New York (N.Y.)—
Fiction. 8. Jewish fiction. 9. Psychological fiction. I. Title.
PS3555.P655L54 2012
813'.54—dc23

2011042395

W. W. Norton & Company, Inc.
500 Fifth Avenue, New York, N.Y. 10110
www.wwnorton.com

W. W. Norton & Company Ltd.
Castle House, 75/76 Wells Street, London W1T 3QT

1 2 3 4 5 6 7 8 9 0

2/12

CONTENTS

ACT THREE: TOD

LIEBESTOD

OPERA BUFFA
with LEIB GOLDKORN

OVERTURE

PILOT LIGHT

*Leib falls into despair, meets a new friend,
and sets off on a journey.*

LOVERS OF MUSIC, friends of Leib Goldkorn: Hail! Also
farewell. You are in the year 2005. Being addressed by a
man born in 1901—momentous not only for the completion of
the Mombasa–Lake Victoria railway, but also for the composi-
tion by G. Mahler of his Fifth Symphony, with, in the key of
C-minor, the celebrated dirge of the dead. Leib Goldkorn: ask
not for whom the musicians parade. It's your funeral.

How old is this gentleman with one foot, sporting a Thom
McAn, in the grave? For this we make a lightning calculation:
2005, the present year, minus 1901. Hmmm. Hmmm. One from
five. Done! Zero from zero. Done! But a nine from a naught?
This is the higher mathematics. See how, like a schoolboy's, my
tongue protrudes from my mouth. The two, hoopla!, becomes a
one; the deficit attaches itself to the nil. Eureka! Leib is in years
one hundred and four. Not exactly young.

Slight correction: we have not reached, on this brisk fall
morning, the ninth of November, the precise day on which my
head, as bald then as it is now, emerged from between the—you
will pardon the expression—loins of my mother. Goldkorn,
Falma. Née Krupnick. Ergo, the present speaker is but, hmmm,
one hundred and three. Sculptor! Carve, please, on the tomb-

stone, L. GOLDKORN, GRADUATE: 11/9/01–10/10/05. Erect it on
the family plot at the cemetery of Hachilah Hill.

Surely the reader now exclaims: "Is not today, this Monday, October tenth, 2005?" It is. Proof: the date of my current
National Enquirer is October 9. Headline: TOP MOB MISTRESS
IN SPANISH HARLEM SHOOT-OUT. SON LEFT UNHARMED. Story,
p. 4." Do you now understand? Has the incandescent bulb
ignited above your head? Your interlocutor will not reach the
day that is not only the anniversary of his hatching but also that
of the famed Kristallnacht, 11/9/38, when the streets of Berlin
were as strewn with broken glass then as are these of New York
with fallen leaves now.

Why such haste to hear the Funeral March, key of C?
Let us speak of the ills of the body. Primo, the coldness of
extremities—a sensation reminiscent of those childhood days
when the family Goldkorn would bathe on the banks of the
Iglawa, emerging from the chill spring waters with ejaculations
of pleasure—*Gott! Gott! Ist das kalt!*—on our blue-toned lips,
much as in America the daring associates of the Polar Bear
Club sport in the surf at Coney Island. It is their belief, shared
by Goldkorn père, that such a frosty dip is a boon to virility.
Virility, ha! ha! ha! Try to find Mr. Johnson now! Once, in
excitement, three and one-half American inches!

The difference between past and present: the Polar Bears,
both shiny-scalped males and broad-shouldered females, wear
bathing costumes of one and two pieces. But in the Iglawa we
younglings, and oldsters too, sported au naturel. On occasion
one had to avert one's eyes from the nativities of let us say Fräulein Minchke—Ja! One's own sister!—lest a fellow experience
a stiffy.

But we were speaking of the frailty of the flesh. Bicuspid
pain. Ringing, key of B-flat, in the inner ear. On the tongue,
fur and tastelessness. Response to blows from Dr. Goloshes's

rubber hammer: nil. Missiles, like half notes, hover in my squinting eyes. Abdominals: distended, obscuring the organs of procreation. From this pouch rise gurglings and faint cries, as if from a drowning man. The excrementas? Do not inquire. Luckily, little comes out since little comes in. No Williams Bar-B-Que Chicken, with side order of half-soured tomatoes. From B. Greengrass, the Sturgeon King, no saltwater treats. Instead of such dainties: Meals on Wheels.

Sleep? On this Posturepedic? Home to silverfish. A congress of fleas. Bite, bite, little ladies! And suck! Not to mention the encounter with a snout beetle. At my age, called by the Bard that of the pantaloon, one does not require forty winks. Instead I sit in my Windsor-type chair and read, a-squinting, page 4 of the excellent *Enquirer*: "The young upper-Manhattan trophy-gal of famed mobster Tony-the-Anchovy-Crappenzo fell early yesterday in a hail of bullets. Karima Castillo, 24, who neighbors described as both fun-loving and a woman who de—"

Here the flame of my candle, like the flicker of life within Señorita Castillo, goes out. What? Candlelight? Like the friar in his cell? What happened to the Sylvania-brand bulb? Intact still, my trusty tungsten. It is the Edison electricity, the running water, and the steam for heat that have been extinguished. Radiators cold, grim, and mute. And my lumberman-style jacket has no longer elbows, my gabardines no longer knees. And look who comes: Old Man Winter, friends.

What happened next? That's what everybody wants to know. Who pulled the trigger? And what of the young lady's fate? These items have had to wait until the light of dawn fell upon the printed page. Only then do I discover that the fun-loving Karima lay dead. Worse. Worse, still. She was "a single mother" who "devoted her life" to her eight-year old son, Jaime, who was "abandoned when the Anchovy sped away in a blue BMW sedan." BMW. This is Bayerische Motoren Werke.

Can you blame Leib Goldkorn—once fun-loving himself—
for wishing to leave such a world? Eight years old! Poor Jaime!
An orphan! Abandoned! And the evildoers still at large. In four
more minutes, or perhaps three—my Bulova has long since been
deposited at the Glickman Brothers shop of prawns—I shall no
longer be forced to think of such cataclysms. *Pantaloon?* Who
am I kidding? I approach the age of childishness. Sans teeth,
melancholy Jacques: sans eyes, sans taste. Sans everything.

Yet it is not the cold, the hunger, or the ache of bones that
will kill me. Nor am I cast into despair by the iniquities of the
world. Leib Goldkorn has already encountered the worst that
men can do. Was he not thrown in ridicule out the doors of
the Wiener Staatsoper? Did he not watch with his own eyes as
his entire family—sisters Yakhne and Minchke; Mother Falma,
née Krupnick; putative père—sailed off on the barge *Kaliope*
not downstream to Budapest and freedom but up the Danube
to Dachau and death? Did he not suffer the scorn, in sunny
California, of D. F. Zanuck? I do not need the callow Kennedy,
President "Jack," to tell me that life is not fair.

Then why does Leib Goldkorn look with longing at the
Magic Chef oven? Into which he will soon thrust his head.
Could it be the absence of *Liebe* und *Arbeit*, the words that my
Coreligionist, S. Freud, employed in order to describe what a
chap needs to find meaning in life?

Love:

Of that I have had my share. We begin, in youth, at the teats
of Madam Goldkorn. An only son, never did I doubt I was her
hero, a Hannibal. Next: the young man who pressed against
me, a mere Jüngling, during a performance of *Tristan und
Isolde*. Let us speak last of the mammalia of Minchke. All here
was innocent, all here was pure. Without effusion.

Far different was lusty manhood. Women! Oh, women! For
them I have had the roving eye. If you have read, O connoisseur,

my first volume of memoirs, *Goldkorn Tales*, you will remember, foremost, my wife: the Litwack. Clara! Meine Frau! Your fingernail polish! Your garter trolleys! With her, in November of 1942, I achieved a definite penetration. Also unforgettable: Hildegard, proprietor of the Steinway Restaurant. Oh, you Stutchkoff! The acrobatics on your feather mattress. With what force did my Jewish-style member burst through the aperture of my S. Klein drawers. Near penetration.

It was in the second volume of my memorials, *Ice Fire Water*, that I described the manner in which I have known, as Abraham knew Sarah, three of the world's most prominent beauties. Miss Sonja Henie, whose ice boot I held in my lap. Miss C. Miranda, whose warming whisper entered my ear:

I yi-yi-yi-yi-yi, I like you very much.
I yi-yi-yi-yi-yi, I think you're grand.

Not least, Miss Esther Williams, who chafed my vegetative organ and breathed with no less heat: *Oh, Leibie, your magic takes my breath away.* Jiggling. A-jiggling. Four fingers and thumb.

I do not claim to be an amorist. Leib is no Lothario. Still, five such mistresses in a mere century, and each of them a knockout: that means I have experienced on average a paroxysm once every, hmmm, hmmm, twenty years. Not bad.

Note that I have not yet mentioned my half-Finn, with whom, since our celebrated "date" at the Hotel Plaza, Court of Palms, I have maintained a relationship that Professor Pergam, of the Akademie für Musik, Philosophie, und darstellende Kunst, would call strictly platonisch. Oh, her pomegranate eyes! The black bun of her hair! What a neck! No, no! Stop! Desist! All such reveries are now streng verboten: strictly forbidden.

Very well, *Work*:

I have always been employed as a musician, with emphasis on the flute. I think with special fondness of the Rudall & Rose model bestowed on me by His Kaiserlichen und Königlichen Apostolischen Majestät at our graduation concert, 1916—only a short time before he, our cherished Franz Joseph, expired in the arms of, of all people, my man-killing Minchke. In truth I have performed on as many varieties of instrument as I have known—to use once more the Hebraic euphemism—different women. Aside from the woodwind family, I have mastered both the Glockenspiel and the Dudelsack at the Wiener Staatsoper and, amidst Manhattanites, the crystalphonicon, also known as the filjam saz. Crowds gathered along 125th Street as upon these musical glasses I played that favorite of the Harlemites:

I'm coming, I'm coming, for my head is bending low.
I hear their gentle voices calling Old Black Joe.

Do you recall, my dear bibliomane, how in my first volume I described my quarter century at the Steinway Restaurant? Upon the piano stool of the Bechstein grand? On this instrument I played with my fellow musicians the following repertoire: Offenbach, Meyerbeer, Romberg, Zemlinksy and Bloch; Dunayevsky, who wrote the inspired "Song of Stalin," and his compatriot, M. Blanter, author of "Katyushka," the hymn to rockets; Henri Hertz, fellow Viennese, composer of the Mexican National Anthem. In short, all the greats. Hélas, the Steinway Restaurant exists no more.

And what of the Steinway Quintet? Salpeter, first violin; Dr. J. Dick, double bass; Tartakower, flautist (poor breath control); Young Murmelstein, second violin: all these artists moved on to the Gumbiner Brothers Bar-Mitzvah Band. And when that band also went up the belly? When its trade was seized by the Litvak, Lester Lanin? Who knows? With the approach of the dread Uncle Al it becomes difficult to remember who is living and who is not. Lenin, not. Lanin? Likely. And Murmelstein? And Dr. Dick? What of the excellent Veronica Lake? Fellow centurians! We live in a world of shadows. Of ghosts.

Let us, on this question of employment, face the terrible truth. Even if I had in my possession the Rudall & Rose, I have not the stoutness of lip to play either "I Loves You, Porgy" or "I Can't Get Started with You." These same lips are too dry even to—TWAT! TWAT!—whistle. No *Liebe*! Dear God, no *Arbeit*! Time, therefore, to become a ghost myself.

HAIL, MAGIC CHEF! I see thine grinning mouth. Thine broad white brow. Soon, dear friend. Soon. No more waiting for long-winded Leib. Open, jaws; open wide. Wilt thou not do for me what Brutus did for Caesar? *F-f-f-f*: the hiss of your breath. We who are about to die salute you. *F-f-f-f*: What, would'st thou speak, venerable Roman range? *F-f-f*: Frank Fingerhut, fils? The Freeholder? Fiend and foe. What? What? Ah. I understand. Why not kill that fraud, the fickle fellow, instead of truly yours, the flautist? That requires a moment's thought.

Why does Leib Goldkorn huddle alone and friendless in flat number 5-D? Why must he read the *National Enquirer* that is on occasion left by the Spaniard from Meals on Wheels, instead of purchasing that lively gazette in our busy, buzzing streets? Who has cut off the Edison current, the pressure for steam, the hot and the cold running water? Frank Fingerhut, fils! One by one he has driven out all rent-stabilized clients in order to make of their simple dwellings the Casa Blanca: luxury units mit marble Toiletten! Self-flushing! Mit Müllhäckslern, which makes all the dreck disappear down the sink. Mit Jen-Air. "Insider" price: Zwei Millionen. Yes, two million dollars. A difficult sum to raise. Of all the tenants, only I remain.

Now the fils, that fathead, has offered me five thousand American dollars to vacate the premises. Should I accept this princely sum? Depart from my lair? But where will I go? All worldly goods—not just the Bulova-brand, but the Admiral "TV" and the tubeless Philco and the non-popping toaster— are in the possession of those Glickman boys, portly Ernest, sinewed Randy. To repeat: Where will Leib Goldkorn go? There are only two choices: Will it be Himmel? Or will it be Hölle? Enquiring minds want to know. Well, dear friends, we are about to find out.

But for a moment: hold. Let us speak, with our last breath, the truth. It it not because of the fils, that falscher Freund, that I am about to place my head in the porcelain noose of the hooded hangman. Nor is it ills of the flesh, the unsold volumes of my memorials, the tiptoes of Uncle Al, or even the loss of *Liebe*, the absence of *Arbeit*, that have driven me to despair. No. No. And once again, no.

Here is the straw upon the camel's hump: an Order of Protection from the constabulary of the City of New York. Would you like me to read it? Word for terrible word? First, sit yourself down. Then draw in a deep breath. Ready? Thus, from the depths of my lumberman's jacket, the missive. Voilà!

I write on behalf of my client, Ms.—

Wait! I cannot allow you to hear her name. Or speak it myself. Let us begin anew:

I write on behalf of my client Ms. NOH [Name Obliterated Here], on whose behalf I have obtained an Order of Protection from the New York City Criminal Court—

Criminal! Mark you that?

—that you must obey in all respects on pain of criminal—

That word again!

—or civil penalties, including arrest and a possible prison sentence. I have sought this injunction for Ms. She-Who [She Who Must Not Be Named] because of your constant attentions and trespasses, including but not limited to your uninterrupted flow of letters—

Guilty, Your Honor! But how else, since I no longer possess a Bell Telephone, could I communicate with my inamorata? Is it possible that for such a simple billet-doux—par exemple, "I dream, my hellion from Helsinki, of the day you will give me, athwart hot rocks, a good twigging. Truly yours, L. Goldkorn, Graduate"—one can be imprisoned in the bastille?

Uninterrupted flow? Might the accused have a word with the court? Postage-poor, it was my habit to fold each of those chitties in the orgasmic style of her countrymen (my inamorata is, as the whole world knows, half a Finn, and half-Nipponese) and then launch such airships out the window to the heavens. Alas! Whether addressed to her news desk in Times Square or to the embassies of her native nations, these feuilletons drew no more response than those of the shipwrecked mariner who places all of his hopes within the bottle that is cast into the indifferent currents of the sea.

But what of the camel? What of the hump?

—of letters, fantasies, and obsessions in published works of fiction—

Fiction? Undoubtedly a reference to my double opus. The second of these, the aforementioned *Ice Fire Water*, described my life in Hollywood and in particular my conjugals with the Misses Henie, Miranda, and Williams, and was no fantasy, no fiction—*I yi-yi-yi-yi-yi, I like you very much.* The first, the *Goldkorn Tales*, a non-bestseller, was praised in print by that same She-Who for its "artistry and ambition," end quote, a remark that created, within its modest author, a definite peppercorn sensation.

—fiction, all of which have created mental distress and fear of bodily harm; taken together, they are an invasion of her personal space, and in the opinion of the court constitute stalking, harassment, and even sexual assault.

Hee, hee, hee. At age one hundred and three? Possibly.

Under the terms of the injunction, and pending a hearing, you are ordered to cease all contact with Ms. YHWA [You Have Withheld Appellation], either at home or in the workplace or in public or private spaces. You may not invoke her name or use it in any written form. Nor are you allowed to communicate with her either by telephone, notes, mail, fax, email, speech, or the delivery of flowers or gifts.

Fax? Is this a gallantry?

Further, you are required without fail to attend a Sex and Love Addiction Seminar and to conclude to the court's satisfaction all Twelve Steps of the program, pursuant to the penalties, both civil and criminal, described above.

Sincerely,

S. A. Lubowitz, attorney at law

S. *A*. Lubowitz? S. No! S.*S*.! Sex Staatspolizei!

An *Addiction Seminar*? For *Sex*? Mein Gott! Are they going to cover Mr. Johnson with leeches? Or worse? I am a grown man. I know how to tame hot-bloodedness. Let us recall, for example, New Year's Day of 1991, when I was a zestful, hmmm, eighty-nine. How better to quench lustful fires than a bracing dip amid frozen seas? Imagine my disappointment upon arriving at Coney Island to learn that the privileges of the Polar Bear Club were for Members Only. Not only that: No Guests Allowed. "What?" exclaimed the still-lithesome Leib. "A permit is required to swim in the Atlantic Ocean? Non-Bears verboten?"

Thus frustrated by swimming anti-Semites, filled still with lubrications, I remained haunted by visions of a Laplandic lass running all ruddy from the simmer of the sauna into the embrace of the floating ice. Only a vigorous hour of Skee ball sufficed to calm the furies. Non-winner of doll. Ha! The last laugh: the earth is warming. All Polar Bears shall soon be extinct.

But not as soon as Leib Goldkorn. Let the municipal court send its Sex Staatspolizei into apartment number 5-D. Too late! But one hour ago I defied the Order of Protection by sending one last airmail—ha, ha, even now I have retained my Hassidic humor—*airmail!*—letter to my favorite Finn. How cleverly I disguised her name! "Dear Miss Okihcim Inatukak . . ." Ha! Ha! Ha! Anyone seeing this would think I was addressing the Queen of the Esquimaux.

In it I did nothing more than utter a fond farewell. Yes, and make one last request: that my paramour not fret upon discovering that her beloved had committed, in her own native nomenclature, hara-kiri.

Twelve Steps? I shall not need that many to complete my task.

STEP ONE: Close all windows. *Check.*

STEP TWO: Turn once more the spigots for gas. Also the knob for roasting. *Check. F-f-f-f.* Again the soft sibilation sounds in my ears.

STEP THREE: A note. Not necessary. What you read now is my farewell. Auf Wiedersehen!

STEP FOUR: Open the Magic Chef maw. *Check.* Darkness. A cave, like that of Professor Pergam's Plato. I drop, like a devotee, to my knees. For in that cavern of shadow and shade one finds the other world, where the ancient Greek maintained all is true, all is good, all is beautiful.

F-f-f-f. Lay down, Leib Goldkorn, your weary head. A fitting end. For did not your own family—sisters, Mutter, putative père—expire from the inhalation of a similar vapor? And your larger family, the Jewish people—were they not killed in just such a kiln? Who am I, a simple panpiper, to avoid a matching fate? Now I understand: all my life, my dears, has been a journey to join you. Sh'ma Yisroel. Adonai Elohenu. Hmmm, hmmm. Adonai Echad!

STEP FIVE: I should have brought knee pads. No matter. I begin to feel a dropsy. A welcome slumber. *F-f-f-f.* Could I really kill Frank Fingerhut instead? Perhaps with a knife? No. No. Away with such thoughts. Fils! I forgive you. *F-f-f-f:* It comes. Yes, it comes. The world beyond darkness. Oh, Pergam! Oh, Plato! You spoke true. There, there: deep in the cave of shadows, a single blue light. Steady. Unblinking. The ray of a distant star. What peace! What joy! For in this beam are gathered all the human souls—Miss Litwack, Madam Miranda, the heavenly Henie—who wish to welcome me to their celestial abode. Mama! Mamele! Your teats! I come! Ja! I come!

But tarry. This flame: Is it not the pilot light of the Magic Chef oven? *F-f-f-f!* Pilot light? But will it not, upon encountering the gas company product, create a detonation? Help! Help! Feuer! Wait. Be calm. Did not the Keystone Corporation shut off the "natural" gas? For flat 5-D and all of 138 West? *F-F-F-F-F!* Then what is this sibilation? The fizzle and fizz? *F! F! F! F!* Look! Adjoining this blue light I see a red one! Also unblinking! A ruby. Ruddy. Rubicund. Save me, Jesus! It is the eye of the devil! *F! F! F! FUT! FUTT!* Ouch! Ouch! The claws of the devil too! Ah: it is the end of Leib Goldkorn! Watch out! Satan! The hellhound! *F!F!F!F! FUTTTTT!*

Hellhound? A hellcat. With a single bound—*FA-FITTZ!*— this feline has leaped onto my head, then onto the tiles of linoleum, and now with a final bound hurls herself onto my window's sill.

A hundred questions bloom. How did this animal enter the Magic Chef? And how long did it make this appliance its home? Do I have, in unit 5-D, a mouse? Is this the pet, perhaps, of Manuel, from Meals on Wheels, who oft leaves behind his copy of the stimulating *Enquirer?* Could he be related to poor Karima? Is he thus caring for the poor orphaned Jaime? And this kitten? Licking with indifference his or her paws? Could I not adopt this outcast as he has adopted the eight-year-old boy? Jaime? My very own Hyman!

Into my hairless head springs the memory of Professor Pergam's lectures on the ancient Egyptians: Were not, to these Nile-ists, all cats sacred? Were they not preserved after death, so that they might accompany their masters on the journey to the afterlife?

Meow!

Dost call, my mummy? *Mummy? Egyptians?* Why so far afield? If I had but time I could relate the customs of our very own redskins, about which I learned when studying for my naturalization exam, Judge Solomon Gitlitz presiding. Would you like, my kitten, to be washed with yucca suds? Should I sacrifice to you, ha-ha-ha, my favorite pony? Come. Come. Together we shall journey to the Happy Hunting Ground.

PLAN B:

STEP ONE: Open window. *Check.*

STEP TWO: Take into my arms the piebald puss. What a creature! A red eye. A blue one. Tail ringed in black, like that of a raccoon. Whiskers on one side only. What's this? A missing leg? A half-chewed ear? You too have been caught up on the wheel of sorrow, darling. Here, pussy, puss. Come, kitty. So, clinging with claws, my companion attaches herself—I see no organ of generation, no sign of spermary—to my lumberman's coat. Oh! With a rough tongue she laps my chin. Such a sweetheart. Together we shall greet the Dawn Mother.

STEPS THREE, FOUR, FIVE: Lift with difficulty—and at age one hundred and, hmmm, three—first one leg, then the other, over the sill. Then duck one's head under the glass. Voilà! No, no: do not tremble, Hymena, honey. Have you not eight additional lives? Example of Hebrew humor: laughing on gallows. Now a last peek at the Jews and non-Jews of the Upper West Side. Their derbies and bowlers. Their neck scarves stretched on the wind. *Look out below!* See? How they stop? How they gaze upward? Look at their pale faces. How white they are. Like milk.

Me-cow!

Ah, Milch. Art hungry? Thirsty too? I have in the Frigidaire nothing but tickets for prawns. Fear not: in Paradies there will be milk, honey, Lindt-brand chocolates. All, mein Liebling, all. Shall we make the jump? Let us count together.

Eins. Yes, yes. Well done.

Zwei. That means two, my tabby.

Und-und: DREI! So, in honor of the tribe of Man-a-hattans, let us cry:

Geronimo!

"Goldkorns! Goldkorns! Pan Leib Goldkorns!"

What? Who calls? Teetering on the precipice, I stare down, trying from among the ambulating pedestrians to pick out the speaker.

"Goldkorns! Says here Pan Leib Goldkorns!"

My eyes have in them crystals, like those in a shaker for salt. Non-twenty-twenty. But Hymena, with her multicolored corneas, has sharper vision than I. She stretches a paw down to where, on the sidewalk by our stoop, stands a large female with a sack over her shoulder and skin as black as what gamblers call the spade of aces.

Mee-who?

"I know not, my feline Freundin. Let us once again attempt to enter eternity together. Eins. Zwei. Dr—"

"Goldkorns! Goldkorns at 138 West! Ain't that this building? Got a special-delivery letter for Pan Leib Goldkorns."

What? A letter for Goldkorns? *Pan?* For panpiper, perhaps? That could only mean that one of my "air" mails was delivered. And now, from the demi-Finn, comes the response. Special delivery too! "Yoo hoo! Madam Postmistress! Here I am! Goldkorn, Leib! Graduate of the Akademie für Musik, Philosophie, und darstellende Kunst!"

A miracle: amidst all the hub-bub and hullabaloo, the Herlemite hears my salutation. "You Goldkorns? Apartment 5-D?"

"Speaking. Have you a love letter from—from—the She-Who?"

"Can't say yes, can't say no. Got a bunch of foreign stamps."

"Aha! Is it from Finland? Or the Land of the Rising Sun?"

The colored looks down at the envelope. "Dunno. Bunch of volleyball players, looks like to me. You comin' down here to pick this up?"

"I fear to make such a declination. What of the Sex Staatspolizei? What if the fils should make a lightning strike, so that on my ascent I find a sign reading EXMITTIERT, which as you know means 'Evicted'? Madam Mercury, would it be possible with your winged feet to bring the valentine to me?"

"Huh? I ain't goin' in there. Ain't got to climb no stairs. I'm a member of the APWU."

"You wish, I see, to play the coquette. What if L. Goldkorn said, Bitte? In English, if you please. What if he said, *Du bist sehr hübsch*? You are a comely thing."

"Don't you sweet-talk me. Don't have to go where there are dogs nor cats."

"Look, Liebchen. I am making with my mouth a moue."

Mee-mou?

"Nein, nein, my Miezekätzchen. Not mouse. Moue."

"No way, Charlie, am I going in that building."

"See here: *Neither snow nor rain nor,* hmmm, hmmm, *gloom of night*— You know the rest of this motto, my dear lady."

"I'm takin' this back to the dead-letter box."

"Wait! For such dereliction I can make to your superior a report."

"Is that a threat I am hearing?"

"No, no! Pas du tout! Look. Do you see? I am blowing a kiss. I like very much the Reubenesques."

"So long, Pan Goldkorns."

"Wait! An idea! Please leave this letter for the gentleman Señor Manuel, from Meals on Wheels. He can bring it to the fifth floor, along with a copy of the thoughtful *Enquirer*."

"Unh-unh. Can't give no special delivery to nobody but you."

"Heavens! I have not heard from this beloved for many a moon. Ha, ha! Tribal jargons. What if she wishes an assignation? Have pity on the heart-smitten."

"I guess maybe I could read it out loud. How's that?"

"Prima!"

"Okay. Let me see. Goodness! A money order. Five hundred dollars. A airplane ticket too!"

"I knew it! We are going to have a honeymoon in Helsinki! Good postmistress, continue."

And here, friends of Leib Goldkorn, are the exact contents of the letter that, in the accents of her native Togoland, this female Hermes now calls up to me:

PAN LEIB GOLDKORNS
138 WEST 80TH STREET APT. 5-D
NEW YORK, NEW YORK 10024

Esteemed Pan Goldkorns:

On behalf of our Lord Mayor, Frantisek Kunc, our municipal council, and the Holocaust Festivities Committee, and all citizens of Jihlava, I send you heart-felt greetings and also congratulations on your long and happy life. Excuse please my school girl English language.

I write you with knowledge of the sufferings of your people in Jihlava, former Iglau. In year 1425 after birth of our Savior, Jews expelled. In 1940, Synagogue burnt down by Teuton invaders. Not yet rebuilt. I make to you assurances that you will not find in our municipality hardly a German person. After the war, we sent them packing! As says Mayor Kunc, "One hundred percent Czech."

Now there are no more Jewish. Except, according to researches, you! Last home-born alive. That is why our Mayor, F. Kunc, requests of me to make invitations. Municipality of Jihlava wishes to honor Israel heritage. Is having Holocaust Memorial Festivity. Noted speakers. Many musics with polkas. Also encouragement of tourism. Is the honor to have last living Hebrew of Jihlava/Iglau for honored guest. All entertainments on first day November.

For you, dear Pan Goldkorns, we have key to Number 5 Valkova, former *Lindenstrasse*. All citizens of Jihlava have desire for you to live out last years—on a personal note may I say Many More!—comfortable in nice boyhood home.

I have in this packet for you one-way airplane ticket, Czech Airline, Flight 0051, New York–Praha, where a Mercedes automobile will be waiting, with skillful driver too, to "whisk" you safely Municipality of Jihlava. Also enclosed: money order for five hundred American dollars for all necessary expenses.

Honored Pan Goldkorns, I send you greetings of my own person and of Lord Mayor Kunc and all tolerant citizens of Jihlava. Welcome home!

With cordialities,

"Miss" Iveta Crumsovatna
Deputy Mayor for Culture, Entertainments, and Sports.
Secretary, 2005 Jihlava Holocaust Festivities Committee.

ACT ONE

LIEBE

SCENE ONE

THE DEDUCTIVE METHOD

*In the town of his birth, Leib meets a lovely lady
and makes, about his paternity, an
astonishing discovery.*

L EIB AT THIRTY THOUSAND FEET. And what do I see, outside the window of my Stratoliner? Fleecy clouds. The whitecapped Atlantic. Behind me, a toddler oft thrusts his McAns into the back of my seat. Insufficient respect for his elders. I have one anxious moment: How am I to make the trek down the heaving corridor to the far-off W.C.? What of the battle with the buttons of my gabardines, not to mention the search for the reclusive Herr Johnson? Not to worry: I am accompanied on this journey by Miss Milada, Checkist attendant, who stands guard for the one-half hour it takes me, with repeated jets, to find the bull's-eye of the target below. Through the closed accordion door, I make out the scent—Is it sandalwood? Is it heather?—of her Tommy Girl perfume. To my fellow centurians I can without reservation recommend this form of travel. It comes with cheese dip. And complimentary knife.

A smooth landing, at which fellow passengers burst into applause. My brand-new Samsonite valise, mit Kunstoffräder, plasticized wheels, goes round and round on the carousel, just out of reach. Three passes. Four. Suddenly the deus ex machina: a gentleman, somewhat froglike in appearance—that is to say, with a broad face and surprisingly protuberant eyes—appears, as if dropped from the sky. Wearing a visored cap. Holding a placard inscribed thus:

L. GOLDKORNS

"Hola, sir! Do you mean Leib Goldkorn?" I cry.

"You are Pan Goldkorns? *You?*"

"Ja. Ohne den 's.'"

"Pardon?"

"You do not Deutsch sprechen?"

"Ne! No speak Němčina! Nikdy! Drive Mercedes."

The brachycephalic face of this chauffeur is not unique. Those gathered at the carousel, the hundreds passing through the lobby, the folk in the fields and streets outside: all have the brown hair, the elfin ears, the high, bone-filled cheekbones of a race long since classified by the famed Carleton Coon. Nose: boxer type. Knees: knocked.

It is not, however, the presence of so many froglike folk—Heavens! Even their eyes are green!—that gives me pause, so much as the absence of the handsome, blond-headed, and pale-eyed Nordics among whom I whiled away the carefree years of my youth. *Where*, I ask myself, *are the good-hearted Teutons?* In truth, it was they who, with their wit, wursts, and Schnapps-bottiche, made of Iglau an isle of Kultur in a sea of Slavs.

Not only have the Němci disappeared, so has their language. *Iglau*, a word that trips from the tongue, has now become the Arabian *Jihlava*. From the rear seat of the Mercedes, my curious kitten and I peer through the window glass: Leopoldgasse, Steingasse, Veilchengässchen, Kaiser Wilhelm Gasse—all these streets have vanished; in their place, Husova Street, Palackého, Skretova, and Komenského.

Gracious! The old Pirnitzergasse, the street on which die Familie Mahler made its home, is now—hmmm, hmmm—Znojemská. And there, at Number 4—slow down, my young amphibian—is their actual abode. "What," I inquire of the Mercedes man, "has happened to the affable Aryans?" But I already know the answer. *We sent them packing.* The words of Miss Crumsovatna, Deputy for Sports.

Speak of der Teufel: no sooner does the chauffeur turn from Bmenska Boulevard onto Masaryko Náměstí, and thus into the great square I always called the Stadtplatz, than I see, standing in front of the municipal hall, a woman without hips, but with a dimpled, pointed chin. Pointed nose too and a head with hive-type hair. More a pole, ha, ha, ha, than a Czech. A *Pole!* Touché, Uncle Al! Could this be the Crumsovatna herself?

What I did not suspect is that my pen pal would turn out on inspection to be such a beauty. Such long legs! Shoulder pads! An endless neck! Mams, true, nothing about which to write a letter home. She smiles, this colleen, and waves a spidery arm. I step from the rear of the sedan.

"Miss Crumsovatna, I presume?"

"Ano. And you are our Honorary Jew? Pan Goldkorns?"

"Non-practicing," I reply.

"Welcome home," says my interlocutress, stepping forward, so that her non-convex chest is touching my lumberman's plaid. She makes a smack at my left cheek, *one*, my right cheek, *two*, and, *three*, at my left cheek again. In certain lands, beyond the Urals, this would signify an engagement. I glance at her hands: each of the fingernails, at the end of her ringless fingers, is painted. Wet n Wild–brand, if I am not mistaken. "Burgundy Frost."

Ringless. Note you that?

"Are you mighty fatigued, Pan Goldkorns? Soon your chamber at Gustav Mahler Hotel will be ready. He was as you know our prominent Jew."

Here I throw the dice, risking all: "Miss Crumsovatna. I request that you call me Leib."

"A pleasure! But you must address me as Iveta."

At such forwardness I experience loss of breath and an unavoidable blush. Gracious! Am I in a chariot rushing headlong toward hedonism? Let us "hold the horse" for a moment and examine this phenomenon. In doing so I shall rely on the analysis of the Coreligionist, who lived in the capital just 120 kilometers to our south:

A maiden sits at the dinner table among company that is mixed. One of the males makes a risqué remark: "I saw Madam X this morning. She has developed große Brustdrüsen." At once the face of the maiden turns red. And why? Because the reference to the mammary of Madam X provides a definite titillation. But because this is a well-brought-up Fräulein, she cannot allow the blood to engorge the cheeks and lips below the table, you know, in the infernal region. Instead she permits it to fill the cheeks and lips above, thus permitting herself both to feel the erotics of the moment and to protect, nay, even to enhance, her reputation as a Jungfrau—that is, as a virginal lass.

"Are you chilled?" asks the Crumsovatna, seeing the rouge spots on my visage.

"No, no, no. Nein."

"Would you enjoy to see our beautiful city and environments? Come, I will be your eager guide."

Now for the first time I lift my gaze from the willowy woman who stands before me to the Stadtplatz I had crossed and crisscrossed innumerable times as a boy. What a transformation! The hustle! The bustle! The motorized vehicles and the stench of their pipes for exhaust. When I was a weenling there was not in the streets of Iglau a single automobile. Mingled with the smell from the tobacco monopoly that hung over our rooftops was that which rose from the cobblestones—I speak of the ejectamentas of good dobbin. The odor of ordure. Ha! Ha! Excellent pun. More wordplay comes to mind: Who was the inventor of the combustible engine? Not Eli Whitney, as mouthed by American schoolboys. No: Nikolas Otto. Hence: *Ottomobile.* Clever. Witty. Antidote to Uncle Al.

This reverie is interrupted by the Crumsovatna. "As you know, here is our main square, named Masaryk, after the founder of our nation. His son, also Masaryk, was thrown by Soviet mad dogs out of window. See big ugly building: this is Tesco Super Store, built by same Soviets. And here, sculpted in 1786, is world-famous Neptune fountain. Notice how the sea god struggles to strike with his trident the dolphin fish. All waters are regurgitated and . . ."

As my guide drones on, the bells of the nearby Jakobskirche begin to strike the morning hour. Had I not heard these identical tones every hour of every day through the carefree years of youth? For an instant I believe I can smell, wafting toward me o'er the vast plaza, the Bratkartoffeln from the dobbin-drawn Schnellimbiss that rolled into the square of a Sunday morn. For a mad moment I can taste the crisps, "mit Salz und Pfeffer!," on my tongue.

"And here," continues the flat-fronted Fräulein, who has linked her sinewy arm in mine, "we have the Vysočiny Museum, and beyond, the Plague Column."

Thus we stroll, she, Hymena, and I, to the city walls, through the Mary's Gate, and into the darkness of the catacombs. At last we arrive at Znojemská Number 4, the home of G. Mahler and now a museum, with non-smoking café, of his work and life.

"An espresso, Pan Gold—my pardon, I mean, friend Leib? Or a teacup?"

At a table intime we share a smažený sýr, Czechist cuisine of fried cheese, and a Lipton mit Zitronenscheiben. Yet even as my companion and I engage in this dalliance—pretend not to notice that she has removed from her weary feet her pumps— my mind grows distracted. What is this soft music about me? Of course! Mahler, muted: the Symphony Number Five, composed, by uncanny coincidence, in the year truly yours was geboren. I sit transfixed through the movements: the Funeral March of the first, and, in the second, the braying brass of the storm.

"More cheese, Pan Leib?"

I pay no heed to this double entendre, or to the toes in their stockings. The hidden orchestra has moved from the yodel motif of the scherzo, to the adagietto, and at last to the ironical rondo-finale, with its celebrated contest between ass and cuckoo bird. What is happening to my intestinals? The sound of this music has sent them a-churning. My heart is pounding and my shoulder hairs rise and fall, as if enlivened by an Edison current. *Cuckoo! Cuckoo!* I feel myself drawn to my feet, looking left, looking right.

"W.," asks my companion, "C.?"

I barely hear her words. The symphony is ending, *Cuckoo! Cuckoo!*; but I sense that hidden in that music, and in these rooms dedicated to its composer's life, lies a mystery, the key to which is about to change my own. Could I, like the great Shylock Holmes, find the solution? In a trance I excuse myself from the table and, leaving the Crumsovatna with tea and tabby, begin my investigation of the Mahler Museum.

THE FIRST THING that catches my eye is a glass cabinet, in which I discover a notice of a Red Cross concert of February 24, 1901. This charity event by the already famed conductor was held at the Rathaus, the same municipal hall before which I first set eyes on the Deputy Mayor for Sports.

I say, Holmes. Why is that important?

Alimentary, my dear Watson: 1901. That is the Wunderjahr of my birth.

I turn next to the adjoining cabinet. In it, pinned under the glass like the wings of a Schmetterling, is a yellow-tinged photograph. Even before the image fully registers on my retina, I feel a tingling sensation on my scalp, as if non-existent hairs, like those on the back of my feline friend, were standing erect. For here is a Foto-fragment of G.M. himself, with white flannels, a sailor's striped shirt, and unwired spectacles on his Semitic-style nose. No hat. A bandage over one ear. In the background, an island-studded sea. All unbidden, my lips form a word: *Abbazia.* I repeat it, as a conjuror will his magic syllables: *Abbazia!* Something about that coastline is familiar to me. With my congenital squint I lean down to read the text:

GUSTAV MAHLER ON VACATION IN ABBAZIA (now Opatja)
Date: March 1901
[Torn half missing]

Did the heart of Shylock Holmes beat with the same force as mine when he closed in on one of his suspects? Would that I had, between my teeth, to calm my nerves, a stout meerschaum. I know these islands and the mountains that rise in a haze at the rear. This is where meine Mutter, Falma, née Krupnick, used to retire each spring for the digestives. Spring? In truth the month of March. I close one eye and peer through the glass case covering the evidence, as if it were the magnifying instrument of the great detective. The "snapshot" is indeed torn, jaggedly, as if in a passion. Still, it is possible to see that the left hand of the composer is grasping the arm flesh of a vanished companion. Look closer: yes, a woman's arm, slightly plumpish. A visible scrap of her clothing. Summer-style attire. On a dark background, white double dots.

Good Lord, Watson! Have I not seen, in a closet, just such an out-of-mode garment? Oh, the double dots dance now before my eyes. Is this a memory of an actual dress on an actual hanger, or something that hangs in the cloakroom of the mind? The other half of the Foto. Who was in it? Who the companion of the composer? The wearer of the polka dress?

Head a-spin, heart a-beating—double dot, double dot—I stagger back from the table, directly into the crucial clue: a pianoforte, top open, with grinning keys.

Bit rum, eh, Holmes, how we could have missed it. After all, the instrument is sitting in the middle of the room.

My dear chap, ofttimes the most perfect deception is the one hidden in plain sight.

I turn to make a closer inspection. This is not merely a piano, but a grand one, concert-style. And more: written above the keyboard, in gold leaf, is the word VOPATERNY. Yes, *Vopaterny!* The same make of instrument that had sat in our drawing room and upon which little Leib Goldkorn had taken his lessons as a child.

I drop, as if in worship, to my knees. Thus no taller than that lad of five or six or seven, I shuffle forward until my nose is opposite the row of gleaming keys. What next? It is not always possible for the resident of 221b Baker Street to rely on the deductive method. On occasion one must act. Ergo, I raise my hands to what Harlemites call the ivories. Ladies and gentlemen, number 265-300e in the Köchel Catalog of W. A. Mozart's works:

> *Baa, baa black sheep,*
> *Have you any wool?*

Non-rheumatically my hands, mit Fingerknöcheln, fly over the keys:

> *Yes sir, yes sir,*
> *Three bags full.*

All about the room, and indeed throughout the museum, people pause. They look up, their round heads cocked the better to hear the tune. And Leib Goldkorn? Torn. On the one hand, I am transported, as if within the time machine of H. George Wells, one hundred years into the past. On the other hand, I apprehend, half with dread, half in anticipation, what is about to come:

> *One for the master,*
> *One for the—*

Here, fatefully, I reached up one octave, to the all-too-familiar key of F.

> *—dame . . .*
> *F-F-F-F!*

In the adjoining café, on the lap of Iveta Crumsovatna, my piebald pussy has begun to accompany the repeated note:

Dame. Dame. Dame.
F-F-Futt! F-F-F-Futt! F-F-FUTTZ!

Aha! Mystery solved! The broken string. The aberrant key. Not once tuned since I had last struck it an entire century in the past! The more I strike it now, the louder the response from the howling Hymena: Dame: *FUTZ!* Dame: *FITZ!* Dame: *FRITZ!*

Now, from every direction, music lovers—both tourists and natives—come running. Attendants too. Some have their hands over their ears. Some have their fists in their mouths. What else can Leib Goldkorn, the virtuoso of the Vopaterny, do? The show must go on:

> *One for the little boy*
> *Who lives down the lane.*

Hymena hurls forward, followed by the Deputy Mayor for Culture, Entertainments, and Sports.

"What is it?" she cries. "Are you in pain? That horrible noise!"

Too late. Rough hands seize me. They lift me high into the air. With a march step they carry me to the door of Znojemská Number 4 and thrust me rudely through it to the ground. My kitten and my companion run forward to comfort me. Calmly, I smile, secure in the knowledge that I possess the key to the puzzle: *This Vopaterny, the very instrument once owned by Gustav Mahler, had for many years occupied the parlor of none other than the family Goldkorn.*

TOOT! TOOTA! TOOT!

Could this be the sound, ever dulcet, of my Rudall & Rose–model flute? No, it is only the moon-faced chauffeur, who sits at the wheel of his Mercedes automobile. The Crumsovatna and I enter the rear and ride through twilit Jihlava back toward the Masarykove Náměstí, where our journey began. But we turn off at Křížová Street and glide the short distance to the entrance of the Gustav Mahler Hotel. Here the sharp-chinned Deputy Mayor explains to me that the Holocaust Memorial Festivity will take place on the morrow. It is here, too, that, taking my hand in her own, she remarks that she has felt much joy during our excursion and, quotation marks are now appropriate, "I hope to see you soon."

QUIET IS THE NIGHT. In all the world nothing is stirring. I lie in my nightcap upon the queen-sized bed of room 68. I am not alone. On the duplicate queen lies my travel companion: on her back, three limbs outspread, the light of the moon falling across her upturned chin, her lip withdrawn, the single fang in her half-open mouth. Slight sound of a snore. Adorable! Sleep on, you sweetheart! Pleasant dreams.

Alas, her master lies awake, tossing, turning. And waiting.

Soon! Hope to see you *soon!* Such forwardness! But there is as yet no sign of my inamorata—though, thin as a furled umbrella, she is surely capable of squeezing through the crack I have left in the hotel door. More saltiness: Did she not, as we parted, place her hand in mine and leave it there, limp, in surrender, for, hmmm, a full six seconds? For a man of the world this is an international signal of assent.

But what is this? There. In the moonlight. A feminine figure. Scant of clothes. Not my evanescent Iveta. Here we have a type more rotunda. With dependable mams. She leans forward. Straining. Sighing. More moonlight magic: a flash of light. Gott im Himmel! A trolley of a garter. It is Miss Litwack! Clara, honey! Are you doing your nails? Look: I have your favorite. CoverGirl. "Plum Perfection." Allow me. Ah. Oh. Ah. Allow me.

Meeow!

What is this? Have I fallen asleep? Dreaming of what was once domestic bliss?

Meee-wow!

It seems that my mouser is no longer in Morpheus. She stands on all-threes, her tailpiece straight back, like that of a pointing Hund. Both eyes stare wide, and the mouth opens either in anguish or in awe.

Futt! Futt! Futtz!

I follow the gaze of the fearful feline down, toward the subterranean realm, where—Mr. Ripley, Believe It or Not!—Leib Goldkorn is in a state of epicureanism! Call the Guinness Records! Lazarus, laugh! Send forth the word to the astonished world.

What is that I hear? Musik? Yes, music. Again the rondo-finale of the Fifth. Are such melodies also circulated through the hotel named after their composer? In the middle of the night? No, no. This concert is in my Kopf. In truth, it was not the prospect of an assignation with my spidery seductress that has kept me a-toss through the many hours of the night. No. My restlessness has been caused by the fact that the mystery of the museum has yet to be solved.

What, ho? Shall we have another go at the puzzle pieces, eh, Watson?

Mee-who?

I assemble the evidence. A Red Cross concert. A torn photograph. A dotted dirndl. And above all, the note, the note, the note—*dame, dame, dame*—the F-sharp that has never been repaired. How was it that the family Goldkorn came into the possession of the very same piano that had once belonged to the family Mahler? I look toward my colleague, who is, while ruminating this question, licking her paw. But it is not her queen-sized bed that comes to the eye of my imagination but the four-poster that I instantly recognize from my parents' bedroom at Number 5 Lindenstrasse, town of Iglau.

Yes, yes, yes: there is the same double-down mattress and the same canopy of Belgian lace that floated above it. And who lies on this inner spring? With arms extended and legs spread wide? Who this bandy Juno? Frau Goldkorn! Mutter! Now, approaching her, like one of Professor Pergam's grinning satyrs, comes not Herr G. Goldkorn but—still wearing specs, and, like the boy in the nursery rhyme, with one shoe off and one shoe on—Herr G. Mahler. About to engage in—diddle-diddle-dumpling—an act of Lustsensation.

As Holmes would oft say to Watson, "Bingo!"

Everything now falls into place. Gustav and Falma were having a flirtation, one that reached its climactic on the night just after the Red Cross concert of February 24, 1901. Suddenly a neglected detail comes into the mind of the subtle sleuth. *The bandaged ear!*

How did the composer receive such a wound? How else than by the hand of the hoodwinked husband, who must have entered the bedroom in time to catch the amorists in flagrante delicto, that is to say, in an act of fertilization. Did he in his rage rip off one of the bedposts and strike his rival atop the cranium? Who can doubt now that the polka-style dress belonged to the former Falma Krupnick and that she is the mystery woman in the missing half of the Foto?

Let us continue. Why did Madam Goldkorn make the rendezvous in Abbazia? Even after her carnals had been discovered? There can be only one reason: she wished to inform her lover that a penetration had been achieved, with pollinization. "Gustav," she surely said, "I carry within me your child."

What a predicament for this pair. How he must have begged

her to flee with him to gay Vienna! How she must have been tempted! To become the consort of the world-famed conductor. To reign as Queen of the k. k. Hof-Operntheater and Empress of all the Monarchie. But no. She already had a rompish daughter, aforementioned Yakhne. She had a husband, Gaston Goldkorn, who owned fields of hops. Above all, she felt the new life growing in her womb: if she was not mistaken, this love child was to become a true Wunderkind, of the sort that is delivered to mankind only once in each generation. How could she bring it into the world under such a cloud?

For every argument there is a counterargument. It is not impossible that the composer even proposed einen Schwangerschaftsabbruch. Hideous thought! And with a coat hanger too. Back and forth the lovers battled, with tears, with oaths, until at last the defeated Mahler tore their photograph in two pieces: if he could not have Falma, he could at least possess her image. And in return, he sent her his beloved Vopaterny—note the witty pun, Wo, *Where*, is the patern[ity]?—perhaps in hopes that one day his offspring would play upon it the very symphony that he at once sat down to compose, the symphony whose conclusion, *Cuckoo! Cuckoo!*, would wreak his revenge on his rival: *Cuckold! Cuckold!*

The final piece of the puzzle: the date of the blessed event. To determine this the detective must know the moment of fecundation, an event oft difficult to determine. We are in luck, however. The pollution on the four-poster occurred on the twenty-fourth day of the second month of the year 1901. To this we must in the well-respected Naegele System add 266 days. Shall we put on our thinking caps?

For February of 1901, a non-leaper, we begin with five days, to which, for March, we add thirty-one more, giving us a total of, hmmm, thirty-six; to which we now add the thirty days of April, rendering a sum of, hmmm, sixty-six; and now the merry month of May, thirty-one. Ergo, ninety-seven. Add the month of June: hmmm, hmmm, 127. The heat of July! The heat of August! May one in such months eat oysters? Uncle Al, I stare thee in the face: 189. Is there milk in the mams? Does the babe kick his wee feet against the belly? Let us hope that the putative père refrains from conjugations. September, October—thirty plus thirty one, equals sixty-one, plus 189, here we must carry the one from the third column, and heft it again from the second, hmmm, *hmmmmmm*, yes, 250! Subtract that sum from 266, and we may calculate there are only sixteen days to go!

But nature has us for a surprise. For only nine days later, on the ninth of November, the early bird arrives. Bald head, ears not yet Dumbo-esque, shoulders non-haired. And look! But look, Gustav! You too, Gaston! And you, fruitful Falma! Let the bells ring from the Jakobskirche! Ja! And from der Kirche des heiligen Ignatius von Loyola! It is a boy! Well, let us look twice. Ja! Ja! Ja! A definite boy!

"HI HO, HYMENA! AWAY!"

Still in my Skivvies, with the ball of my nightcap a-flutter, I leap off the bed and dash to the door. "We have not a moment to lose!"

Down the hallway we trot. Down the stairs. To the lobby, where the clerk sits with his round head propped sleeping on his chubby Czech hands. Onto Křížová—née Kreutzergasse—go Leib and his kitten. Where to? What next? I move a few steps to my left, then turn right onto Dominikánská. We take the angle, against the traffic—two lazy hackneys—onto Husova, then right on Křivá. Whoops! On this former Krammergasse, a dead end. My breath comes now visibly from my mouth, my heart beats like a drumstick on the drums of my ears.

Meee-OW!

Pardon. A misstep upon the tattered tail and—what's that ahead? Heavens! We are at Frauengasse, a.k.a. Matky Boží: in other words, right back at the square named for the man whose son jumped from the window. Oh, woe: I almost wish I had jumped from 138 West Eightieth Street myself.

What's this? My wondercat once more stands rigid, like a puss pointing at a partridge. Then she stares at her master, closing a red eye, gazing with her blue one, almost as if she were a traffic signal bidding Leib Goldkorn: *Go!*

Instead, she runs off herself, making a U-turn and heading west, always west, bounding across the main boulevard of Dvořáková, then a left, and a loop, and a right again. I have lost all grasp of the compass. I see no street signs. All my senses are trained on the fleeing feline. Mein Gummibärchen! Slow down! But she speeds off even faster: this way, that way, this way again.

Who knows where we are going? Hymena does! She gives a last look over her shoulder, breaks into a three-legged gallop, and, hoopla!, leaps onto a wall. On two legs I come stumbling after. What's this? A gate, with the branches of a candlestick emblazoned upon it. I push forward. Unlocked. And so I step inside what I now know was my destination all along: the Jewish cemetery of Iglau, by the living called Jihlava.

S. WERNER, L. FERNBERG, J. J. UNGER, a rabbi. TAUSSIG. SCHICK. ZELENGASS. These are the names etched on the tombstones, some tumbled, some standing. I plod onward, peering as best I can by the light of the moon and the stars:

GRISSMAN, FRANZ: Ach, only a boy of, 1877–1880, hmmm, three. The family MILRAR, Little ANTOINETTE, hardly a breath taken in the year 1904. SONNENFELS, a professor. TORBERG, WERTHEIMER, DUSSL. Dust. All dust. And Leib? Living, though near his own date of expiration. I sink in weariness to the ground.

Tombs to my left. Tombs to my right. But nowhere the graves of the family Goldkorn. With each breath I inhale tiny particles of Falma, Minchke, Yakhne, the putative père—all of whom were sent into the system of atmospherics by the invaders. They exist in that mausoleum of molecules, not the tumbled tombstones of Iglau.

Meee-now!

A ghost? A specter? A shade risen from its crypt? No, only Hymena, who has jumped to the top of a tall gray slab. There she sits, blinking, lanternlike, her ruby-red eye.

With the last of my strength, I rise once more to my feet, which only now do I realize are unshod and unstockinged. Painfully I stagger to the upright stone. Blank. I circle around it. What are these names on the reverse side? MAHLER, BERNARD. MAHLER, MARIE. Parents of Mahler, G. I squint to read more. Ah! The tragedy! Both perished in 1899, just two years before that annum mirabilis—transmission by Marconi, for example, across the broad Atlantic—in which I had been born. I drop once more to my knees. I stretch out my arms to the granite.

"Grossmutter!" I cry, my voice echoing back and forth among the mute monoliths. "Grosspater! *Hier ist dein Kleiner Junge Leib!*"

SCENE TWO

HONORARY JEW

*As Leib's life is celebrated, he meets many
old friends and one new relation.*

THE DAWN OF the next day: the Secretary of the Holocaust
Festivities Committee arrives, together with the frog-faced
chauffeur, to transport me the few scant blocks from the Hotel
Gustav Mahler to what looks like nothing more than a high
wall of charred bricks.

"What have we here, Miss Crumsovatna?"

"Here is known as Benesova Street Synagogue."

Instinctively I return to my native tongue: "*Was ist das für
eine Tragödie?*"

"The invaders. They burned it to the ground."

"Wann?"

"*1939.*"

1939! When Gaston and Falma, Minchke, and Yakhne, had
already sailed in the *Kaliope* up the Danube. And I, having fled
across the Bodensee, was singing for sous among the frugal
French.

A tear must have fallen across my cheek, because the Deputy
Mayor is dabbing there with her handkerchief.

"Do not be sad, my dear Leib. Give Iveta a smile. This is for
you a happy day."

My dear Leib! Did you hear that? Yet I cannot smile. For in truth I stand not only before this wall of burnt brick, where in youth I heard our Rabbi Goldiamond declare to me, *Hayom Leib ben Gaston Ata Bar mitzvah* (Perfect Hebrew! A near-century later! Get thee hence, Uncle Al!), but also before the other wall that looms before me at the age of one hundred and three. Peek around *those* bricks, friends. Dark. Dark. Dark.

"What's that, Miss Crumsovatna? Gardenia? Could it be L'Air Du Temps?" Indeed, the scent from her handkerchief, like salts in the nostrils of a pugilist, is already restoring my spirits.

With a thin-lipped smile she answers; I cannot hear her words because, from the far side of the ruin, a band has started to play what I know to be the "Radetzky March." J. Strauss, composer. Part-time Jew. The Crumsovatna takes my left arm; the no-necked chauffeur—Uncle Al exercise: All toads are frogs, but not all frogs are toads—takes my right. Thus supported, with Hymena trotting behind, I walk around the old synagogue wall.

What a sight greets my eyes. The band, in flower-white uniforms, is toot-tootling away. A crowd of citizen Czechs, at least a hundred or a hundred and fifty, sit in rows of chairs. Their round heads nod to the beat of the music, like green-colored balloons in a breeze. In the actual wind a large banner chuffs against the synagogue wall. On it, the following words:

WELCOM HOME! LEIB GOLDKORNS!

In front of the crowd, a rostrum and microphone. To either side, small boys play with dogs and slings. A stand sells ices. Suddenly the music stops and a cheer, Huzzah!, rises to the cloud-filled sky. I look around, but Iveta, leaning toward my ear, purses her lips, behind which I know a tongue is lurking.

"Is for you."

Now the multitude are on their feet. Tremendous applause.

More huzzahs. A voice rings out in electrical amplification: "Welcome to Holocaust victim Goldkorns!"

I see that a square-shouldered, square-jawed gentleman is speaking into the microphone. "All Jihlava says many halós to native son."

Slick hair too, like a count.

"Is handsome mayor," whispers the deputy, her elbow point stabbing my ribs. "Frantisek Kunc."

On the other side of me, the Mercedes motorman says a single word, "*Pozor.*"

"Pardon? *Poseur?*"

Both my companions release my arms. Alone, I totter forward, while the band begins to play the very piece I once recorded with the NBC Orchester: Overture to *Il Segreto di Susanna*. More cheers. Am I mistaken? Are not a dozen caps, like floaters in eyeballs, flying through the air?

Suddenly all rise from their seats as musicians start in on J. P. Souza's "Star-Spangled Banner." This must be in honor of the fact that in 1943 I passed the difficult nationalization exam, Judge Solomon Gitlitz presiding. A serenade for a citizen.

We continue at attention while all sing the Czechist anthem, "Where Is my Home?"

To je Čechů slavné plémě.

"That is the glorious race of Slavs." Slight exaggeration. Now come the final notes.

Mezi Čechy domoy můj!

"Among Czechs, that's our home!" Sobs from the ladies. Several bald-headed gentlemen give a stiff-armed salute.

"Honored Mayor Kunc, I am presenting Leib Goldkorns, Holocaust Žid." So says the Secretary of Festivities, with a curtsy to her square-jawed superior.

"Haló!"

"Greetings, sire."

"Haló! Haló! Haló! Haló!"

These salutations come from those whom the Crumsovatna introduces as the deputy mayors for housing, for education, for public works, and—another square-jawer, with what seems a broken nose—the policejní prezident, Pan Broz. With a bone-crushing grip, he guides me to a chair. All sit save the shiny-haired Kunc, who begins to speak into a microphone. All in Czech, often vowelless, as in the related Pomeranian tongue. Here is a sample sentence with which we young German-speakers used to torment our knock-kneed countrymen:

STRC PRST SKRZ KRK!

Ha! Ha! Ha! "Stick a finger through your throat!" Is it any wonder that, in spite of all, I harken for the happy Huns?

No sooner does the mayor conclude his remarks than a dozen young ladies of Gymnasium age appear and arrange themselves in two lines in front of the synagogue wall. They are dressed in white and yellow, with leatherette straps crossed over their budding parts. Hmmm. That lass with Haarzöpfen, pigtails. Has she not a perky nose? With a start I notice she is making a wink, yes, a definite nictitation, directly at me.

"Go. You must go," hisses Iveta, with a halo of Gardenie hovering above her. "Perform ceremony."

Again the schoolgirl, with her sky-blue eyes, performs her come-hither. So I come. Now I see that she holds, in her plump-ish hands, a velvet cord. I draw near.

"Hello, Honigkuchen. What's the name?"

"Hanna. Hanna Nechvátalová."

How many years separate us? Ninety? Well, perhaps only eighty-eight or eighty-nine. Shameful, the thoughts that occur as I notice the sweet hair part on her head—and more shameful still what I call up from the depths my charm:

"A pretty name for a pretty girl."

Ach! I feel the Freudian flush. Vile pantaloon!

"Thank you, Jew Goldkorns."

She places the cord in my hand, I give it a—here is a pun on my citizenship—yank. On the wall the WELCOM HOME banner falls to the ground, revealing, affixed to the scorched brick, a bronze plaque. The text is in four languages: Czech, Hebrew, German, English. Four tragic tongues. English, then:

> **On this site stood Benesova Street Synagogue**
> **Destroyed by Nazi Invaders—1939**
> *Here worshipped the Jews of Jihlava*
>
> **We shall—**

(What is this mist over my eyes?)

> **We shall not forget them.**

Great applause from all, though I believe I can detect from the group of hatless, hairless pánové (Can you guess the meaning of this word? *Gentlemen?* Gold star!), a rude sound that I hope the schoolgirls—and in particular my little cupcake—do not hear.

"Řeč! Řeč!" cry the others. "Řeč!"

The Crumsovatna: "You must make speech."

Taking a breath, I turn to the crowd. "Dámy a pánové—" I stop, stymied.

"Meine Damen und Herren," I stammer, and stop once more.

"'גב'דות וּרְבות'" Stumped again. Struck mute, just as I had been before this standing wall four score and ten years earlier, on the day of my bar mitzvah. My subject then was Tamar, and Hirah the Adullamite, and how Onan spilled his, um, seed upon the ground. On that occasion, too, the words stuck in my throat until our rabbi, S. T. Goldiamond, stepped forward, put his hands on my shoulders, and told the world that Leib ben Gaston was a man.

"*Siman tov, u'mazal tov! Mazel tov, u'siman tov!*" The entire congregation was shouting and chanting and pounding me on the back. "Mazel tov!" The next thing I knew, a volley of hard candies flew through the air, pelting me on the head, the back, the torso zone. I fell, scavenging, to my knees.

And now, in the fall of 2005, who should I see coming toward be but Samuel Taylor Goldiamond himself. Yes, the yarmulke on top of the white locks of hair. A flock of Leberflecken across the forehead. The undershot jaw.

But how can this be? True, in 1914 our rabbi was but a young man of sixty; to approach me now, with a cane in each hand, all a-tremble, he would have to be—hmmm, hmmm, two becomes a nine, carry the one: Gott im Himmel! One hundred and fifty-one! Call Mr. Guinness! Hello, Mr. Ripley!

I look again. That yarmulke: verily, it is a bald spot. That undershot jaw: caused, as in so many musicians, by the chin rest of the violin.

This ancient drops both his walking sticks. I open my arms. We toddle across the space that divides us.

"Leib Gladstone!"

"Is it you? Young Murmelstein! Second violin!"

We clasp each other. A touching moment, even though, from his body parts, there rises a smell of kumquats.

"I flew in an airplane," he announces.

"Me too. Did you meet Miss Milada? D-cup? 'Tommy Girl'?"

More questions flood my mind. Who else is alive? Who is not? For example, fellow members of the Steinway Quintet. Salpeter, first violin. J. Dick, with his double viol. But, as if he had been reading my thoughts, Murmelstein shakes his hoary head.

"Gone? All gone? What of Mosk? The waiter. Looks like a penguin."

To this inquiry, the violinist only shrugs.

"Řeč! Řeč!" The cry of the heartless horde. But it is to Mr. Murmelstein that they are directing this command.

He takes, from his breast pocket, a paper, which he unfolds before the microphone. "Leib Gladstone played the Bechstein instrument for many years in the Steinway Quintet. I am from the town of Nasielsk. I played violin. How come I don't get a celebration? The end."

Applause, of the polite variety. I too have heard better speeches. Now Pan Kunc returns to the microphone and says— I don't know what: *Strk prst skrz krk*, or some such Slavic silliness. Hard to imagine how such a vowel-challenged folk could produce melodious works like the "Hippodamia" of Zdeněk Fibich or the tuneful arpeggios of that mad genius, Stich-Punto.

The Secretary of the Holocaust Festivities Committee, with whom I have established suggestions, rises to make an announcement. "Now arriving before us is a special lady friend of Honorary Jew. Can he make a guess to who is such a woman?"

From the crowd there comes a tittering, and among the non-follicled strongmen a sort of sucking sound. I even hear, from the direction of the single-fanged feline, a mocking mew. Needless to say I am in a maelstrom of anticipation. Who could this past personage be? A paramour? The one, the only Hildegard Stutchkoff? On whose Sealy-brand—please see *Goldkorn Tales*, whose author the half-Finn called "an exuberant writer," end quote—I had achieved an expostulation? At the thought of that double bosom there occurs in the hinterland a stir of hedonism. Ja! It must be the Stutchkoff. Hilda, honey!

But who should now come from around the edge of the wall, and in a wheelchair at that, but a woman—neck bent, head shaking, tongue hanging too, who is definitely not the former proprietress of the Steinway Restaurant, but, but, but: Aha! Madam Schnabel, the contralto, formerly of 138 West Eightieth Street, with whom I oft fought for possession of the W.C.

"Greetings, Myra," I say.

To my surprise the voice that issues from the shrunken sack before me is just as I remember it when—*Yoo-HOO! Yoo-HOO!*—she attempted to invade my refuge within the cabinetto.

No need for a microphone now. The busty Brünnhilde belts out her line:

THIS IS YOUR LIFE!

I turn to the Crumsovatna: "Madam Schnabel was not, you know, an inamorata."

"Patience, Pan Leib. Soon you shall hear from the lady of your dreams."

But it is not a dream damsel, or any sort of lady at all, who next appears. Instead, imprisoned within an aluminum walker, comes a gent who looks nearly as old as the guest of honor. And, with his pale face, dripping nose, and what appears to be a single strand of jet-black hair coiled on top of his head, a stranger. Wait! Wait! That short stature; the corner of a trembling lip raised in a mischievous smile: Could it be?

"Willi!" I shout. "Willi Wimpfeling!"

"Den leibliche Leib!" he answers, in a voice that twangs like the viol he once used to play. "Leib Kornfeld!"

Yes, here was my fellow Akademician—like L. Goldkorn, a prize graduate.

"*Goldkorn*, I reply. "Class of '16."

"Ho! Ho!" laughs my classmate, with something of the old twinkle in his eye. "Do you remember the time we spied on Fräulein Minchke? Splitterfasernackt!" Which means, stark-naked.

I turn once more to the Deputy Mayor for Sports.

"Miss Crumsovatna. This playmate was not, you know, a significant other."

"Ah, but he carries a message from one that was."

A message? With a trembling hand my classmate removes from his breast pocket an envelope with Old Glory stamps— thirteen stripes, Judge Gitlitz, for Delaware and the twelve original states.

"Okihcim Inatukak!" The name bursts involuntarily from my lips. The Esquimaux Queen! She has received my "air" mail. She has scriven in return. A sacrilege that her words are about to be spoken by this aged sybarite:

My dearest Leibie—

To my ears, music!

> I am so very very sorry I can't be with you on your big day. Think of it! Honorary Jew! Of course, I discovered your heritage on that magical night beneath the moon, the stars, the palms.

Palms! The Court of Palms. Our date at the Hotel Plaza. There it was that I yearned—as you may read in my not-yet-remaindered *Ice Fire Water*—for my bountiful beauty.

Alas, I rarely fly now because of my broken eardrums. My punishment, Leibie, for spending so much of my youth underwater.

Aha! The Finnish baths. Pressure of the sauna.

So all I can do is send you my words and tell you that I will never forget our night together. You were more a man than Victor Mature.

Victor: Yes, I have beaten all rivals.
Mature: Here we have Asian-style delicacy: not someone *old*, but a gentleman of such-and-such years. Fit as a fettle. All marbles intact.
More a man: Could this be a reference to, you know, the American inches?

Always yours,

Always!
Yours!

Esther.

Esther?
Mayor F. Kunc seizes the microphone. Dámy a Pánové, you are hearing tribute from Hollywood film star of *Pagan Love Song*. The famed Paní Esther Williams!"

Tremendous applause. Vocal approval.

"Would our Honorary Jew make response? Say some words?"

"But, but, but—" I cannot help stammering. "She ran off with Fernando Lamas!"

At once the Bohemia-Moravia band strikes up yet another trademark tune: "Bells of St. Mary's," oft played to Harlemites in return for Roosevelt dimes. Now old acquaintances—young Murmelstein, Madam Schnabel, wee Willi Wimpfeling—shout in unison:

THIS IS YOUR LIFE!

At these words who should come striding forward but the plump proprietor of the shop of prawns. The next thing I know, he is hugging against me his non–Charles Atlas bosom.

"Larry Goldkorn!" he exclaims. "Repeat customer!"

Once more, His Honor takes charge. "Jew Goldkorns. Here is the man who has helped you in time of needs. Pan Ernie Glickman!"

Fanfare. Huzzahs.

The lord mayor turns to the American. "Do you not have for us a gift presentation? Made possible by generous Jihlava citizens?"

Ernest picks up from his feet a cloth valise. "Yes, yes. On behalf of my brother, Randy, and thanks to the contribution of this municipality, I am very pleased to return to its owner—"

"Bulova! Gift of the Zanuck!"

"No, no, no, no. Not the Bulova. No tickie. Ha, ha, ha! No watchee!"

"Hee, hee," chuckles Murmelstein. "That's funny."

Glickman: "As I was saying, I am pleased to return to you—" Here the prawnbroker breaks off to unhinge his jiffy and rummage inside. Simultaneously a Czechist cloud moves aside from the sun, whose rays fall blindingly onto the object within the bag.

I squint, shading my eyes from the silvery glare. "What is it? What can it be?"

Wimpfeling has better vision than I. "Gott im Himmel! Die Flöte! Der Preis der Akademie!"

True. Before me I see, shining, glittering, all a-sparkle, the Rudall & Rose. Nine decades fall from me like so many old clothes. I am the lad of fifteen who, on the occasion of our Graduation-Day Concert, accepted from His Apostolischen Majestät this First-Place Prize.

It is not from the hands of the emperor, but those of the broker of prawns that I receive the beloved instrument. Instantly hundreds of Czechs, in a Slavic gesture of joy, clap their hands over their ears.

"Nehraju!" they cry. And again: "Ne! Ne! Nehraju!"

Obviously, they wish to hear a ditty. Madam Schnabel has clasped her hands together. "Leib! Leib! I am begging you!"

"Well, friends, since you insist . . ." Does my dear old instrument leap to my lips, or do my lips descend to that open mouth I have so often kissed?

"Auch das noch!" cries my fellow Akademician. "Bitte! Bitte!" Why, there are tears in his eyes!

Murmelstein, too, holds out his hands in supplication. "Please, Gladstone! Think of my heart!"

Even Hymena, who has adopted the Czechist manner, has a paw over her half-eaten ear.

"Ladies and gentlemen," I declare, with my fingers already on the E, the B-flat, the F. "The Scottish Rhapsody."

"Zavrete ho!" So cries Pan Broz, the chief of police, who runs toward me holding what seem to be silver bracelets.

But before he can bestow upon me this additional gift a dozen voices cry out—

THIS IS YOUR LIFE!

—and a familiar figure steps forward to join us.

"Hello, everybody!"

I cannot believe my eyes. This man knows the fifth floor of 138 West Eightieth Street only too well. Frank Fingerhut! The fils!

"Help!" I cry, and position myself behind the policeman. "He wants his rent!"

"No, no. Nothing could be further from the truth."

What's this? On the freckled face of F.F. not a frown? But an actual smile? This causes discombobulations, like the day, at the Steinway Restaurant, a cheese blintz was mixed with the Roumanian broilings.

"*Nothing? Further?*"

"That's right! I come not to take away your old home but to give you a new one!"

At this the fils produces a piece of paper and begins to read the following words:

"Leib Goldkorn, 5-D, stabilized. It gives me great pleasure to announce that you will now be able to live out your days amidst familiar surroundings, indeed in your very own boyhood home, Number 5 Valkova. May you live there in happiness and health for—heh! heh! heh!—many years."

"Heh! Heh! Heh!" echoes the crowd. "Mnoho Let!"

"Pardon. *Valkova?*"

"Psst. Pan." That is the Sports Deputy, leaning forward in her chair. "Was before Lindenstrasse."

"Former tenant Goldkorn. Here are the keys to your home. They are yours. Take them."

Your home. Instant reverie: The tile roof. The pool for carp. The staircase that Yakhne ran up three steps at a time, and the banister down which, rump foremost, Minchke used to slide. Our Persian-style carpet. Our cage of budgies, hopping from stick to stick. The rainbows in the lozenges of our chandelier.

Ah, the bathing tub, with its lion's claws, its dolphin snout. Once, Minchke and the present speaker—

His Lordship, the mayor: "Is a problem, Pan Goldkorns? Why not take happily keys?"

"My sisters! My mother! The père!" My voice in a wail resonates among the ruins of the Benesova Street Schul. "Even budgerigar birds! Gone! The house is empty! Alone! Leib alone! The only survivor at Number 5!"

The Deputy Mayor for Sports leans close with a smile. "No, dear friend Leib. You will not be alone."

"What? How can that be? Even the poor yellow carp!"

As if in answer the cry goes up yet again—

THIS IS YOUR LIFE!

—and into the ruins of the temple steps a child of perhaps thirty-one, perhaps thirty-two. Her black hair is in ringlets and, in spite of the chill, a bodice of frills cannot disguise the pneumaticals. Also high heels.

I squint. I stare. But the coquettish Czech cloud has moved once more across the face of what has become the noonday sun. Still, I note that these eyes, with dark irisis; these cheeks, with disappearing dimples; that leftward bosom, with its spot of perfection—all these things are somehow, to me, familiar.

"Tell me!" I say to the mysterious minx. "Who are you? What is your name?"

Instead of answering, she takes from the front of her dickey a white handkerchief and, turning away, begins to dab at her eyes.

I wheel about to address the Deputy Mayor for Culture, Entertainments, and Sports. "Who, Miss Iveta, is this damoiselle?"

But she too has buried her face in a Kleenex-type tissue.

"Excellency," I say, bowing to the lord mayor—then notice that he, like the others, is shedding a tear.

"Pan Goldkorns." This is the head of municipal police. "Pan Goldkorns—" But he also breaks off and begins to rub ten thick knuckles into the sockets of his eyes.

Why, even Frank Fingerhut, the fils, is fighting against his feelings.

In the end, it is my colleague, young Murmelstein, who manages to get out the words: "Leib Gladstone: Do you not recognize a member of your own family?"

I gasp. I gape. "You are mistaken. I have no family. All were at Auschwitz ermordet."

Now the Schnabel rolls forward, the tears glistening on her cheeks. "Not all."

What is this? What can it mean? The dimpled darling who stands before me is no more than a babe in her fourth decade.

"Alas, alle. With my own eyes I saw older sister, younger sister, Mutter, and dubious dad: all sailed on the *Kaliope* to Dachau. Auschwitz next. None escaped. None returned."

"Ano. Pravda," says His Honor. "Our researches have made the confirmation. All perished."

"I knew it. Poor sisters. Poor Mutter. And the père."

"Except—"

"*Except*, my lord?"

Iveta Crumsovatna: "Was one of your sisters not a famed beauty?"

"Not Yakhne. Absence of brisket. Plus Adam's apple: the same as a man."

"And the other?"

"Minchke? A peach. But why do you ask? You don't mean . . . ?"

"Ne. Ne. You must not hope. But she did live more long than others. Until January 1945."

"Ach. Not even forty-three years of age. Little more than a schoolgirl."

"And is it not true," continues His Excellency, "that she was . . . in our language, *svůdný*?"

"Enticing," translates the Crumsovatna, with a slight reddening of her rouge.

"Sexy," adds the chief of police.

"Ja. True. At the Graduation Concert, 1916, I won from his Apostolischen Majestät the First Prize; but she won his heart. It is rumored that, just months later, in the joint act of, you know, conjugation, he kicked over the bucket."

"Well, Pan Goldkorns," says His Worship. "Is it not possible that Mademoiselle Minchke outlived her family by using those same charms to make a . . . we say a *svádění*?"

"A seduction." That from Chief Broz.

"Ano, a seduction of a high officer among the Němci. The Germans. The Nacisté."

"What? Do you mean Minchke? And a Teuton? That they . . ." And here I made the international symbol of a finger fornication.

The Deputy for Sports—at what game does she excel, I wonder? Volleyball, as on her nation's stamps? Bowling? Boules? The deputy gestures toward her vacated chair. "Perhaps, dear friend, you might wish to sit down?"

Dear! Friend! And such a long neck! "No, no. Nein. Are you suggesting that my sister and a Nacistický made together an eructation?"

Pan Broz: "Not only that: we have proof that there were consequences. Do you know what is meant? A chlapeček. A baby boy."

At these words I do sink onto the hardwood chair—only to spring up again, with the sort of joy one receives from a schnapps shot. "What? Can it be true? Leib Goldkorn, Graduate, ist ein Onkel!" But no sooner are the words out of my mouth than I droop down once more. For there can be no doubt as to the fate of this poor little chlap. Never the chance to play Köchel Number 265.

"Sad," I say.

My "dear friend" leans down, so close that I pick up anew the sweet scent of Gardenie. "No. Please. Do not feel despairs. The father, the tata: he was big man. Hauptsturmführer. Also a doctor. He made arrangements of escape."

"This is not, Miss Crumsovatna, cheery news. Better if this Nordic had been killed. Shot. Hanged. Executed with the others."

"You do not understand. Yes, he made escape. But he took with him his child. They crossed the ocean together. And together they landed in Jižní Amerika. First Argentina. Then Brazil."

This time I almost fall off my uncushioned seat. "*Zusammen?*" I murmur. "Together?"

Chief Broz: "Let us get move on. Do you see that the sky becomes dark?"

I do see. Overhead, the clouds are rubbing shoulders. The bulb of the sun dims; the breeze, in response, grows stronger.

"Please, Pan. This suspense. What happened to my kleiner Neffe?"

"I will tell." Thus does His Honor take charge. "This boy, Josef Juniorsky, grew and thrived. At the age of twenty-seven he had a child of his own. A dívka. 1977. São Paulo. Honorary Jew Leib Goldkorns: this girl baby stands before you now."

A tremendous cry arises, not just from the figures in my past, not just from the Holocaust Festivities Committee and the band members and the assembly of round-headed Czechs, but, so it seems, from the gallery of stratocumulus clouds:

THIS IS YOUR LIFE!

I stand, thunderstruck, dropping my flute to the ground. I turn toward the double-breasted maiden. Those irises. Those dimples. Minchke's eyes! Minchke's cheeks! The mark of beauty: I could have sworn it was on the leftward mam. It seems now to have drifted to the right. The movable mole!

"Meu tio!" These words burst from the red-painted lips. Portuguese. Her native tongue. "Meu tio Leibie!"

She flies toward me, arms outspread, the wind-whipped tears springing from her eyes. I also open my arms. The next instant my own flesh, my own blood, in a silk skirt and open blouse, is inside them.

Bliss. Not to be alone. To know that some part of you, of the Goldkorn-Krupnick line, will survive. I cling to the lovely lass. I bury my head, with its horseshoe of hair, its still-growing ears, its woodwinder's lips, into the nest of ringlets. And she? She, all weeping, with both arms draws me to her. Now, methinks, let these clouds hurl their bolts of lightning. Let this heart of mine cease its own *Boom-de-Boom*. This is the moment to die.

Then, in less than that moment, all happiness turns to horror. Down in no-man's-land I begin to experience, yes, a salty sensation. Rabbi Goldiamond! Help me! Is there in the Talmud a taboo? Against a Hebrew and, in high heels, his Grossnichte? Now what? This mammary pressed to my chest. These abdominals against my own. Haunch to haunch. Ham to ham. Pan Johnson: Down, sir! Down at once!

"*Ay-eee*," cries—what *is* her name? *Karima*, like her fellow Hispanic? *Josefina*, like her dad?

"*Ay-eee!*" Again that cry as, jumping backward, she stares wide-eyed at the netherlands.

"Please. My dear, please. In the saga of the *Kalevala*, lusty Kullervo has his way with his, um, sister. And among the Pharaohs of Egypt—"

"Safado! Homem velho safado!"

"Ha! Ha! Ha!" The laughter comes from the Honorable Frantisek Kunc, who now rushes forward. "With such touching reunions our festivities are complete. Welcome, Pan Goldkorns, to your boyish home."

Now comes the chief of police, waving some kind of paper. "I have agreement. The Jew signs here."

"Here is excellent pen, already filled with ink." His Honor withdraws the implement from his breast pocket and hands it to me.

I take it. "Very good. Waterman-brand. L. E. Waterman, founder. You require my John Hancock?"

Of all people, we hear now from the feckless Frank Fingerhut, fils. "It's just, you know, paperwork."

Madam Schnabel: "A mere formality."

"Ano," comes the shout from the crowd. "Formalita!"

Ernie Glickman: "You can even keep the pen."

I lean over the paper, which turns out to be a multicolored map of our town. "Look, friends," I declare. "We are standing here."

Chief Broz places a fat finger on a paragraph of consonants, followed by a signature line. "You write name there."

His Honor points too. "You can do it. The *l*. The *e*. Then the *i*.

"But it's all in Czech."

Iveta comes close. "Don't worry, my dear Leib. A formalita. Is no problem to sign."

Those gardenias! "All right, missy." I unscrew the top of the Waterman and place the tip to the paper. "If you say so."

"*Pozor!*"

Again that word. Again from the Mercedes man. I glance to where he first shakes his head and then wags his finger. The message is clear: *Beware.*

"Sign! Sign!" All my old friends, my old colleagues, are in unison declaiming this word.

"Označit! Označit!" The crowd echoes the same demand.

Just then I notice something on the map. The municipality of Jihlava has in the course of the twentieth century spread far beyond the borders of the old Iglau. "Look, fellow citizens. This stadium for sports. These houses and streets. Even this railway depot. Why, in my day all of this territory was nothing more than fields of hops. You know, Hopfen. Oft as a child I would lie among such female flowers, watching the white clouds float by, like the marble busts of Mendelssohn, Mahler, Mayerbeer—the three great musical *M*'s. Just think! My father, Gaston Goldkorn, would now own half your town!"

A hush. And then, as if from the intestinals of some invisible giant, a far-off rumble. Thunder? The approach of a storm?

Or was it a growl from the part of the crowd without Haar on their heads? Could these chaps be part of a local Polar Bear Club? Perhaps, in January, in February, they take a bracing dip in the Iglawa. Now I see that they have raised their fists in the air. "Ne reparace! Ne honorář!" What are those things in their hands? Sticks? Stones? "Označit. Špinavý Žid. Nečistý Žid!"

What to do? I turn back to where the automobilist was standing, but I see that he is now surrounded by the Polars, who—to swim all the faster—have shaven their heads. They have pinned his arms behind him. One fellow, in a demonstration of British calisthenics, has crooked his own arm around the good man's throat.

The sky darkens further. *Boom-Boom-de-Boom!* The percussion of thunder. A single drop, a raindrop, emerges from the heavens and falls onto the atlas, at a spot, lower left, that is familiar to me: Židovský hřbitov. Jewish cemetery.

"Meu tio. Meu querido." It is my Grossnichte, granddaughter of sister Minchke. Her dark skin has turned somewhat pale. "Meu amado. Won't you sign? So we can live happy together in new house? I want to take care of you. Like your filha. Bring you café com leite, eh? You like? Bring you porridge. Sign. Okay?"

A second drop. A third. "Ha, ha! Not coffee. Maybe a slivovitz? Made from plums!"

To my surprise, and delight, the little darling goes up on her toes—and I cannot help but smell distinct notes of oak moss—and plants on my cheek a kiss. Do I blush? Ho, ho: we know what *that* means.

"Assine seu nome," she murmurs, directly into my ear. "Sign, Leibie Goldkorns."

How can I, with such blandishments, resist?

"Oh! Oh! Pomôžte mi!" That cry comes from my former chauffeur, as the Polar Bears perform a folkish kick-dance on his back. "Pomôžte mi!"

"Easy, lads!" I cry. "Queensbury rules!"

With that the fraternity—I see they wear tattoos, an art form forbidden to Yiddish speakers—abandons the driver and instead comes striding toward me. One of them throws smartly against my shins a sharp-edged stone. Another raises his stick. A third repeats what seems to be their password. "Označit! Označit, Žid! Ne reparace!" A fourth makes the translation. "Sign, Jew! No reparations!"

All fall upon me. They seize my lumberman-type jacket; they pull at my beltless gabardines. A raindrop on my neck?

No, an expectoration. Can it be? In the twenty-first century? Pogrom!

Ow! Ow! Ow! These cries come not from my own lips but from a spot some yards away. *Ow! Ow! Meeee-ow!* It is Hymena. Now she bounds toward me with, clamped in her jaws, my Rudall & Rose.

The crowd—let us call them by their correct name: Cossacks!—They fall back as the feline dashes to my feet.

"Ne! Ne! Nikdy!"

I stoop. I grasp by its silver shank my beloved companion.

Now all repeat the gesture of throwing their hands to their ears, perhaps in this instance against the tremendous thump of the thunderclouds.

"Ne! Ne!" from the Czechs.

"Nicht!" from the German speakers.

"No!" from those who are either naturalized or native-born citizens of the USA.

And from Leib Goldkorn: "And now, ladies and gentlemen, for a change of pace: *Borscht Capades*, J. Rumshinsky, composer."

Splat. Splat. Splat. It has begun to rain in earnest. Is that why the multitude seems to flee? Just as our concert begins?

TWAT-TWARP-TWAT!

There go the pogromchiks, as rapidly as if they had been mounted on their steeds of the Steppes.

TWEET-TWAP-TWARPT!

And there fly all the figures from my past. What's a little rain, friends? Why this fear of getting wet?

TWANK-THRPPT-THWUPPT!

Farewell, Festivities Committee. A pang at the sight of the Deputy for Culture, Entertainments, and Sports. Hopscotching from sight, while hiking her skirts above her spindleshanks. Stay, dear Iveta. Do not miss the Dance Divertimento.

TWIZZLE-TWAZZLE-THWONK!

Wave goodbye to the bowlegged Czechists. All disappear, seeking shelter from the downpour. *Thump, Kerthump!* The thunder has driven everyone away, save for the Mercedes operator, clearly a music lover, who remains at his spot on the ground. And, of course, my own flesh and blood, who stands with her inner elbows over her ears. Who knew that she was a fan of Rumshinksy?

A-one. A-two—

TWANG-TWIPPLE-TA-ROO!

The face of F. Kunc, Lord Mayor, appears from behind the remnant of the synagogue wall. Hair bangs plastered to forehead. Droplets dripping from chin.

"Pssst! Madam Mengele! This way! Over here!"

And in a flash, she too is gone.

I must play now to an audience of one, who accompanies me with his musical moans. No: two. For at these well-known tunes, spun forth in a sprightly D-major—

TZZT-TZZAT-TZAAM!

—the clouds themselves seem to hasten away, also carrying their skirts behind them, leaving only, over all of what had been the former Czechoslovakia, the round smiling face of the sun.

SCENE THREE

DER MUSIKSALON

Leib has a drink, or two, in the Musiksalon, recalls his audition with the famed J. J. Epstein, then falls asleep on his boyhood bed.

OFF I GO the next afternoon on the brief walk from the Hotel Mahler through the Masaryk Square and on to my boyhood home at Number 5 Lindenstrasse. *Brief?* Mayhaps for Sir Charles Atlas, into whose face an earlier pogromist once kicked the sand, or for Plum Warner, outstanding cricketer. But I must pull in arrears my Samsonite valise—over cobblestones!—while balancing my kitten in her pet hostel. *Lindenstrasse?* No: Valkova. Named, mayhap, for some famous gent or other: perchance inventor of the portable W.C. or, a Czechist specialty, the open-toed sandal. Or—who knows?— the five-pronged fork.

Arrival, breathless. A pity: gone are the Lindenbäume that gave the street—no, no, Miss Hymena, not a *mews*—its former name. Except there, in the middle of the block, a single specimen: bent, bowed, older even than the present speaker. No sign of those blossoms that on a summer night could intoxicate a bookish boy. Only, eins, zwei, drei, four pale leaves, all of them a-tremble in the November breeze, fearing deportation. Aha! Subtract one! Now, poor things, only, hmmm, three.

But look: at least our house has not changed. The same green shutters at the windows. The same green door. Let us take out the gift of Fingerhut, fils: the silvery keys. *Open sesame!* says me. Ho. Ho. Good one.

I stand motionless in the foyer. Goldkorn agog. It is as if I have been whisked on our old Persian carpet one hundred years into the past. In spite of past Slavic or Teuton occupants, all about me remains the same. In the niche to the left, Hermes of yore; in a niche to the right, strong-chinned Athena. Zones of generation draped. Ahead, the debouchment of the spiral staircase. Here sat a lad upon the bottom step as his sister hurtled down the banister, knickers non-draped. Interessant!

Look leftward: the salon for dining. There, as if the family Goldkorn had sat around it only last night, partaking of a robust Rheinischer Sauerbraten, is our Bavarian-style table. If I close my eyes I can see steaming before me a particular favorite, Schlesiches Himmelreich—yes, Kingdom of Heaven, the fruit pieces covering the forbidden bacon.

Look, Hymena! This was my seat à table. Look up: Do you see how our chandelier, of Prague manufacture, has trapped in its prisms the rays of sunny days past, just as the crystal of the nighttime sky discloses stars that have long since expired? Pardon poetics. Now, my honey bear, look down: Do you see that rubber button? The master of the house, and here we speak of Gaston Goldkorn, had only to press it with his foot, and at once a peasant girl, plump Eliska, would appear with a bowl of Leberknödelsuppe. Excellent trick: she would cross her sirloins and with a pumping motion produce the sound of a trombone. Dare we summon her now? I press the semi-sphere and—yes! A far-off chime: but the ghost of Eliska, with her swollen ankles, does not appear.

Let us turn to the right—that is, to the parlor, or, in American vernacular, the "living" room. Identical sensations. That sofa? Ours! The twin leatherette chairs? Ours! The curtains at the windows? Ours as well! And there, as aforementioned, our Persian-type rug. How oft as a child did I imagine that, while lying upon it, I would be borne off to the faraway places in the pages of my books, just as Solomon on his flying carpet could breakfast in Damascus and sup at Medina. Pumped with pride was I, flitting through the clouds like the Hermes in his niche, with wings on my feet and the wind in my hair. *Carpet!* I cried, with a snap of my fingers. *Take me to Bialystok!* Foolish child. Only God is perfect, both Jews and Musselmen agree. Thus the weaver in his tent deliberately drops a stitch or leaves, among his myriad of knots, one untied. Thus does he demonstrate the imperfection of man. And how!

Here, Hymena, and here, and also here. Regard depressions in the silk, the threads that are bare. That is where stood the casters of the pianoforte, a Vopaterny grand. Gift to meine Mutter from—well, we know from who. *Only God is perfect:* thus on that keyboard we find the fateful F-sharp flaw. From this excursion into the past we might learn one other lesson: There is one house in a man's life—to wit, from the days of his youth—that he will always own. All the others who have lived in it since are only renters.

What is that smell? A sniff. A second sniff. Is this not the fragrance once generated by the Imperial and Royal Tobacco Monopoly, an aroma that hung not only over Iglau but Humpletz, Budwitz, and far-off Tábor? Such fumes were not absent from Lindenstrasse Number 5. Sister Yakhne, on feminist grounds, would enjoy a Dutch Liliputano. At times the playful Eliska would make the smoke from a cigarillo come out of her ear. But I know that what I smell now is the residue of the putative père. His habit was to sit with feet up in the music room, lost both in the clouds of his Trabucco D.D., or Doppeldezimeter, a terrifying eight American inches, and in the newsprint of his rustling *Prager Tagblatt*.

And so, as Hänsel und Gretel followed the Brotkrumen, I follow my Jewish-style nose. Through the parlor, a leftward turn, and voilà! Der Musiksalon! With, at its rear, the schnapps bar. Oho! Here are all my old friends: Goldwasser, Edelkirsch, Becherovka, Himbeergeist; also Jägermeister, slivovitz, Spätburgunder—all arranged by decree of G. Goldkorn in the order of the spectrum, from the blue-violet Curaçao on the left to where the rainbow ends, at the right, with the ruby-red Campari. At once I spy the same bottle of Fernet Stock that, with a tumbler of Mr. J. Walker and a thimble of Signor Cinzano, I turned into a first-rate Rob Roy. How many times, as a pubescent, did I tiptoe down the staircase as the père, the mère, and les deux soeurs lay all abed, and mix together this excellent digestive.

"I say, Hymena, dost care for a drop?"

Mee?

"Verdammt! This cap is tight. Aha! There!" I pour a "finger" of Fernet into a glass and place it before my fur-bearing friend. "On guard. This is not Milchwasser. Fourteen herbs. Eighty-proof!"

Fitz! Futz!

"Ha! Ha! Did I not warn you? It puts a hair on the chest!"

For myself, two "fingers." Maybe three. "In your eye—" Up goes the glass: "Mud!"

Of a sudden there falls on my head the nightstick of a policeman. The blow is only partly caused by the forty percent alcohol in my drink. The true shock comes from the sight of the Monarch-model machine that gave this room its name.

It is just as I remember: a consul-type, with windup motor and metal horn skillfully painted to look like wood. And there, above the Grammophon, lined up on open shelves, are the ten-inch discs of the Fonotipia-brand. With a cry of joy I peruse the labels with their angels and lyres. Here is Léon Escalais, as Eleazar in *La Juive*, J. F. Halévy composer. And here? Vannutelli in selections from Oscar Straus. Also *Gli Ugonotti*, of Monsieur Meyerbeer. Fear not: in this collection are works by non-Jews. Par exemple, Gounod. Elisa Petri (what a dish—a pretty pun, Uncle Al) sings "O mia lira immortale" from the opera—well, am I not a grown man? May I not disclose without blushes the name of this work? *Sappho!* Yes, the perverse Poetin from the isle of *Lesbos*! Hee-hee.

"What? Is my glass empty? Signor Cinzano, welcome. Did I mention that Rob Roy was a hero of Scotland?"

Fittz! Futtz!

My feline is once again imitating a Spürhund—ridge fur fluffed, tail stump erect, one paw, of the three remaining to her, raised. To what does she direct my attention? Ah! It is the Fido, a.k.a. "Nipper," on the label of *Die Stimme Seines Herrn*.

Fizz! Footz!

"Ha! Ha! Ha! Silly little Kätzchen! This is only a painting of a dog. He listens to His Master's Voice. Look: he is on every disc of the Deutsche Grammophon collection."

So speaking, I pluck to my bosom a disc of the k. und k. Infanterie Regiment Nr. 4 Band. How lively their "Toreador Marsch." What next? Here is an old favorite. The Tanzpalast Orchester playing "Oh, You Beautiful Doll." Room in my arms for one more: the Grammophon Orchester in the stirring "Arabische National-Hymne." Oh! Musik! Gods of Musik! These tunes that come to me now are not embedded in the shellac of the recordings but within the crevices of my cranium.

What do you say? A few fingers more? Down to the hatch!

Time to dance, darling! Turning and turning, as fast as a disc on the Plattenteller of the Monarch itself. Eighty-two revolutions each minute. Round and round! An interesting factotum: shellac comes from a beetle. Tanz, Leib Goldkorn. Tanz, Hymena. Young again!

Für Weh und Wunden
gab sie Balsam

What? Who's there? Who utters these words? Looking this way, looking that, I see no one, save for Hymena, mouth wide, palette pink, singing in what is my native tongue.

für böse Gifte
Gegengift

Clever cat! To have learned these R. Wagner words. Does she know those that come next?

für tiefstes Weh
für höchstes Leid

What is this? I hear not only the cadence from this talented tabby, but the sonorities of an entire Orchester. Are these the delusions of a man who has imbibed, I confess it, a fistful of fingers? What's next? Rosen Elefanten? Wait! It is not the room that is spinning but the disc on the Monarch-model machine. In my dance I have bumped against it. It is not my Liebchen who is singing but—Ja! This vibrato. This crystal tone: the great Lilli Lehmann. *Tristan.* Act One. Scene Four. Isolde orders Brangäne to—

Heavens! The voice drawls to a stop. I leap to the machine. I grasp the—what do you call it? Oh, addled Uncle Al! The crank. The handle. *Der Kurbelgriff!* There! A turn! There! Another!

gab sie den Todestrank

The death potion! Worse than absinthe! In the golden goblet!

Der Tod nun sag ihr Dank!

Futz! Fwatz!
No, no, honey-heart. Do not fear. You'll see! This is not a
death drink. No, it is a Liebestrank! Love! A drink to love! I
have seen it in person. I played a part. Listen! Listen, my kitten,
to my tale.

THE YEAR IN QUESTION is 1907. In that Jahr, Lieutenant
General R. Baden-Powell founds the Boy Scout movement. In
America, Oklahoma becomes—hmmm, just one minute, Judge
Gitlitz, Your Worship—the forty-sixth state. Inhabitants, in
spite of late entry into the Union, known as Sooners. Also intro-
duction, in the state of Pennsylvania, of Hershey's "Kisses."
Mee-yow!
Ha! Ha! She knows these are made of *milk* chocolate.
Now let us fly on our magic carpet all the way to the capital
of our beloved empire: 1907, Vienna, where Jews and gentiles—
not to make any comparisons—have just been given the freedom to vote. It was in that same city ninety-eight years ago that
I saw a *Tristan*, whose Isolde was sung by the same fair-haired
soprano whose voice—let us wind up the Monarch motor once
more—comes back to us now from the land of the dead.
On the day of this event, a bright and sunny one, a father
and his large-eared son could be seen riding along the Schubertring in an open-air tram. On a youth from provincial Iglau,
what an impression! The many ladies in hip hoops and puff
sleeves, with visible chests. The men in caps and derbies and
fezzes. The lurch of the red-painted car on its metal tracks.
Where are the horses? This question the boy put to the man.
"Ho! Ho! Diese Trambahn ist elektrifiziert!" True, as evi-
denced by the lightning bolts that snapped along the wires

above, and the smell of lightning, like burnt cork, that wafted down from those same taut strands. Through the glassless windows anyone could see—two, three, five, ten: too many to count—the many Personnenwagen, weaving back and forth along the streets, leaving here a cloud of white steam, there a cloud of black smoke. Poor horses! Goodbye, fair dobbin! The century to come belongs not to you.

A clang. A double clang. The car came to a stop. The father took the son by the collar, as a cat might a kitten, and the two passengers stepped from the platform to the ground. Surprise: it is I, little Leib, on my first trip to Vienna, and the gentleman with the moustache and woolen waistcoat is none other than the putative père. We left the Schubertring and turned onto a street named for Pestalozzi, whose educational principles I had already encountered in my kindergarten class, and then on to a small side street that took its name from the confirmed bachelor Immanuel Kant.

At the third house, a tall, narrow one, I squinted up at the brass nameplate: J-U-L.—I spelled out, only to have G.G. speed through the words. JULIUS J. EPSTEIN: HERR PROFESSOR DOKTOR.

All musical Vienna, and all Iglauans too, knew of this famed friend of Brahms, mentor to the greats, and professor of piano at the Conservatorium, now retired.

"Teacher of Ignaz Brüll!" I piped. "Who composed *Die Bettler von Samarkand*!"

"Ja," answered the owner of hundreds of hectares of hops. "Also teacher of Gustav Mahler."

Something in the way he ground his molars at the word *Mahler*, and cracked his knuckles too, made me shiver. With his thumb pad he pressed the button beneath the name of the pedagogue-pianist and, at the answering signal, led me into the building.

Up we went on the stone staircase, one flight, then another;

suddenly, silently, and smoothly too, the lift came down. I heard, from the père, a gasp, like a puncture in a rubberized tire, and just had time to see a blond-haired woman—wide, black-rimmed eyes, long nose of the aristocratic type, and manly chin—press the palm of her hand against the cabin glass, before she dropped away. On the landing, Gaston Goldkorn paused to mop, with his handkerchief square, his brow; then we walked onward to the topmost floor.

The man who ushered us into his rooms was small, bent, semi-bald, and as white as the keys he had depressed for much of his seventy-five years. "Aha," he declared upon seeing Leib in lederhosen. "Here is the Wunderkind!"

Proud putative père: "This Junge plays two-handed piano and is known throughout the town of Iglau for woodwind expertise."

Here G. Goldkorn squeezed my shoulder, a signal that I should remove from between my suspender straps my instrument, a panpipe similar to the pinkillo of Peru, on which I could produce six notes on the diatonic scale, the last of which would cause die Hausfrauen of the Jewish quarter to run to their kitchens, certain that their kettles were a-boil.

Julius J.: "This is a fine, sturdy lad. Such ears! Such lips! And from Iglau! I remember the day, it was more than thirty years ago, that another boy from this town arrived at my studio to audition for the Konservatorium. And tonight that former fifteen-year-old will at the Hofoper conduct the *Tristan* of Richard Wagner. Question number one of my exam: Of whom do I speak?"

L.G.: "Hmmm. Hmmm. Humperdinck! Composer of—"

J.J.: "Ha, ha. I mean little Gustav. Gustav Mahler."

The molars ground. The knuckles cracked. The père pushed me forward. "Herr Professor Doktor. I leave you this afternoon my precious treasure. My only Sohn. The Moravian

Mozart, people say. I return at five p.m. Here, a small token"—impossible not to see how a thousand-Kronen banknote passed from one hand, tanned, to another, pale. "And now, goodbye. Make music! Auf Wiedersehen!"

My father, the good Gaston, moved to the door. I meant to trod after, but he quickly closed it behind him.

"So, my little woodwinder, we shall now hear whether you can play for J. J. Epstein the way the famed J. J. Quantz played for Frederick the Great. Please to follow me."

Here the pianist led the way into a small room overlooking the Kantgasse. The afternoon sun streamed through its open windows. A black-lacquered Bösendorfer took up most of the space, along with a small round table, covered with a rug and a piece of the white lace named for the Englishman Doiley.

"Gieselinde!" Herr Esptein called. "We shall have a tea. Mit Butterkeksen!"

"Ja, ja, Herr Doktor," answered a female voice, from deep within the apartment.

As the snow-white foot of a woman slips into her patent-leather pump, so did the professor slide onto the bench of his piano. "What should we play together, eh? Perhaps the Sonata in E-flat Major, Bach-Werke-Verzeichnis 1031." So saying, the maestro ran his hands over the keys in an impromptu cadenza: *Glissando, Bruscamente, Furioso.* I stood, immobile, the pipe at my lips. Then the pianist paused, *Smorzando,* and into the hum of the fading notes I threw back my head and cried:

> *Fly in the buttermilk,*
> *Shoo, fly, shoo—*

Da capo:

Fly in the buttermilk,
Shoo, fly, shoo—

"Fantastisch!" exclaimed my accompanist, bringing all ten fingers down on the proper G-minor chord. "Ein amerikanisches Volkslied!"

Then into my panpipe I blew with all my might:

TWORP! TWIPPLE! TWAPFT!

"Gott im Himmel!" cried J. J. Epstein, whose skin, impossibly, grew a shade lighter.

TWAZZIP! TURUPPPT!

From outside, on the Kantgasse, on Christengasse, and even on the distant Beethovenplatz, a variety of canines began to howl. On our own block schnauzers and dachshunds, two boxer-types, and an Affenpinscher ran through doors and leaped from first-story windows. Behind my back I heard a shriek and a crash: Gieselinde, the servant, had spilled the tea service, with shortbreads, onto the hard wooden floor. There was a second crash: the fallboard of the piano had slammed down on the keys. The piano itself, like a living beast, was trembling and making a *sospirando*:

Cow's in the cornfield
What'll I do?

Da capo:

Cow's in the—

"Halt! Bitte! Halt!" The Herr Professor Doktor, seeming, like certain peanut worms, to have not a drop of blood in his body, was crawling beneath his instrument.

Suddenly the entire sky went dark and there was a clapping sound: Had the sun fled from the heavens? No. Flights of crows, numbering thousands, were wheeling over the roofs and chimney pots of Vienna, creating an artificial eclipse. It was then that I noticed something in that unnatural shade: a man and a woman, huddled in a doorway, holding their hands over their ears.

The septuagenarian regained his feet. He leaned out the window—so far, in fact, that, like a desperate man in a burning building, it seemed he would jump. Instead, he called toward the couple on the Kantgasse:

"Zurückkommen! Now! At once! Do you hear me? Kommen Sie schnell!"

The man and woman turned; each looked up. To my amazement I saw that it was the lady in the lift and the putative père.

"Bitte! Bitte! I beg you. Look. Look! See what I am doing! I am destroying the Geld! I don't want it! I refuse to take it!"

True to his word the professor was tossing pieces of the thousand-Kronen note into the air like so much confetti. The père, adjusting his waistcoat, blinked upward, against the sun that had just come out from the cloud of crows. His mouth was open, though he said not a word.

"So hören Sie doch! Listen!" J.J.E. cried imploringly. "The audition is completed. Come back at once. I make a promise. I take an oath. I shall recommend him to the Akademie. I swear it! Once at age fifteen, he will be admitted. Woodwind section. One hundred percent guarantee. In Gottes Namen! Take this child away!"

Two things occurred: the blond-haired woman ran up the street in the direction of Johannesgasse, and Gaston, glowering, moved back toward our building, inside of which the Herr Professor Doktor, the maidservant in black skirt and white apron, the Bösendorfer, and the boy all stood motionless, listening to the heavy tread of his feet upon the stairs.

ON LINDENSTRASSE LILLI LEHMANN has fallen silent, as if the potion she had swallowed were poison after all. The motor on the Monarch model once more needs winding. The centurian ignores the crank. Instead he addresses Hymena, who cocks her only ear to hear Her Master's Voice:

"And that, my dear, is how Leib Goldkorn came to enter, and become a Graduate of, the Akademie für Musik, Philosophie, und darstellende Kunst."

IT HAS GROWN dark in the Musiksalon. The sun, it seems, has set on the Czechs and their republic. In response, Hymena yawns, and in a friendly reflex I yawn back. I feel of a sudden the weight of my years: fatigue, hunger, and bladder twinges. First things, as my fellow New Yorkers say, first. The W.C., I know, is in the far wing, off the kitchen. With Hymena at my heels I retrace my steps to the johnny, where the Tiefspültoilette is just as I remember it, with a tank and chain at the top and a pattern of roses along the circumference of the seat. Suffice to say that in mere minutes I stand with Pan Johnson wrested from the depths of my S. Kleins and held in what since earliest adolescence has been an overhand grip. Yet nothing occurs. The urge is great—mein Gott!, like a tide pulled by the strength of the moon—but not a drop appears.

Mee-now?

Ah: the cause. Impossible to make excretions when another pair of eyes, especially female ones, looks on. A case for Krafft-

Ebing, Baron von. I put out the little miss. Consummation achieved. With finishing touch.

And now to bed. The stairs loom above me as the Himalayas once did before Sir Edmund Hillary. I surmount them. At last, the upper floor. To the left, down the hallway, is the Hauptschlafzimmer, where, on the four-poster, under a cloud of gauze, G. Goldkorn and the former Falma Krupnick engaged in connubials. Once only: note Yakhne. But on the second occasion, Ha! Ha! Ha! Instead, it was G. Mahler who performed that act of pollination. Mad for love!

Let us turn our backs on this scene of Fleischeslust and move down the hall to the right—past the door of that older sister, beneath which the exhaust of the Liliputanos oft curled; past the door of younger sister, Minchke, behind which she transposed her beauty spots; and past Eliska's closed portal, which, though stout, could not muffle the nighttime moans of self-befriendingness. Thus we arrive at the room of the home's only youth.

My heart is a-quiver as my hand touches the knob of the door. "Open," *says me*. No longer funny. Odd, how a joke can be told only once. Let us think of a new one. *Confucius say: Woman who fly upside down have crack up.* Ha! Ha! Ha! Get it? *Crack up?*

Alas, I can no longer with digressions put off the moment of entry. Voilà! My boyhood room is no more changed than the parlor below. There is my bed, a Biedermeier, with its spread of taffeta nubs. Wearily, I fall upon it—Whoops! Hoop-la! You too, my tabby?—and stare in wonder at the two poster images that after all these many decades remain affixed to the opposite wall.

There, to the left, the reproduction of Old Shatterhand riding atop Halatitla, *Lightning*, while beside him gallops his blood brother, Winnetou, upon—amazing how this name has lain in storage among my cortex coils—Iltschi, *Wind*. By these two "Westmen," an Apache with a feather in his hair and the German paleface, I was taught a lesson not available in the Akademie: We are all, Gentile and Jew, Afrikaner and Esquimaux, Trobriand Islander and Swedish masseur—all, in this adventure of life, Blutsbrüder.

And to the right the rotogravure depiction of RRS *Discovery*, locked in the grip of Antarctic ice. She was launched in that year of note 1901, commanded by the greatest of all heroes, R. F. Scott. Beaten to his prize, the southern pole, he and his men suffered as few had before them: frostbite, snow blindness, scurvy. Exhaustion of provisions: the meat of the ponies, the meat of the dogs, Pinguinfleisch, and plum duff. The final storm: marooned in their tents, day after day, night after night. *Gentlemen! Do not fall asleep! Pinch each other's cheeks!* Alack, all strength ebbs away. Last written words by Scott to his wife: "What tales you would have had for the boy." And for all boys, in all nations, including the one in Iglau who has all his life admired such English pluck. God save the Queen!

> *Westwärts*
> *schweift der Blick*

What's this? Who's there? Someone is singing. Has the Monarch model self-started again? No. Not possible. This is the voice of a lusty young man.

> *Ostwärts*
> *streicht das Schiff*

Das Schiff? What ship? The *Discovery? Der fliegende Holländer?* Is Leib Goldkorn a-doze? *Gentlemen! Do not fall asleep!* Our pemmican is buried nearby. Ach: I am confusing past and present, one ship with another. So, Hymena, honey, as the commander staved off that drowsy death by telling his tale, so I shall complete the story of that fateful day in Vienna when, after my successful Julius J. Epstein audition, the putative père rewarded his supposed son with an excursion to the kaiserlich-königliche Hof-Operntheater. The opera that night was *Tristan und Isolde.*

Frisch weht der Wind

Yes, *fresh blows the wind* that takes the lonely sailor and the kidnapped Isolde away from her beloved Ireland, home of *Book of Kells* and *Book of Records* (most number of bikini waxes in four hours: 262, but, ha-ha-ha, who is counting?). Potatoes. And Jewish mayor of Dublin. Believe it or not! But we are speaking of an ancient land in ancient times.

Irische Maid
du wilde, minnige Maid!

Yes, the tenor misses his wild Irish maid—as do I my frolicsome Finn. Let us climb back on our Persian rug. *Carpet! Take me to Vienna! To the Hofoper! Away!*

SCENE FOUR

TRISTAN

*At the opera Leib enounters first a youth, who
offers him sweets; and then his natural father,
who puts him and his panpipe onstage.
Whether or not it was a dream, he wakes
in the arms of his kissing cousin.*

OUR SEATS THAT night were in the two-Kronen Promenade. Here we have a manner of speaking, since in this all-male section it was required to stand, as if in tribute to Franz Joseph, whose Imperial Box was directly over our heads. Yes, His Apostolischen Majestät was just three meters above me, though of course he could have no inkling that the prizewinner on whom he would come to bestow a Rudall & Rose model was but three meters below. In similar fashion, how could I have known that all the things that so dazzled the child—the crush of the crowds, the tuning of instruments, the gleam of the Kaiserstein staircases, the gold and ivory and ruby-red plush of the boxes—would become commonplace to the already-balding Graduate, once he arrived daily at the Staatsoper to perform his duties as Glockenspieler and Dudelsackpfeifer.

Ah, that triple chandelier! Its thousand lights! Would that the Americans had dropped their bombs on Dachau, on Auschwitz, thus freeing many families along with my own, instead of on the same front railing at which Gaston Golkorn had cleared enough room for me to see the ship that was carrying the Irish princess across the sea.

"Das Schiff, Papa! Das grosse Schiff!"

"Shhhhhhh!"

The Viennese about us began to hiss, even as the stout lady on the stage asked a musical question:

Sag, wo sind wir?

"On a big boat!" came the piping reply. "With a sailor!"

Again the hissing sound, as if from faulty steam pipes.

I looked at the singer—white-gowned and bejeweled—who was praying that a sea storm would wreck her ship and drown all aboard: those fair locks of hair, parted in the center; the charcoal rings around the eyes; the meat-eater's jowls—

"Look, Papa! It's the lady in the lift!"

The whole Promenade seemed to erupt:

"Throw him out!"

"Who let in that beknackter Jude?"

"Das ist ein Skandal!"

Even the Leutnante and Oberleutnante, who only had to pay ten hellers for admittance, began to bang their scabbards against the brass rods that separated their section from ours.

"Arrest him!"

"Wo ist der Platzanweiser?"

"Ja! Ja! der Platzanweiser!"

But the usher, an old man whose thin neck rose from a stiff collar, was already on his way. "What's this? Speaking? Speaking ist streng verboten."

Here a young man, still in his teens, addressed me. "What a pretty boy. Does he want sweets? Here they are." From the pocket of his topcoat he withdrew what turned out to be a

Kaiserschmarrn with raisins and powdered sugar, which he unwrapped and held out in the palms of his hands. Immediately my mouth filled with a syrup. "Now hush. Be still. Fill up your lovely little mouth."

Like an Eichörnchen, a sort of chipmunk, I did. Lost in that sugary trance, I paid little attention to the dispute between the soprano in white and the tenor in chain mail: She wants to speak to him, he won't speak to her; she's going to marry his uncle, but instead she forces her maid to prepare a Todestrank; and then the princess and the knight have a big argument, all the time with violins sawing and a hullabaloo in the horns—in short, not the sort of story that would capture the imagination of a boy who had already read the tale of how Old Shatterhand killed a grizzly with a single blow of his fist.

Nun wieder nimm das Schwert

I lifted my head. What did this Tristan say? Ein *Schwert*? A sword!

und führ es sicher und fest

"Papa! Help! He wants her to kill him!"

Once more: the hissing Huns; the angry soldiers; and, from what seemed a continent away, down in the orchestra, the conductor turning, shading his eyes, staring up at the source of the disturbance. Then the young teen—he had a forelock that fell across half his brow, though he was too young to grow, under his nose, more than a few hairs of a moustache—invited me to dig into the jacket pocket of his salt-and-pepper suit. What a treasure: half a Salzburger Nockerl. Light as air! Not only that, but it seemed that my outburst had caused the couple onstage to change their minds, since the Isolde took the sword from the Tristan and drove its point into the planks of the ship instead of the ribs of his body.

Auf das Tau!

That was the cry from the shipboard sailors, much like that of our own naval cadets when they sing their own C. Zimmerman anthem—

Den Anker lichten!
"Anchors away!"

Now came the moment of terror. The lift lady persuades the bold knight to drink a goblet of forgiveness, which, with an interesting rhyme, he brings to his lips:

Vergessens güt'ger Trank
dich trink ich sonder Wank

"No! Herr Tristan! It's poison! There's poison inside!"
The whole crowd began to shout louder than claqueurs do for their favorites. This time the conductor actually lowered his baton, while His Majesty's Armeeoffiziere rattled the brass bars, as if they meant to leap into the two-Kronen section and throttle the miscreant in their midst. Now the teenage youth drew closer, holding open the pocket of his speckled trousers. "Here, my handsome friend. Your treat is inside."
With eagerness I groped in the depths. Yes, something was there, warm and tubular, like a quark cheese strudel, though in consistency resembling a Thüringer Wurst.

Süsseste Maid!

This exclamation rises from Tristan, who has not been poisoned after all, unless one counts as venom the potion that forces one to fall in love.

Trautester Mann!

Thus answers Isolde, as they drop into each other's arms.

At that instant my own arm was seized. It was the elderly usher.

Der Platzanweiser: "You. Troublemaker. Provokateur. Come with me."

He sought to pull me away, but my right hand remained clamped on the delicacy, from which Schlagobers had begun to ooze.

Now not two, but three voices cry out in ecstatic joy:

Tristan:

Isolde:

Young Wagner fan:

Liebeslust!

The Imperial official—for that he was, if only a lowly usher—yanked me away. The putative père, who all this time had not removed his gaze from the two-chinned soprano, started to come after.

"Nein," said the Platzanweiser. "The boy. Not you."

Onward sails the ship, into the port. Down goes the gangplank.

Kornwall, heil!

shouts the crew.

To the sound of the trumpets and the rumble of the descending curtain, the old usher and the young boy—not yet six years of age—abandoned the Promenade.

ZWEITER AUFZUG

Or, in plain English, Act Two.

One night, while King Mark and his knights are off on a hunting party, the lovers meet beneath what appears to be a gigantic lime tree.

Tristan: *Isolde! Geliebte!*

Isolde: *Tristan! Geliebter!*

And so forth and so on, mit Küssen, mit Umarmungen, the sort of kisses and hugs that Old Shatterhand would bestow only on an Apache blood brother or, from time to time, his horse. Nor were the melodies what we might call toe-tappers, with the peppiness of a tunesmith like V. A. Bely, winner of the Stalin Prize.

Still, I was not for a single moment bored. This was because of the bespectacled conductor, who had arranged for me to sit, half hidden, at the side of the stage. From there I could see him waving what seemed a half dozen arms, demanding more power from the brass, less volume from the strings, shaking his baton at the errant tympanist, and now and then pronouncing for the two lovers the words they had forgotten: *Der Liebe nur zu leben*—"to live only for love."

Strange, the laws of genetics: Were there ever a man and a boy less alike than the conductor in his armchair and the lad on his three-legged stool? Thin-lipped and thick. Elfin-eared and Dumbo-esque. A full head of wild-streaming hair and, even at that tender age, a telltale thinning of the downiness, precursor of the Laufflächenauswaschung—let us not mince words: *bald spot*—to come. Nose: aquiline. Nose: button. Yet here were—have you guessed it?—father, G.M., and, L.G., son. What linked them ran far deeper than appearance: a river of musicality, a heart filled with song.

Of course, I did not know of our kinship at the time, though I believe I can say, one hundred years later, that I had a premonition. Yes, I sensed a greater fellow feeling with this stranger, his passion, his hypnotic baton, the flash of light from the lenses of his pince-nez, than I had ever experienced with the putative père, even on those occasions when, at a good harvest, he played see-me, see-me-not among the noble hops, or, in the icy Iglawa, playfully held my head under the water.

Uh-oh: the dawn is coming—and with it Mark, the King, who discovers that he has been betrayed by his most faithful friend—a moment that could not but recall to me the scene in which Old Shatterhand was tricked by land-grabbers into thinking that his Apache brother had led the massacre of a family of Anglo-Saxons. Luckily, my hero soon found out the truth; but when King Mark confronts Tristan, demanding to know why he has brought on this disgrace—

Warum mir diese Schmach?

—the tenor tells the bass he cannot answer:

O, König, das
kann ich dir nicht sagen.

Suddenly the villain, Melot, challenges the knight:

Verräter! Ha!

"Watch out, Tristan!" comes a childish treble from the wings. "He's got a sword!"

The brave youth hears the warning cry and draws his own weapon:

Wehr dich, Melot!

There is a terrific fight, which might have come from the pages of *Winnetou, der rote Gentleman*—except in this battle it is our hero, Tristan, who falls wounded to the ground.

The shrill voice of a child: "Help him! Get up, Tristan! Get up!"

Alas, instead of the knight rising, the curtain of the k. k. Hof-Operntheater came slowly down.

Bravo! Bravo!

For the first time in my life I fell beneath the sway of the crowd. What force it had! What magnetic power! Under its spell, I slipped from my stool and began to make my way forward, and still forward, toward the hypnotic sounds.

But first I bumped into Isolde. She alone had remained behind the curtain, though the audience was now shouting her name: *Lilli! Lilli!*

She paid no heed until a single voice, arising from the wings, made her turn. "Lilli! Meine Liebe!"

I turned too. It was the putative père! I started to run to him, as did the lady in Isolde's gown. A hand, however, gripped my shoulder. It was the teenager, the youth in the salt-and-pepper—and now sugary—suit.

"Time for more treats," he said, while brushing the forelock from his rightward eye.

Then another hand knocked his away. "Who allowed this fellow to enter? Wächter, take this gentleman out."

The speaker, I saw, was the conductor of the opera. Now he put both hands on my suspendered shoulders.

"Guten Abend, my little friend. What is your name? Wait. Let me guess. *Leib,* is it not? My geliebter Leib." He smiled down on me, his glasses winking in the light. "I cannot tell you what a joy it is for me to meet you at last. Goodness, you have a head exactly like an egg! And a musical prodigy too! No, no: do not deny it. *The Mozart of Iglau.* I see you have your panpipe. It will give me much pride to hear you play it tonight."

"I want my Vater. Papa! Gaston!"

But the grip of the conductor remained firm.

"Nein, mein Kind. Everything is arranged. Your, ah, Vater will remain with our Sopran until the morning. You and I will spend those hours getting to know each other. Lilli . . . !"

Here he called out, over the sounds of the shifting scenery, to the woman I had first seen in the lift.

Then he turned once more to me. "Leib, I want you to meet our wonderful Isolde—"

"Ja!" shouted my new friend, the pastry provider, as he continued to struggle with the attendants. "Eine Jüdin! A Jewess!"

The blond-headed soprano, with a half goiter, came forward.

"Lilli, I have told you about our famous prodigy. You will perform together tonight. My child, this is the famed Lilli Lehmann. You will be the Shepherd who summons her from afar with the notes from your flute."

Here the maestro hummed a rustic melody, a C-sharp, a B-flat, a D. A simple tune to charm wayward sheep. "Have you committed it to memory?" he asked, and started to hum once again.

I put up my hand to stop him. "Alles ist hier," I answered, pointing to my oval dome.

"Such a genius!" cried the singer, bending to give me a hug.

Lost in her arms, half overcome by the oak-moss smell from her "Jicky"-brand perfume, I glanced offstage to where the père was watching the two of us with strangely glittering eyes.

The next thing I knew, a stagehand had thrown a shepherd's cloak over my back, and a second such Bühnenarbeiter plucked me from the boards and deposited me on a huge rock that, I could not help but notice, overlooked the distant horizon and the sea. I gazed about me in the dimming light; everyone had disappeared. I was alone with the wounded Tristan. From the far side of the curtain I could hear the string instruments beginning the prelude to—

DRITTER AUFZUG

—that is to say, Act Three.

The curtain went up to reveal a second sea—of faces, thousands of Viennese, some with moustaches beneath their noses, some with pearls around their necks. Just below me the Direktor of the kaiserlichen und königlichen Hof-Operntheater slowly beat his baton, with one finger, to emphasize the pianissimo, at his lips. That baton slowed further, and further still. It stopped.

Still in his armchair, the conductor was staring at me. A pause. My instrument was in my hand, but it felt as if the entire weight of the Bösendorfer Grand that had accompanied me only hours earlier was pressing down upon it. What was that first note? My mind had gone blank. The pause grew longer. As all of those men and women ranged below and above me, tier upon tier, with impatience cleared their throats, it was as though the flock were calling the Shepherd, *Umäh, ummäh-h, mäh-h-h,* rather than the Shepherd, C-sharp, B-flat, D, calling the sheep.

The Direktor lifted his face toward the boy on the rock and, just as he had prompted the forgetful singers, he now, by soundlessly moving his lips, prompted me:

Du spielst schöne Musik, mein herrliches Kind.

I raised the panpipe to my lips.

TWA—

"Pssst. Pssst."

What was that? It sounded like eine Schlange among the sheep.

"Pssst!" Once more that hissing. I glanced down. There, hidden by my plaster promontory, a figure was slithering toward me on its belly. Was this the reptile from *Das Rheingold*? Or one of the snakes from *Die Zauberflöte*? I looked again. It was the professor of piano! Epstein! Julius J.!

"Nicht! he hissed. "Don't play! Not a note! There will be a Katastrophe!"

My breath, as you can imagine, caught in my throat.

"Mein Sohn." That was the conductor, who rose from his armchair and aimed the point of his baton at the shepherd boy. "Spiel Musik."

Again I brought my instrument to my lips.

TUF—

"Look. Look what I have for you." Those words came not from the spot where J.J.E was still squirming forward, but from the other side of the rock. "Komm zu mir." The teen! The young Wagnerian! He was crawling toward me on his hands and knees. "Palatschinken! Krapfen! Rum balls! Nut kisses!"

The pianist grasped one of my legs. The youth clutched the other. Both pulled in opposite directions.

"Hilfe!" I cried, for fear of being torn in two.

The dying Tristan, on the far side of the rock, raised his head. "*Was ist hier los?*"

Then the familiar rumble of the descending curtain drowned out every word.

Difficult to describe the chaos that ensued. A stagehand ripped the cloak from my shoulders. Another stagehand pulled me from my perch. Epstein, a Brahmsian, and the Wagnerite were swinging their fists at each other. A bass player ran across the boards, dragging his viol behind him. From out of the wings the prow of the ship nudged forward, then drew back again. Suddenly Herr Mahler, the conductor of the orchestra, strode forward and threw up his hands, as if demanding a diminuendo from all.

"Ladies and gentlemen, I have endured my last insult. I announce for all to hear that this will be my final season in Vienna. I have decided to accept a position with the Metropolitan Opera of New York."

"Gut! Exzellent!" So cried the fellow in the salt-and-pepper suit. "Let the Yid go to the Yids. We shall create a Vienna that is judenrein!"

G.M.: "It is true, I shall not miss such Antisemitismus. What I shall miss is not seeing this lad"—and here the Direktor pointed to none other than the five-year-old version of myself— "grow up to be hailed as the musician he was born to become. Yes, I would have liked to hear such a great artist. But my solace is that he, and he alone, shall bring to the world the only opera I have ever attempted. Yes, he alone!"

With that, the composer moved directly before me, holding a thick leather-bound book in his arms. "Here is my life. Here is your life. Here is the life of our people. Take it, my prince.

Guard it. It is the only copy that exists in all the world." So saying, he thrust the weighty volume into my hands and moved back to the pit, where, only a moment later, the violins and violas, and then the violincellos, took up the notes of the prelude once more. I barely had time to glance at what was written on the cover—*Rübezahl*, or *The Turnip Counter*—when Herr Salz-und-Pfeffer wrenched himself free of his captors' grasp, ran forward, and snatched the manuscript score from my hands.

"Stop him!" everyone cried.

"Don't let him get away!"

I saw the père dash forward and begin to wrestle with the youth for the prize of the book.

"Give it to me!" I cried. "Give it to me! It's mine!"

In my short pants and peasant shoes, I struggled to join the fray; but before I could do so the Isolde, L. Lehmann, enfolded me once more in her full-fleshed arms.

"*Great artist*," she said. "Did you hear the words of our maestro?"

"I heard: *great artist*."

"Leibie," she said. "Acordar. Wake up."

"*Accordion?* No, panpipe. *A born musician.* That's what he said."

The great soprano's golden hair fell over my face; the fair ringlets tickled my nose.

"Ah-h-h," I sighed, even as I noticed that some other musician had begun playing the Shepherd's tune. "*Chooo!*"

"Bom! At last you wake. You have been having em sonho."

What? A dream? How could that be? I felt Isolde's hair on my cheek, my brow. I smelled her "Jicky" perfume. But hold: this hair was not blond but black. I sat upright. I was not at the Royal and Imperial Opera House of Vienna. I was on Lindenstrasse 5. Beside me Hymena lay on her back, eyes rolled upward, three limbs extended, with a pink tongue hanging from her mouth. Cat nap.

"A dream?" I echoed. "Ein Traum?"

"Sim! You say, many times, artista excelente, artista excelente. And Músico nato. Born musician. Músico nato."

"A dream?" I said once more. No, no: it could not be a dream. All these things actually occurred: Gustav Mahler departed the k. k. Hof-Operntheater that same year. Indeed, anyone can check the date of the famed L. Lehmann *Tristan*, an event still talked about in the coffeehouses of Vienna: the twenty-seventh of May, 1907. There are almost certainly fellow centurians, like myself not under the spell of Uncle Al, who to this day recall the little Shepherd Boy too frightened to play his pipes.

But then who is this woman of Latin mien? Is she seeking, with the Graduate, an expurgation? And why the patois in Portuguese? Could it be the Bombshell?

Why, why, why, why, why when I feel your touch

Madam Miranda?

My heart starts to beat, to beat the band?

No! A similar Senhorita. Madam Mengele! Minchke's blood in her veins. The grandniece of truly yours. Ah, ah, ah: these Goldkorn family lips! Ooooh: these distinguishable mams. No doubt. No dream. It is my kissing cousin!

SCENE FIVE

KINFOLK

*Leib discovers more survivors on the
Krupnick side of the family.*

IN THE SAGA of my favorites, the Finns, the hero Kullervo
experiences an eructation with his own sister. Such infatuations are common throughout all the folk of the world.
Among my own people, Rebekah, "a virgin, neither had any
man known her"—note how scripture oft says the same thing
twice—married Isaac, her cousin. Ditto, as Rabbi Goldiamond
taught us, with Jacob and Rachel and also Jacob and Leah, who
was not a looker like her sister.

Need I mention the fun-loving Greeks? The Coreligionist
has brought much attention to Oedipus and his dam, though
one must admit that cohabitation did not end well. On the
other hand—and here we rely on the lessons of Professor Pergam at the Akademie für Musik, Philosophie, und darstellende
Kunst—we have the example of the joyous marriage of Zeus
and his sister Hera, who so quickly pulled her breast from the
nursing Hercules that she created—ha, ha, ha, how my still-
living classmate, Willi Wimpfeling, laughed at this tale—the
Milky Way.

Oh, you playful gods! But is it not on earth as it is in heaven?
What of Cleopatra and her multiple brothers? Caligula and all
three of his sisters? Olden times, you say? Close to my heart we

have Franz Joseph I, bestower of the Rudall & Rose, and Elisa-
beth of Bavaria, a union of first cousins all too likely to lead, as
with the whole Hapsburg line, to such inbreeding, with larger
and larger lips, that Charles II of Spain could not chew his own
food. A sudden thought: perhaps this is why our own Bonnie
Prince Charles turned from a Number 10 like Princess Di and
in a fit of hereditary madness wished himself to be a Tampax-
brand inside the privies of, let's face it, a plain Jane.

What are we to make of such shenanigans? Many readers
will in disgust turn away. That is because of the teachings of
the muftis and monks and mother superiors. I do not exempt
my own religion: "None of you," writes the hapless (see Isaac,
see Jacob) Reb Leviticus, "shall approach to any that is near of
kin to him, to uncover their nakedness." All these thoughts,
pro and con, race through my mind in the few seconds it takes
my relative from Rio to perform on my body what is either a
Brazilian rhumba or what my own half Finn would call a Laplandic dance.

What a dilemma for Leib Goldkorn! On the one hand is his
epicurian nature. On the other are the deeply ingrained teachings of the mother superiors, along with the Goldiamond doc-
trine. In such a situation what is a man, and one with hair on
his shoulders, to do?

"Oh! Oooo! Ohhh! You the pai! Meu papai. Big poppa!"

Answer, friends, to the enigma! My *papei* was not the père.
That is, Gustav was not Gaston. Ergo, Minchke, the grandmother of this busty Bombshell, was only my *half*-sister. That
means we have the green light! Gracious: it seems that Senhor
Johnson has gotten the message too.

"Oooo. Muito grande! Imenso!"

"Sim, senhorita. Ha! Ha! Ha! Quatro Americano inches.
Almost."

"Volumoso! Oitenta milímetros! Enorme!"

"Let's see, that's, hmmm, twenty-five to the inch, divide the—"

But before I can complete the exercise in arithmetics, I begin to experience, believe it or not, Mr. Ripley, an indisputable peppercorn sensation.

"Meu herói. Meu namorado—"

What a busy bee, this Brazilian. Down go the Stutchkoff gabardines. Away with the S. Klein drawers. Now she opens the gates of Hades above me and begins to lower herself, bit by bit, as a cloud might descend upon the steeple that rises above a Christian town.

"Ha, ha, miss. I see London. I see France—"

What's this? A pause? A hesitation? Fear, no doubt, for the maidenhead.

"Tío Leibie, you do what I ask? Um pequeno favor?"

"Anything!"

"Sign esto documento."

What was that in her hand? The parchment! Yes, the map of Iglau. With the fields of Hopfen. A bit irregular, this: to introduce, during the throes of romance, a moment of mercantilism. What say, Watson: time for caution, eh?

"Yes! Ja! I will! Sim! Where? There? Show me die gestrichelte Linie. That means, auf Englisch, the dotted line."

All the while I am in desperation patting the pockets of my lumberman-type jacket, and patting them again, until I find the Waterman pen.

"Here it is!" I cry, and with my teeth tear off the cap.

"Prenome" she says leaning forward so that our infernals actually came into contact. "E sobrenome."

Action in the Netherlands; simultaneously the implement for penmenship and that for propagation run out of ink.

"Tolo! Bobo! Idiota! Velho impotente!"

The maiden, it seems, is concerned about the status of her

Jungfernhäutchen. "Calm yourself, my dear. In spite of emanations, all is intact in the zone of the hymen."

At the mention of her name, my feline companion awakens. She rubs herself in affection against the Bombshell, who is engaged in repacking her mams into her bustier.

Mee-owwww!

With a kick of her high-heeled shoe she sends Hymena flying. I see in her eyes a coldness, in the line of her lips a hardness, which in the whirlwind of passion I have not noticed before. Sharp incisors too.

"Senhorita Josefina, do not think I was yesterday geboren. No wonder you wished me to sign the document. If I had, you would be the sole heir to the hops. The Queen of Jihlava. I am on to your game, missy."

"Not sole heir."

"What? You have in Brazil einen Bruder? Eine Schwester? Is she"—once a charmer, always a charmer—"as nubile as you?"

"Nao. There is no one. I am uma filha único."

"Then I am the master here. Lord of all the manors. Ha! Ha! Not one of them rent-stabilized!"

At that moment I hear, from outside my old bedroom, a sound—a knocking, a murmur of voices. I cover my nakedness, as the author of Leviticus might say, and make my way to the window. Hymena is already there, standing on her single hind leg. We both note that a crowd has gathered in the dark of night. Some have electrical torches, and by their light I can see the familiar round heads and verdant faces. I can even make out—there, and there—the features of the Polar fraternity.

"Siga-me, velho," commands the ravisher from Rio. "Old man, follow me."

Together we mount the back staircase to the attic, a vacant space around which, in winter months, Yakhne used to run laps and perform physical jerks, and where once I remember opening the door to see Eliska on all fours and the putative père on his knees behind her: "Ha! Ha!" laughed Herr Gaston Goldkorn. "We believe we heard eine Hausmaus!"

A sudden thought: The *Rübezahl*, sole opera of the great Gustav Mahler. Who succeeded in taking it? The putative père? Or the youth in the salt-and-pepper suit? If the former, would he not have wished to safeguard it, dedicated as it was to his supposed son, for posterity? And where else secret it but in this very attic? In some old trunk. Tucked in a rafter. Under a floorboard. And was this, a world treasure, not my true inheritance, more valuable far than all the thousands of hectares that surrounded the town of Jihlava, once Iglau?

Eagerly I follow my grandniece, or Halb-Grossnichte, up the stairs. She raps three times smartly on the portal and then throws it wide. What do I see but a group of men, and one woman, all wrapped in rags, all bearded—no, not the female— and all chanting in a foreign tongue and banging their heads on the floor.

"Zigeuner!" I cry. "Gypsies! Hausbesetzerinnen! Squatters in my house."

The Bombshell: "Nao é sua casa."

"What, madam? Not my house? Am I not the last of the Goldkorns?"

"Sim. But not last of Krupnicks. Krupnicks of Kopitshinets."

With that the entire clan leaps from the floorboards—were they, too, seeking the elusive mouse?—and rushes toward the Graduate. Some kissing my hands. Some clutching my ankles and kissing the uppers of my Thom McAns. "Cousin! Cousin!" is their accented cry. "Our American cousin!"

Can it be? Is this the family of Falma? My mind races back a full one hundred years. Was there not oft a visitor at this very house, a bachelor with his hair combed to the side? Yes! I remember how he used to put his face against the cage of the

budgerigars and attempt to teach them a few simple words:
Flanschdichtung, for example, or *Rohgewindeschneide-*
maschinen. What was the fellow's name? Falco? Fieke? No, no:
those were the names of the parakeets. Come, Uncle Al: release
thine horny hand. *Rufus!* Rufus Krupnick! Brother of Falma.
Potato farm owner. Onkel Ruffie.

Who one year arrived on Lindenstrasse with a shy, thin
woman and a baby boy, my first cousin—now memory flows
through the broken levee—Kaspar. Over the years he proved
himself to be a typical Krupnick: humorous and tuneful, capable of playing, with his full, blood-filled lips, arias on a blade
of grass.

After my departure for Vienna and enrollment in the Akademie für Musik, Philosophie, und darstellende Kunst, I lost
touch with him and all die Kinder von Kopitshinets—until one
day in March of 1938. That was when this same Kaspar arrived
at the orchestra pit of the Wiener Staatsoper just as I was greas-
ing the ram's horn with which I would that night accompany
Abdul Hassan Ali Ebn Bekar, which, I don't have to tell you, is
the title role in *Der Barbier von Bagdad*.

"Kaspar!" I declare, staring at the man who stood before me
in a cap and patched trousers, and with shoulders so thin they
could support only one suspender at a time. "Is it you?"

He nods.

"And these—" here I directed my gaze toward the young
boy, aged perhaps eight, and what appeared to be his three
younger sisters. "These are your children?"

My cousin nodded again. Then he dropped to his bony
knees. "Leib. Mein Blutsverwandter. Hilf mir!"

My blood relation wished my assistance. The potato crop
had failed on the collectivized farms. The Ukrainians were
stealing what they could from the Jews, and from force of habit

killing and raping them too. They did both to the mother of these little tots, each of whom now began to spin and wave their arms. "I thought," said my erstwhile playmate, "they could dance in *Der Nussknacker* ballet."

Perhaps, with the Goldkorn clout, they could—except that three days later the Germans raped a quite willing Vienna. You know (not too late to read *Goldkorn Tales*, "a superb work," the excellent *San Francisco Chronicle*) how the family Goldkorn embarked on the *Kaliope*, which—another lesson from the pedagogue Pergam—had been better named the *Charon*. As for L. Goldkorn, I fled over the frozen Bodensee to La Belle France and then to the Golden State, motto, *Eureka!* And Krupnick and Kinder? Back to Kopitshinets and—what else could one imagine?—oblivion. End of the line, folks.

Or so I thought. But then who is this chappie, swarthy of skin tone, with a split beard to his belly, who stands before me? "Thanks to the help of the Almighty, blessed be his name, we meet again. Greetings upon you."

"Huh?"

"You do not remember? The little boy? With his little sisters? Who had his hands over his ears in case you started to play the ram's horn?"

Can it be? Is this bearded man, a septuagenarian in his prime, the wee lad who had auditioned for *The Nutcracker* in the former century? It is:

"Rabbi Yitzhak ben Kaspar. At your service."

"And Kaspar himself?"

"A ditch at Chortkov. May he rest in peace."

"What of the three little Fräuleins? Your sisters?"

"They met, sad to say, the same fate. Yet, praise be to G-d, they are replaced by my three sons."

I look at the three striplings, each, like his father, of a dusky hue, mit einem Schnurrbart on upper lip, and with chin beards of varying vigor. One after the other these youths step forward and, with palms placed together, make a small bow.

"Cousin, I am Arik," says the one.

"Cousin, I am Anat," says the second.

Says, lisping, the third, "Couthin, I am Abdi."

I turn toward the woman, who has, on her lip, a slight and not-unappealing Schnurrbart of her own. "And what is the name of your sister?"

All three put their hands before their mouths. They titter together. "Not thithter," says Abdi.

"*Mother*," the two others simultaneously declare.

I look more closely: though her head is covered by a shawl, I can make out the touch of gray in her hair. In addition, beneath the folds of her cotton robes, the mams possess the heft of "butternut"-type squash. At the rear, a detectable maturity of the natatorium. In short, a Leib Goldkorn type. "Pleased t'meetcha," I say, holding out an eager hand.

The Brazilian—do I detect a note of jealousy here?—intervenes. "This is Zipporah, wife to Yitzhak, um Judeu Ortodoxo."

The holy man speaks for himself. "I see that you are surprised by our presence in your home. Surprised, even, by our existence. I shall try, G-d willing, to explain."

What little illumination there is in the attic comes from a gas lamp in the far corner and the patch of electrical light created by the open door. The patriarch of the Krupnicks remains on his feet, while his family reclines beneath him on the worn wooden planks. Josefina squats on her heels. And I, after a difficult maneuver, sit stiff-legged, with the furry feline on my lap. The rabbi folds his arms beneath what I now understand is his caftan, and begins to address us.

"I will, dear cousin, be brief. You know that Kaspar brought

us back to Kopitshinets and that from there we were transported
to Chortov, from which only I escaped alive. I spent the years of
the war wandering through the forests like a beast. When peace
came I returned to our village, where my former playmates met
me with pitchforks and brands of fire. Once again I fled for my
life and wandered the earth."

"But why," asks L. Goldkorn, "did you not sail like so many
others to Israel?"

At that word all five of the Krupnicks, parents and children,
turn their heads and, like the faithful Jews of Fifth Avenue
when passing St. "Pat's," the irische Kathedrale, spit three times
over their shoulders.

Yitzhak ben Kaspar: "Cousin, I have been to the Holy Land.
I arrived in the year 5707—1947 to the heathen. There I began
my studies in the charitable house of the Charedim and met the
great Teitelbaum, king of the Satmars, may his name be writ
forever. It was from him that I learned the reason for all our
sorrows—yes, why Kaspar and my sisters and all the Jews of
Kopitshinets and all the other towns and cities had to die. It was
because of the Zionist heresy."

"Ha, ha! I am myself a non-believer. Though sometimes I
imagine that somewhere, perhaps on the moon, or some other
planet, my beloved helpmate, the former Clara Litwack, waits
for—"

"Calar a boca! Listen to the narrativa, por favor."

"There is little more to say. One year after my arrival, Palestine became Israel—" Once again the patriarch and his family pause to make an expectoration. "Then I knew I could not
remain. To take the land before the coming of the Merciful
One, to do so by force—that was a violation of the oaths of
Solomon, may his merit protect us, who in his song adjured the
daughters of Jerusalem never to arouse love until it is desired."

"Arouse? Does he mean מר Johnson?"

"The mighty Rambam has taught the meaning of this text: that it is a sin to be impatient for G-d's love. Thus the Holy Land must wait until the coming of the Anointed One. The new Jewish entity was illegitimate and the source of all our suffering. I had no choice but to flee. Once again a wanderer, searching everywhere for my fellow Satmars, in Manchester, in Antwerp, and in the ruined little towns that could not form even a minyan. It was in just such a Roumanian village that I met the rebbetzin."

Here I turn toward the downy-lipped female, whose cheeks redden under my gaze, an indication, as previously discussed, of an inundation of the Southern Hemisphere.

"But why, Reb Yitzhak, have you come now to the Lindenstrasse?"

The patriarch makes a smile. "My dear cousin, it is because of you."

"Moi? I am only an Honorary Jew."

"Yes, there are on this continent few genuine Jews—few who do not recognize, indeed worship, the Zionist state. The true Jews are in America. In the borough of Brooklyn. The Williamsburg section."

"Mas, rabino," says my relation from Rio. "Why do you not travel to the Estados Unidos?"

"Impossible! It was easier for me to sail through the British blockade of Palestine than to enter America now. I have tried again and again, but one hurdle always remains. A living family member, a blood relation, to guarantee my employment and a place to live. Imagine my delight, then, to hear that this Goldkorn, a world-famed musician, would soon come to my great-aunt's home in Jihlava. We traveled northward at once."

"*World-famed?* True, I have made a 'Red-Seal' recording with the National Biscuit Company Symphonia, A. Tosc—"

"Listen to me, Leib Goldkorn. I am now three score ten, and more. I want to die among my own people."

"*Die?* Why *die?* You are little more than ein Jüngling."

"I shall speak plain: take me with you to your home in New York."

"What? This is a misunderstanding. I am no longer a New Yorker. I have the keys to the former city of Iglau. Besides, at 138 West Eightieth Street there is but a single W.C."

"Do you see this document?" With that my distant cousin motions to the Bombshell, who hands him the piece of parchment. "I too have a claim on the lands owned by my great-uncle and great-aunt."

"Scheisse!" I cry, struggling in centurian fashion to my feet. "Verdammt! I knew it. You want the Hopfenfelder."

The rabbi: "Not at all. Have you a pen? I shall be happy to sign. No hops. No hectares. The Krupnick line will cede everything to the Goldkorn branch."

"Here! Here! A Waterman-model. What a nib! Take it, bitte."

"Gladly. But in exchange, you must agree to take us with you to America."

"What? America? Sorry: no more ink."

Mee-wowwww!

Hymena, spilled to the floor, now paces in an agitated manner beneath the high dormer window of the attic.

"Was ist los, mein kleines Kätzchen? Have you perhaps discovered the Hausmaus?"

Yitzhak, tall for a Krupnick, stands on tiptoe to see out of the dusty panes. When he turns back, his dark skin is perceptibly paler; even his forked sable beard seems to have grown streaks of gray.

"Kopitshinets!" he cries, in tones of despair. "The Ukrainians. Once more they want to kill us."

"Pooh, pooh. *Dies ist nur dein Fantasie*. My dear fellow, we are living in the twenty-first century."

There is a loud thud, followed by a crack. The hair on the back of the tortoiseshell tabby stands on end.

"Ay-y-y-y," cries Josefina, in Portuguese. "Proteja-me!"

The three sons of the rabbi race to the window, crowding together to look out. Seeing them thus, I cannot but help trace the genetic ties to their progenitors. The one, Arik, is tall and willowy, like his père. An ectomorph in the W. H. Sheldon system. Nervous type. The other, Anat, takes after the rotund rebbetzin, with amplitude in the nativities. Endomorph. Phlegmatic type. The last, Abdi, is a blend of the mère et père, without a neck, as if that couple, in their conjugals, had produced a refrigerator. Mesomorph. Active type, with lantern jaw. Now he, with his confreres, turns from the window. Their faces have also been bleached of their Ukrainian tans.

Arik: "We are surrounded. We cannot escape." This is the sort of exaggeration one might expect from such a neurasthenic.

But what of Anat, of indolent nature? "We are going to die!" That's what he is shouting. "Die like dogs!"

Uneasy, I ask: "What is going on, gentlemen?"

Here the man of action crosses the attic, picks up the present speaker as easily as if he weighed no more than a Staubwedel, which I don't have to tell you is a feather duster, and holds me up to the window.

What a sight meets my eyes. The crowd I had seen earlier has multiplied fourfold. They have built, in their midst, a large fire. A dozen of the Polar Bears are dancing about it, waving flaming sticks. Two more have climbed the branches of the linden, so that I am staring directly at their ribald tattoos, their glistening scalps. Yet others run toward Number 5 and hurl missiles toward the facade. Now comes another thud, with this time the sound of breaking glass.

With surprising tenderness, the mesomorph sets me down. "Pogrom," he whispers.

Then all the Krupnicks, as well as the far-flung Brazilian, drop to their knees and knock their heads on the floor.

"Sons of Abraham!" they cry, in an appeal to our fore-fathers. "Save us!"

Hymena, the darling, looks at me with despair in her red eye, hope in her blue. I kneel beside her.

"Be calm, my Gummibärchen. Did we not meet in the maw of death? Be calm. Once again we shall face our fate together."

SCENE SIX

BESIEGED

Surrounded, harassed, and starving,
Leib gets two birthday gifts.

WELL, MY DEARS, here I am: alive. I have not yet played on my Rudall & Rose the song of the swan. I lie on this Biedermeier, with the taffeta-type nubbins pulled to my chin. Hymena huddled, as always, beside me. The door, following custom, is open a suggestive three inches, lest the Bombshell or even—here we think of butternuts—the rebbetzin wish to make inquiries. From far off come the pleasant sounds of Hebrew prayers, punctuated by the devout knocking of heads upon the floorboards. And what is that? From the zone of the master bedroom? These are the connubial cries—the grunt of the male, the ululations of the female, as the married couple labor in the vineyard to produce a fourth male heir.

Why, simple son, is this night different from all others? One week has passed since, on the first day of November, we took part in the Holocaust Memorial Festivities. Add seven to one and we get, hmmm, hmmm—alas, I am too weak of mind, too weak of body, to make this lightning calculation. Let us simply say that at the stroke of midnight, the pages of all the calendars in the former Czechoslovakia shall turn to 11/9, or, in the continental manner, 9/11. November ninth! That's right, folks: Leib Goldkorn is about to become, hmmm—older than Lester Lanin!

The question of questions: Will I survive these brief minutes to the witching hour? I feel the pulse beat drop. A coldness rises from the toes. Each breath, departing the nose, makes the wheeze of an oboe. And why? Because from the moment I discovered my kinfolk in the attic to where you now see me prostrate on the non-Sealy, I have had nothing save an occasional carp ball to eat. Starvation, friends! They are starving us! Even if one of my inamoratas should slip through the door—What's this, darling? You wish to blow out the candles?—I fear that all would remain shiftless in South America.

To see how things have come to such a pass, let us return to the moment at which our enemies, ringing the house, clinging to the linden tree, threatened the inhabitants of Number 5 with catapults and fire. At what might have been the climactic moment we Jews in the attic heard the sound of approaching sirens.

"My dear cousins, dear relations," declared L. Goldkorn. "I am a naturalized citizen. Since the year 1943. Solomon Gitlitz presiding. Now comes the American ambassador. To protect its people, our government sends in the Marines."

But it was not the ambassador. Nor was it the commandant of the army or navy. It was the Policejní Prezident, in his black and red policejní automobil. This was soon followed by a policejní vagon, out of which jumped twenty troopers, with helmets and sticks. The crowd, at this show of force, fell back. Pan Broz stepped forward and raised a megafon to his lips.

"Leib Goldkorns. I cannot with such few polices make protection guarantees. You must sign dokument."

The mild-mannered mesomorph lifted the feather duster,

that is, truly yours, to the dormer window. Through which I then raised a shout:

"And then, Pan Broz? What next?"

"Then you come out. With safe passages to America."

"You have to sign," said Anat.

"Yes, surrender," said Arik. You remember, he was the ectomorph, a nervous type.

The rebbetzin: "Then we will go to the Williamsburg section."

But I replied as follows: "Policejní Prezident Broz. Examine, please, the map of Jihlava, former center of Teutonic culture. Notice the new policejní stanice. It seems to have been built on our family shire. Yes, on the hops hectares. Ergo, you and your excellent policisté are at work in Goldkornopolis and are employed in a manner of speaking by me. Fall back, sirrah! Back, I say! I shall not sign."

The threat that night was over. When we woke the next morning we saw that the crowds had withdrawn to the far side of the road, and that the police had erected a series of barricades between those who wished to practice Hooliganismus and ourselves.

Now began, between the besiegers and besieged, the game of Katz und Maus.

Mee-mau?

"No, no, my gummy bear. I am speaking as might a poet. I do not mean a mouse to eat."

First, our foes shut off the pipes of water. We thought in advance to outsmart them, drawing a supply into that same lion's-claw tub in which Minchke and I used to bathe at opposite ends—until on one occasion she reached for the non-Ivory brand of ein Stück Seife, only to grasp instead what was an undeniable stiffy. From this reservoir we had plenty to drink.

Next, the members of the Lední Medved Klub—Polar Bear

Club, L. Goldkorn translation—turned off the electricity. With this we also coped, and even provided ourselves with musical merrymaking, for instance with a Deutsche Grammaphon disc of the Ungarische Zigeuner-Kapelle in their celebrated "Dorflump Potpourri." *But you said there was no electricity*: that is undoubtedly what you are thinking. Ha! Ha! Forgetful reader. The Monarch model possessed a Kurbelgriff! We spun the tunes by hand.

Then came the third attack. Those on the other side of the barricades turned off the heat—a serious threat in the month of November. Gathered under our eiderdowns before the crackling fire, we managed to pass the time in what were, for Jews, high spirits—for instance, in Ukrainian pinochle, in which aces are low and the contestants are required to wrestle with thumbs; or in philosophical discussions, as in, *Who was the greatest composer of the modern era, Offenbach or Meyerbeer?* At times the Krupnicks sang the Gypsy songs of their homeland, superficially lively but with that undercurrent of melancholia so familiar to me from the recorded works of the estimable Ink Spots. I offered to play, on my silver flute, the peppy *"Shche ne vmerla Ukrainy,"* or "Ukraine Is Not Yet Dead." But for some unexplainable reason this was not encouraged.

Thus, all in all, and if only for a few brief days, it might be said that this old pantaloon was, with his new family, and the prospect of vast wealth too, living the life of Riley. Until the next McAn dropped.

It came on a particularly cold night, a night when "Jack" Frost was truly a-nipping. We threw extra chairs and a leaf of the dining room table into the flaming hearth. Then, huddled beneath our Daunendecken, like lads in the Baden-Powell movement who watch the rising sparks and hear the snap of the saplings, we began to tell stories of goblins and ghosts.

First the three sons told their hair-raising—or, in my case, scalp-tingling—tales: the mysterious Ukrainian potato thief; the headless Chinaman; and the casket maker of Medzhybizh, who dug up his grave sites in order to use the same coffin again and again—until one night he pried open the lid only to have the corpse sit upright and with his bony hand haul him into a crypt that then closed forever.

Then came the turn of Reb Yitzhak ben Kaspar, who began to tell what experts agree is the greatest ghost story of them all: that of Rabbi Loew and how he wished to save the Jewish people by creating the Golem of Prague. I need not repeat to you, sophisticates in such matters, all details. Even though I knew them myself, I could not suppress a shiver at the description of how the great mound of clay began to glow when a Mr. Levi walked around it right to left and a Mr. Cohen walked the other way, left to right.

So chilling was this tale that I felt Hymena crawl to me beneath the eiderdown and snuggle for warmth against my gabardines. But then, just as the magical words from the *Zirufim* caused the monster to—mein Gott!—grow hair on his head and, on his fingertips, nails, I happened to notice the tortoiseshell tabby stretched out before the hearth. But if not Hymena, who thus sought comfort by cuddling against my trousers? The answer so shook me that I paid no attention to the homunculus as, with a terrible groan, he drew into his nostrils his first breath of air. For, lying just to my left, and groping with a hidden hand ever upward toward unmentionable zones, was the rebbetzin! I kid you not.

On spoke the heedless husband, poor chap. Little did he know that as he spun his legendary tale the fingers of the Jezebel were approaching the sirloins and—what was this? Zipporah was manipulating the zipper! The great creature, made from the clay of the Moldau, was stirring. He was starting to rise. But so was Leib Goldkorn. Inch by American inch. Peppercorns, friends? On the skittle.

At that moment, just as the Golem heaved himself upward, Arik, the ectomorph, and Anat, the endo, began to clear their throats. Then the rabbi, hacking and hawking, stopped his tale. Now all the Krupnicks were coughing. The Bombshell pointed to the fireplace.

"Fumaça! Fumaça vindo do fogo!"

True: smoke, thick, black, laden with ashes, was pouring from the hearth. It filled the room.

Rabbi Yitzhak: "It's the goyim!"

Anat: "They have stopped up the chimney!"

Arik: "They want to smoke us out!"

Both lads jumped up, sending goose feathers flying. Imagine my shock upon discovering that the eager palm, and all five fingers, belonged not to the person on my left but to the one on my right: Abdi, the muscular mesomorph! He smiled at me, in truth rather sweetly, and batted the lengthy lashes of his eyes.

The rebbetzin fell to her knees before me and began to plead. "Surrender! The paper! Sign! Help us go to America!"

Anat: "Otherwise they will kill us!"

Yitzhak ben Kaspar: "It's worse than the pogrom of Kopitshinets!"

I got to my feet, crying out a message of reassurance.

"Be calm. These are Fingerhut tactics. I know what to do."

So saying, I groped through the coils of smoke to the telefon.

"Hello? Pronto? Hello? Connect me *pronto*, ha, ha, with the American Embassy. American Embassy? Greetings! I want to speak to Madam Rice. Hello? Hello? Madam? I am a citizen! Since 1943! *Fifty-four forty or fight!*"

"*Hello?*"

Was it she? The Secretary of the States?

"Hello, with whom am I speaking?"

"Amerikanischer citizen! *Remember the Maine!* Ha, ha, ha! *To Hell with Spain!*"

There was nothing but the sound of breathing.

"Hello? What happened to Madam Secretary? Who is this?"

"This is Ambassador Cabaniss. Bill Cabaniss. Vanderbilt, 1960. Rotary Club. Alabama Academy of Honor."

"Ha, ha! Capital, Montgomery. State bird, yellowhammer. Cattle, poultry, soybeans, nuts."

"With whom, sir, am I speaking?"

"Leib Goldkorn, Graduate, Akademie für—"

"Gildenstern! Thank God you called. Things are getting out of hand. You've got to come out of there. The Czechs are rioting in the streets. Sign their papers. We'll make it worth your while. People are marching in the city of Prague. The secretary is concerned. This is starting to become an international incident."

"Motto: *We Dare Defend Our Rights.*"

"Listen here, son. You sign what they want you to sign. This is an order from—from the highest authority."

"Do you mean President Busch?"

"We've got to get you out of there. Will you sign?"

"First, you must with your cell phone—or are you, as you said, a Rotarian? Get it? Ho-ho. This is quick wit. No sign of Uncle Al—"

"Who?"

"Call, please, His Majesty Frantisek Kunc. Make him stop the smoke attacks."

"Will you sign if I do?"

"Maybe yes. Maybe no. Noncommittals."

There was another pause, with more heavy breathing, followed by a definite click. Two minutes later, as if someone had thrown open all the windows, the smoke, and with it our despair, suddenly vanished. And a few moments later, the heat came back on.

Did I say our despair had vanished? And did I say we were the "Leben von Riley" living? Do not believe it! Even at the best of times we were afflicted by the embargo on foodstuffs. As the days went by, and our supply of jellied Karpfengbällen ran out, poor Anat, once so round, so roly-poly, grew hollow of cheek. And Arik, slenderous to start with, passed like a wraith among us. Hunger, my dears! The constant rubbing and rumbling from the abdominals, like the rocks that in the conical belly of a Betonmischmaschine, you know, the mixer of cement, are being unceasingly tossed about.

Observe how under such duress even the strictest dictates of religion will melt away. The Catholic, in extremis, will eat on Friday a fish. Would a Jew in similar straits consume—run, run away, Liebchen—a cat? Kosher? Hmmm. Poor Hymena! She soon came to resemble one of those wires, with bristles, that housewives use to clean bottles. Was it possible that in her hunger she had begun to eat the hind end of her tail? Who can blame her? I oft caught myself looking with appetite at the uppers of my McAns. Like Scott shivering in his tent, I would gladly dine on a penguin. We are not, fellow Americans, as distant from the Zulus as the alphabet might suggest.

HERE I AM, friends, Biedermeier-bound, just where I was when we abandoned the present tense. Hymena snores still at my side. Hungry! Hungry, my dears! I suck on the tafetta tufts as if they were toffees. Though my Bulova is in the shop for prawns, I know it is now past the hour of midnight. That means that I am one hundred and, hmmm, four years young. Happy birthday, Leib Goldkorn. Happy birthday to you. And now I might close my eyes. Fifty-fifty if they ever open again.

What is that noise? That whispering wail? Are my coreligionists once more at their daily devotions? No, this sound comes not from the attic above but from far below.

Hei-i-i. Vav-v-v.

Rise, you birthday boy, and shine. Oh, these aching bones. My feet, non-shod, suffer from Goldkorns. Do you hear that, Uncle Al? *Goldkorns!* Wit: one hundred percent. With candle, in nightcap, I go into the hallway and down the stairs.

Wee Willie Winkie
Runs through the town
Upstairs and downstairs
in his nightgown.

Vav-v-v. Zayin-n-n.

Yes, there is that chant, still rising from below.

Zayin-n-n. Cheit-t-t.

More chanting. It's coming from under my feet. Where could the source be?

Cheit-t-t. Teit-t-t.
Teit-t-t. Yod-d-d.

Of course! The catacombs! From the old mining shafts. Where the family Goldkorn would store its surplus hops.

Yod-d-d. Kaf-f-f.

I hasten to the stairwell that leads to the cellar. Down, down, down the creaking steps. Now the sound of chanting has grown even louder:

Kaf-f-f. Khaf.

Here is the door trap to subterrania. I open it. I continue my descent, an Orpheus who has—foolish, forgetful fellow—left behind his Rudall & Rose pipe.

What's that? A definite smell of hops! It draws me down to the final step. Now all is as black as the darkest night save for, in the direction that I take to be north, a dim and flickering light. From that direction, too, comes the droning of human voices. Both grow in intensity as I move forward until, at a sudden bend in the rocky corridor, the tunnel expands into a large chamber lit by a hundred burning candles that are ranged along the open rim of what seems to be a stone sepulcher.

And there are my cousins, like the Nibelungen, hard at work on their mysterious tasks. Each seems to have dressed himself in a white sheet, like a Greek or a Roman or, as is the custom in my adopted homeland, a child playing ghost upon All Hallows' Eve.

Everyone except for Yitzhak ben Kaspar is on hands and knees. They have formed a circle, and all are bent forward, kneading what looks from my vantage to be a large mound of dough. And as they do so, each chants the strange syllables I have heard from afar. Not so strange: I suddenly realize that these are combinations from the Hebrew alphabet, with the last letter of one pair becoming the first letter of the next, as in a kind of round:

Khaf-f-f. Lamed-d-d. Lamed-d-d. Mem-m-m.

The voices go on and on, rhythmically, hypnotically, so that, hidden behind a pillar of rock, I feel myself falling into a trance. Then, while the chorus of consonants continues, the rabbi kneels and with a wooden stick begins to inscribe something on the surface of the dough.

*Mem-m-m. Mem-m-m. Nun-n-n.
Nun-n-n.*

Suddenly my eyes fly open, and I wake from the spell of sound. Of course! I know what my family, at such an hour, and in such a place, is preparing. A surprise party! Oh, the dears! The darlings! How daring they were to smuggle into our refuge this yeast, this flour, and perhaps even an actual egg. How they must have conspired, with a wink, a nod, a finger to the lips, to keep their secret. Now I can tell how many candles are burning gaily on the ledges of the ancient oven. Not one hundred. One hundred and four! No! With one to grow on, hmmm, one hundred and five! Will I have in my lungs the power of breath to blow them out? And what would I wish for? Eh? A Finnish frottage? From You Know Who!

The recital of the alphabet has come to an end. Now Reb Yitzhak directs his children, along with the Bombshell, to walk in a clockwise circle around the unbaked cake, while he and the rebbetzin walk in the opposite, counterclockwise, direction.

This is, methinks, an unusual recipe. Not found in Fanny Farmer. But are these not unusual times? Thus the birthday boy watches in silence as all come to a halt.

"Kneel," intones Rabbi Yitzhak.

All do so, leaning forward and sliding their hands under the doughy confection.

The rebbe: "Now, on this happy anniversary—"

Anniversary! Note you that?

"I ask you to rise."

As one, they get to their feet, lifting their creation into the air.

In my hiding place I let out a gasp. How did they know? My favorite! Pfefferkuchen! A gingerbread man!

And what a big fellow he is, a six-footer and more, with a head the size of a Wassermelone, thick sturdy legs, and feet that would require a T. McAn number 12. Oooo: anatomical correctness, though from my angle of observation it seems the spermary contains but a single sphere. The nose: potato. The mouth: tight-lipped. The eyes: like any statue's, wide and unblinking.

Like pallbearers now, the cooks carry their plump patisserie toward the waiting oven and with a great heave lay the Pfefferkuchen inside it.

Suddenly, and all unbidden, the candles begin to glow more brightly and more brightly still. It is as if they are trying with all their strength to provide enough heat to do the baking. A moment passes. Then another. Yes, this blinding blaze will surely raise the temperature high enough to fricassee a chicken or bring a crawdaddy to the boil.

A pity: all too soon the tapers burn down and begin, one after the other, to go out. It is as if they are being snuffed by an invisible hand. Only a half dozen left. Three. Two. One last doughty little chap: then he too succumbs. A puff of blue smoke and the darkness is complete. Out of this blackest of nights comes a familiar voice. That of Reb Yitzhak ben Kaspar:

Ve Elohim barah et ha adam m'efar hadamah vsam—

What? What did he say? I know these words. From where? From when? Avaunt thee, Uncle Al!

Ruach chaim b'appo y'adam nasah baal chaim.

Aha! Goldiamond! Give me a honey spoon! Goldkorn gets the gold star!

And the Lord God formed man of the dust of the ground, and breathed into his nostrils the breath of life; and man became a living soul.

Now an amazing thing occurs. Though all the candles have been extinguished, the interior of the oven begins, faintly at first, to glow. How can this be? Had the heat within the sepulcher become so intense that the human-shaped dough had somehow caught fire? Was it possible that the stone walls themselves had started to burn?

My cousins range themselves around the glowing kiln, which shines ever more brightly, so much so that I am forced to shield my eyes. All the Krupnicks look away too.

Reader, you are at liberty to disbelieve what I tell you now. I can hardly believe it myself. From the depths of the sepulcher, a figure slowly starts to rise. Hideous sight! It is human! The skin is pale and stretched across the bones. Scraps of clothing—a black collar, a brown shirtfront—stick to the skin. The eyes, closed at first, now open. Pale they are, and staring. Alive! It is alive! And across the brow, under the hank of loose black hair, one word, אמת, *EMET.* Truth!

I know what this is. And so, if you will but recall the ghost story of Rabbi Loew at the Moldau, do you. Reb Yitzhak ben Kaspar has learned the secrets of the Satmars. He has passed it on to his family. All together they have created a Golem. The one who has come to save the Jews!

The Krupnick clan steps back, forming, with their right arms in the air, a kind of arch. But the Golem is not looking at them. With his glittering eyes, he is staring directly at truly yours. Am I mistaken? Or is that, under the brief bristles of moustache, at the corners of colorless lips, the smallest twitch of a smile?

In spite of everything, I smile back. There is something about this aged face—is it the shock of hair, the Schnurrbart between nose and lip, the unblinking pale eyes?—that reminds me of someone I have known in the distant past. Of a sudden my salivaries begin to pump a sweet substance, vaguely reminiscent of a Kaiserschmarrn, into my mouth. I feel the syrup spill from my lips, onto my chin. Now I have it! This decrepit figure before me, old as Methuselah, is the Wagnerian! My friend from the k. k. Wiener Hofoperntheater! The youth in the salt-and-pepper suit! Involuntarily I take a step toward him, as if he might yet have, in the pocket of his tattered brown shirt, another such treat.

But before I can take a second step, the phalanx of Krupnicks, and Miss Mengele too, click the heels of their shoes together and, still with their arms in the air, cry out the word, *Führer!*

Führer? Have I heard correctly? My ears, as described in the opening pages of this memorial, are no longer A-number-one. *Foyer*, mayhaps? Or *Femur?* I look once again at the figure that has come out of the grave. Not only have I known the youth, I realize, but I recognize the man. Have I not seen a hundred portraits in the *Movietone News*? And in the pages of the *Herald Tribune*, to which I was once a loyal subscriber? Did not the cloth-covered speaker of the Philco-brand writhe in agitation as it broadcast the sound of his voice?

Hold, sir: according to the "March of Time" this man had killed himself in a bunker at Berlin. Three times dead: a bullet, a capsule of Zyanid, and the flames of a pyre. Unless that had been a trick? And the charred corpse had belonged to some other poor chap? Could such a thing be? The whole world fooled? And I, the sole American citizen, albeit naturalized, to know the secret?

About my brains: for even if the suicide in the bunker had been staged, the supposed victim had been geboren in, if I am not mistaken, 1889—by coincidence the same year that the Jew C. S. Chaplin, who was to impersonate him in the cinema, drew in his first breath. No doubt about it. He must be defunct. If not, this Furrier would be, hmmm, hmmm—a difficult calculation, the one must jump two zeroes to the five—one hundred and sixteen years old! "Gracious! A Guinness World Record!"

In my excitement I cry these last words aloud. Hearing them, all wheel about.

Yitzhak ben Kaspar: "You!"

"Ho-ho! Should I not be here, fellows? Too many cooks spoil the broth?"

As one, my cousins begin to move toward me. On their faces, not a single smile.

Behind them, with creaks and cracks in his bones, the Golem leans forward. All stop and turn. He is digging within the marble walls of his tomb. Then he sits up, holding a ragged sheaf of papers in his arms. Hard, in the dim, green-tinged light, to see. Everyone screws up his eyes. The cover of the manuscript is stained, dusty, torn. Still, I manage to make out the letter *R*. And then, with umlaut, the letter *ü*. Heavens to Betsy! It is the score of *Rübezahl*! Snatched from my arms. And that means—

"Ladies! Gentlemen! This *is* the Furor!"

The creaking and cracking resume. The limbs of the Wagnerite are moving. His hands grip the side of the sarcophagus. He pushes upward, so that the entire zone of the torso appears. After that, a foot and a shin, and then a length of leg drapes itself over the marble edge. The Fowler is getting out of his tomb! Look! There is shank number two! Still holding the *Rübezahl* score, the centurian-plus stands on his own two feet upon the ground. He takes a step forward. The others fall back. He takes another and yet another. Gott im Himmel! He is coming to me!

I put one arm up and another arm out, like a policeman ordering the traffic to stop. But he comes on nonetheless. There is another creaking sound. The hinges of his jaw are dropping open. Oh! Oh! My skin is covered with gooseberries. Now mouth gapes wide. Not a sound, however, comes out.

"Ha! Ha!" I manage a doltish laugh. "Have you more rum balls?"

I see the teeth. I see the tongue, blood-red in the black cavern of the mouth. So close has he come that I can smell, like sulfur and patchouli, the stink of his breath.

Suddenly there is a shriek—*Futtttz! Frittttz!*—and a ball of spit and fur and sharp shining claws flies through the air.

Hymena! Honey!

Under attack, the Fueler throws an arm before his eyes. *Feets*, I tell myself, *do your stuff!* In my halting gait I attempt to run. At that instant, all hell, if you will allow this mild explication, breaks out. I move with raised knees first left, then right, now this way, now that. My cousins dash helter-skelter in the attempt to head me off. Here is the corridor to safety. I no sooner achieve it than who but the mesomorph should appear.

"Thith way," he hisses. "Come with me."

I whirl about and lope in the opposite direction, holding my ears against the echoing din.

"Get him!"

"He's over here!"

"No, over here!"

"Impeça meu tio!"

"What a runner!"

Futz! Fwatz! Fwwwitz!

Everyone is shouting and groping his and her way through

the dim light. I look back over my shoulder in time to see the Golem moving off along the northward corridor, toward the heart of the town. *To think that he of all people might save the Jews!* No sooner does that ironical thought flit through my mind than my left foot trips on the edge of the stone slab and I hurtle Hals über Kopf into the stone sarcophagus. How deep the tomb! Will it be the grave of Leib Goldkorn, Graduate?

And, in fact, as my cranium, with its many thoughts and memories, strikes the bottom of the sepulcher, darkness descends, and all lights on earth go out.

WHERE AM I, FRIENDS? Alive or dead? In heaven? Or is it hell? Let's look on the bright side. See, see there: it is Winnetou and his noble steed, Iltschi. There is no doubt that redskins are welcome in paradise. And even Afrikaners of good repute. Hmmm. But a horse? Which can barely think or speak? And if a horse, why not a guppy? And if a guppy, why not a radish? Ha! Ha! Or even a stone?

Wait: Is that Indianer not part of the Shatterhand poster? And Iltschi too? Could it be that I am, after all, in my upstairs room? And just where you left me, athwart my boyhood bed? Taffeta tufts to my chin? Was it all a dream? No birthday party? No Golem? No gingerbread cake? But then why do I suffer from such a Kopfschemrz? Why is there a bump—goodness, just feel it—on the side of my head? Did I trip into the sepulcher? Or did I in my dreaming thrust my head against this beam of the Biedermeier?

All I know is that, in the depths of this special night—one hundred and four! Older than Xavier Cugat!—all is still, all is quiet. Wait. I hear a sound of rustling, just outside my door— a door that, as you know, I always leave open a crack. Just in case. Now, pushing through, comes a slippered foot, plump, and the five plump fingers of a hand. Zipporah! The rebbetzin! Back for more! But I do not allow myself to anticipate the joy of nuptials. When the full figure of the rabbi's wife enters my chamber, I calmly address her:

"Begone, madam. You are nothing more than a fig of a dream."

She does not vanish. She comes toward me, speaking thus: "Oh, dear man, look at you! Such a nightcap! With a ball at the end."

Still I resist. "Madam, Leib Goldkorn can be fooled once, but not, in one night, twice. Be off! To horse!"

But she does not go off. Instead, in her tentlike caftan, she draws closer. "Permission, if you please, to sit?" She points to a corner of my feather-filled mattress. I nod. "Cousin Goldkorn, I have for you certain feelings. Look, I will show them to you." And with that she pulls both halves of her robe aside.

Like many a youth, I took much interest in the operations of the Deutsche Luftschiffahrts-AG, particularly the LZ 4, which I once saw sailing over the Bohemian-Moravian Heights, and the LZ 11, the *Viktoria Luise*, named for the Duchess of Brunswick, who with her hair in a bun was for the lads of Iglau a hot ticket. What the spouse of Yitzhak ben Kaspar did when offering to show me her feelings was release from the hanger of her opened caftan two such Zeppelins, which, in this windless atmosphere, now hang motionless before my gaping eyes.

It was on this very bed and on that very spot that Falma, an original Krupnick, had perched when reading to her only male child a Silesian fairy tale; or rocking him in times of illness; or, on more than one occasion, shedding with him a tear as she complained of the attentions shown to Eliska by the putative père. The Coreligionist might say that was the reason that I in the grip of primitive instinct now throw off my nightshirt and lurch forward on all fours, taking the leftward mam in my mouth and suckling there a full moment before changing objects and beginning to nurse at the mam on the right. And in the dark continent? Stirrings.

Suddenly, a crash, a bang, and the door flies wide. The Bombshell!

"Meu Leib! With another amante!"

"Ho, Ho. It is not what you think. Nourishment only. A drop of milk for a starving man."

"Não!"

Uttering that cry, Josefina dashes to the non-Sealy and begins to climb aboard. "Not her. Me! I know what Leibie like. Eh? He like the sapatos. Sapatos com salto. With heels."

By this she means not any old McAn but her own five-inchers, red with black shiny stilettos. But my grandniece does not allow me the pleasure of examining the buckles, the straps, or the ankle knobs trapped inside them; instead, in an athletic maneuver, she leaps to my back, upon whose spine she begins to trod.

"Ha, ha. I have hirsute shoulders. This has been from child-hood an embarrassment."

Olha que caisa mais linda—The Bombshell is singing the lyrics to "The Girl from Ipanema," while doing a samba across the short ribs.

Now occurs a moment that is even harder to believe. Through the open door strides the Deputy Mayor for Culture, Entertainments, and Sports.

"Leibie, milácek, it is I, your Iveta."

Not only that, she is barefoot. Barefoot, comrades! And through the loosened top of her waistcoat the pink eye of each non-convex mam comes a-winking and a-peeking. Is it at that sight, or the smell of gardenia, that my Jewish-style member decides to explore the world outside its S. Klein drawers?

What happens next is the sort of event one finds in the rearmost pages of R. F. von Krafft-Ebing. There one might read of the man who drank his own urine, or of another man, of the upper classes, who achieved transports with a rope. Prepare yourselves, friends: The Crumsovatna joins the jamboree. Without hesitation she begins to slide on her back to where I remain on my hands and knees; with skill she maneuvers downward and still farther downward, until she lies with her head beneath my sirloins. Then, opening her mouth, she takes all eighty centimeters of Pan Johnson inside it. Never in my lifetime, and probably not in yours, has such a thing occurred.

My feelings are mixed. On the one hand, there are in proximity teeth, molars, and bicuspids, which causes a certain alarm; on the other there is a feeling of warmth, and a hominess, such as a snail might experience in the safety of its shell. *Glücksgefühl*, that is what we call this sentiment in German.

> *Fala que não vai*
> *Sente o que interessa*

Thus sings the Brazilian beauty, while continuing to trod with heel points up and down my backside. March on! March on, missy! *Le jour de gloire est arrivé!*

> *Ma-ma-ma-ma—*

That is the Crumsovatna, who with tongue and glottis is creating a sensation by humming the Act Two aria from *The Bartered Bride*.

Picture in your minds Leib Goldkorn, centurian: a damsel in front, a damsel on top, and a damsel below. Might it not be said that, suckling and being suckled, while the armies of Napoleon cross and recross the dorsal plain, I have accomplished what many men dream of but few achieve: the ménage à quatre?

Pashas amidst their harems, Musselmen with their virgins, Mormons and their many wives: none can match in their fantasias what I have grasped in the flesh. Is this the pinnacle? Can man aspire, in the sphere of the carnals, any higher? Nein! Or so I think until I hear the door to my bedroom slam open again.

Who is the eager visitor? A pleasant thought: Miss Williams, star of *Pagan Love Song*, has changed her mind! Better late, madam, then never!

Come with me where moonbeams
Light Tahitian skies
And the starlit waters
Linger in your eyes.

Or—do I dare dream?—is it the She-Who? Heavens! Do they have such origamies in Japan? I try to call her name, not yet forbidden, but my mouth, as described above, is full. I try to search out her Finnish form in the dim-lit room: but the lighter-than-air ships block my view. I feel the goose feathers of the non-Sealy sink by the foot of the bed. Welcome aboard, stranger! I can sense the mystery woman approach from behind. Something brushes against the crupper. There is a fumbling at the rectals. Oho, so that's your game, is it? Tomfoolery? Bring it on! Now I hear a voice, one that is not unfamiliar, declare, "Hold thtil. Pleathe. Hold thtil!" Abdi! The mesomorph!

On the horizon, ladies and gentlemen, the storm of a expostulation is gathering. In the atmosphere there rises a mist of perspirations, oak moss, gardenia, and, from the gentleman at my rear, Shocking, by Schiaparelli. Within my own body elasticized cords, growing tighter and tighter, pull at each joint and limb. The peppercorns are hopping on the griddle. And a spicy sauce, like a mole poblano, pours over my skin. Yet one thing is missing before the storm can break. Above, below, fore and aft, every inch of my body is receiving pleasure except—yes, you have guessed it, the bottoms of my feet. And no sooner does this vacuum become apparent than, with warm, soft motions against my insoles, and the sandpaper swipes of a tongue, it is filled. Hymena! She has joined the hymenals.

Ekstase. From the currents in the Straits of Magellan it is clear that Pan Johnson has grown to what I believe is a personal best. The elastics are at the breaking point. The spermary at the boil. Now the top of my head, with its hair-horseshoe, is about to fly off. Oh, Moses! SH'MA YISROEL! Suddenly, among all these stridencies, the slappings and shouts and mewings, the cascade of the songfest, one cry rings out above all the others:

Pozor!

Everything stops, as if a bevy of beavers have felled a mighty oak across flowing waters. All the forest animals raise their heads, alert, aware.

Pozor!

This time the word—*beware*—is accompanied by a tremendous thump. Fists upon the Lindenstrasse door!

"What wath that noithe?"

"He will wake the husband!"

"We must to hurry!"

"Oh, Deus! Cristo!"

Frist! Fssst! Futst!

Disengagement. Withdrawal. Silence and shame.

Once more the thuds; once more the anguished cry:

Pozor!

As one, we rush into the hallway. Reb Yitzhak, head of the family, and his two other sleepy sons, meet us on the stairs. We all tramp down together, trailing nightwear and undergarments behind us. *Thud-thud-thud.* Thus the sound of desperate fists.

Rabbi Yitzhak ben Kaspar flings open the door. Before us is the Mercedes man, his chauffeur's cap askew on his bulbous head. He takes one step forward, toward where I sagging stand.

"Pozor, Goldkorns! Pozor! Is not what you think. Warning! They are podvodníci. Podvodníci!"

Behind him, and behind the barricades, the crowd of Czechists has swollen in size. They are shouting and swearing. They wave their flaming torches in the air. The Krupnick clan moves protectively around him, but the chauffer pushes through and holds out his arms toward "L. Goldkorns," the man he met—it seems a lifetime ago—at the airport. What's this? What has he in his hands? A book. A manuscript. Bound in leather.

Leaning forward, I take a closer look. *Rübezahl!* My father's only opera! The greatest of all birthday gifts! In amazement I address him: "Where, my good man, did you find this treasure?"

Suddenly his green, exophthalmos eyes bulge even farther, so that I fear the balls will fly from their sockets, and he wheels round. There is a knife in his back! Bubbles, blood-filled bubbles, form at his lips. He opens his mouth. I strain forward to hear his words:

"Židovský hřbitov. Jewish cemetery. Pogrom. At Mahler family tomb. This. Underneath tombstone. Pozor!"

Then those same eyes turn entirely white, and without another word, either with vowels or without, the poor man drops lifeless to the ground.

INTERMEZZO

*How Leib is persuaded to give up all claims in
Jihlava and return to his home in New York.*

HOW, INDEED, DOES such a persuasion take place? Brute
force? The ministrations of Police Chief Broz? Or will, after
all, the Secretary of States send in the Marines? I shall employ
this brief intermezzo in order to explain.

At first nothing occurs within Number 5 Lindenstrasse.
A day passes. A second day. A third and a fourth. The only
change is that our abode is filled with a new odor, one that
schooners of Schiaparelli, tumbrels of Tommy Girl, and jars
full of "Jicky" cannot disguise. A combination of banana and
burning rubber, with notes of salt herring. You have guessed
it: flesh decomposing. The chauffeur, now a Brunswick-green,
lies propped against the downstairs Tiefspültoilette, swollen to
twice his normal size and bubbling with springs.

His death has become what Frenchmen call a cause to cel-
ebrate. Who hurled the fatal dagger? That, my dear Watson, is
the nubbin. The goyim have given their answer. On their signs,
their placards, across the banner stretched down the length of
what they call Valkova Street, and in the cries and curses that
reach our ears day and night: *Ti Židé jsou viník!* Yes, we, the
band of the besieged, are the murderers, accused of seeking a

Christian body for our sacred rites. The blood libel, friends! In the twenty-first century of our Lord.

As you might expect, all of us have drawn closer than ever to starvation. We talk, like the men on Scott's expedition, of nothing but food. I dream through the night of lychee nuts. Though none speak of it, I think that in each of our minds there grows hour by hour the one forbidden thought. Goldiamond: look the other way. Professors Pergam and Epstein, Julius J., mentors of my youth: forgive me. But is it not an indisputable fact? Does there not, athwart the Tiefspültoilette, and fermenting nicely, like, say, sauerkraut or naw-mai-dong, lie a fine repast?

What? What's that you say? Kannibalismus?

No, no, no. Not at all. Pas du tout. Ha. Ha. Ha. Just kidding.

On the fifth night I know that I, that all of us, are truly at the rope's end. Lying on the Biedermeier, turning over in my mind whether the chauffeur would object if I took just a nibble of a purple pinky, I hear a voice cry out:

"Jew Goldkorns."

I rise from the field of taffeta. I crawl to the window. What do I see below but a young maiden whose blond hair shines in the Lindenstrasse lamps. She stands in that no-man's-land between gentiles and Jews, besiegers and besieged. There she remains, like Fortuna and her cornucopia, with a chicken dangling from one hand and a smoked ham in the other. I know her. Paní Pigtails! The Nechvátalová! Her virginal lips are parted in a smile. Oh, that perky nose! And the hint of a mammary too. She gives to me a definite come-hither. Though I suspect this is another dream, or the last thought of a dying man, I nonetheless go thither. And once in the street, drawing close, I address her:

"Is that a ham?"

"Ano," she replies. "Gift from American ambassador."

Now the handsome mayor steps from the crowd behind her.

"And," he says, "from town of Jihlava."

L. Goldkorn: "Does that come with gherkins?"

Mayor Kunc replies: "We know you have hungers. Little girl brings food. Offers smiles."

"But what of the, hmmm, death of your countryman?"

"About this we must ask Policejní Prezident Broz."

On cue, this square, stolid figure moves forward into the lamplight. I greet him:

"Someone else did it! Innocent! Not guilty! He was only a chauffeur."

"Not to please worry," the chief answers. "Official verdict of investigations: Obvious case of sebeobrana. Self-defense."

"But what about the Jews? The ritual murder? Blood in the matzo?"

"Ho, ho," laughs the lord mayor. "This does not often happen."

Chief Broz: "All is forgiven."

"Forgiven? Forgiven? Give me that Hühnchenbrust! Give me that Schinken!"

"With happy cordials," says the mayor. "But first, will you please to—"

Wouldn't you know it? Out comes the parchment paper once more.

"Nein!" Do I have second thoughts? Is not that ham glazed? "Nein!"

His Majesty, the mayor: "But why not, Honorary Jew? Do you not have restored to you *Rübezahl* book, heirloom treasure? Is property owned by Jihlava. By mighty Czech State. Should go into G. Mahler Museum."

"*Your* property? But this belongs to truly yours."

"Located in cemetery for the Jewish. Town property. Is finders keepers."

"But do you know how this treasure got into the tomb?"

Here the Police Chief Broz, with his fat forefinger, makes

on his chest the sign of the Jesus Christ cross. "Is the d'ábel. Is d'ábelský power. Our angry peoples knock over Mahler grave headstone. Out comes a strange light. Out from the tomb!"

For a moment my mind goes a-reeling. *Was* it d'ábelský power? Had the Golem burrowed through the town sewers and left the manuscript in the grave of my Grossmutter, my Grossvater? Childish superstition. A more likely explanation: one century earlier the père had won the battle for *Rübezahl*. Perhaps he had indeed hidden it in the attic for a time. But the fact that my true father, the composer himself, had given the manuscript to me must have been hard for him to bear. It was he, a jealous human being, and no Golem, who had buried the manuscript in the Mahler family tomb.

"Ha! Ha! You say *finders keepers*. But I know another folkish expression: *Possession is*—hmmm—*nine-tenths of the law*." I shall keep it forever."

Mayor Kunc: "Is good. Excellent. We give as gift to Honorary Jew. Now Honorary Jew will sign."

He holds out the document. All eagerly crowd round. Even the not-homely Hanna gives a little lick of the lip. But I cannot be swayed. I shake my head: No.

At this a complete stranger, tall, silver-haired, and of a type Anglo-Saxon, strides out of the gathered masses.

"Leib Gildenstern! Graduate! How are you, sir?" This he booms forth in the voice of the old South. "Bill Cabaniss, American ambassador. I believe you and I have had a little conversation on—" And here he holds up the small, gleaming instrument, no thicker than a Roumanian broiling. "The phone."

"Ja. The non-rotarian."

"Someone very important is eager to speak with you. All the way from America, I don't mind giving you a little hint. She is also an Alabamian. And an Academy of Honor inductee."

"Could this be Miss Tallulah Bankhead? Cameo in *Stage*

Door Canteen. Suspected of conjectures with women of same sex."

The ambassador: "Certainly not. I am speaking of—"

Suddenly the Bell telephone breaks into song:

I wish I was in de land ob cotton—

"Oh, that's our call now. Coming in from Washington, D.C." He flips open the front of the device. "Madam Secretary? Secretary Rice? Yes, he is right here. I'll put him on."

The instrument is now in my own hands. "Hello! Hello! Excellency! I am also a member of the Akademie. Class of '16!"

"Am I speaking to Leib Goldkorner?"

"Ja! Das bin ich!"

"First, may I express my very best wishes, and those of the President, on your recent birthday."

"I almost got a Pfefferkuchen."

"One hundred and four! According to our researches, that makes you the oldest living American Holocaust survivor."

"You call this living? Ha, ha. Forgive the humor, Your Grace."

"You poor, brave man. What you must have gone through. I am proud that our country provided you, and so many others like you, a safe refuge."

Note you: she said *poor.* She said *brave.* This gives room for thought. Is not my interlocutor a well-known Nubian beauty? Has she not a sensuous gap between incisors? With a beguiling sprinkle of Sommersprossen, like a cadenza of eighth-notes, across cheeks and nose? Charmant! But let us resume our tête-à-tête:

"Do you recall, Your Serenity, how when the first Pilgrims came to America they would have starved had not the Indianer shown them how with a fish to grow corn? A true tale.

Similarly, when planters in South Carolina, state beverage milk, attempted to raise rice, they failed—until slaves from Afrika taught them the best way to do so. To this day we pay homage to their skills in the portrait of beloved Uncle Ben. Do you not think it possible that, just as I am named for those golden kernels, you might take your moniker from these polished grains? Do we not thus share a common heritage? Hello? Hello? Friends: the line has gone dead. Hello?"

A faint voice comes from the Bell telephone. "*I am still here.*"

"Good! Here is a difficult historical question. What do A. Pushkin, and A. Dumas, and A. Hamilton—the three great A's, ha-ha-ha—share in common? And also with *you*! Hickory-dickory-dock: Can you Beat the Clock? Too late! Here is the Antwort: each has in his veins the blood of a darky! And, as with you, Miss Phi Beta Kappa, each has an excellent intellect. Hello? Hello? This instrument has not been perfected."

The voice comes through again, even more weakly. "*Mr. Goldkorner. We at the State Department, and at the American Holocaust Museum, wish to honor you as our oldest survivor of the Shoah. We have arranged a special celebration. I hope you will agree to return home as soon as possible. The American government, and that of the Czech Republic, have agreed to provide transportation and all expenses.*"

"But, Your Magnificence, will there be a home to return to? The fils is creating the Casa Blanca. All private residencies. Non-rent-stabilized. I do not have a Condo-leeza. Ha-ha. A Condo-*leeza*. Get it? This is true Jewish humor."

This time there is an audible click, and the phone goes dead.

I return the instrument to its owner and address the three officials. "My regrets, gentlemen, but I cannot accept the offer of this Southern belle."

The ambassador: "But did she explain? There is going to be a premiere."

"A premiere?"

"Ano," says Mayor Kunc, "World premiere. Of the *Rübezahl*."

Old times dar am not forgotten—

At this Ambassador "Bill" flips open his instrument again. "Is it Miss Rice?" I inquire. "The Madam Secretary? Love the dimples!"

Apparently not, for the Alabamian shouts as follows: "Hello? Hello, sir. We've been expecting your call. Yes, I'll put him on." Once more the phone is placed in my hands. The ambassador whispers in my ear: "It's the manager of the Metropolitan Opera. In New York City."

I shout into the receiver: "Hello? Hello? Pronto! Sir Rudolph? The Jew? Sir Rudolph Bing? This name is an example of onomatopoeia. Here speaking is your fellow Viennese. We share the same age. *Bing!* Ha, ha, ha! How is it we are both still alive?"

Mayor Kunc reaches out to cover the mouthpiece. "Fool! Is Joseph Volpe! New director of opera."

I press a button on the slim device, so that only I can hear the reply to the following words: "Hello? Joe? How about that Renée Fleming? Ha! Ha! Ha! What a pair! I do not refer to tonsils. What? *What!* Begorra!"

I turn to the others. "He wants Leib Goldkorn to translate the *Rübezahl*. Into English language. Also to direct the world premiere. Joe! Listen, Illustrious One. Why have you chosen a mere Glockenspieler at the Vienna State Opera for such an honor?"

Ambassador "Bill" provides the answer. "Didn't you read the manuscript? Those are that Mahler feller's instructions."

At that instant my cousin, Reb Yitzhak ben Kaspar, steps from the door of Number 5 Lindenstrasse, holding the copy of *Rübezahl* in his arms.

Little Hanna nods her head up and down, so that her Haar-zöpfe, or pigtails, go flying. "All Jews real smart. How come you don't know what is wrote?"

Police Chief Broz takes the manuscript and opens the first page. I squint down and read aloud: "*Für meinen Sohn Leib*—ha, ha, the cat is out of the sack—*ein musikalisches Genie*. This means, *a musical genius*. But how could he know? At that time I played only the panpipe. Well, of this German text I shall make a lightning translation. *He and he alone*—why, these are the very words he spoke to me at the Hof-Operntheater—*he and he alone shall direct the* Rübezahl, *my only opera. Viel Glück, mein Sohn. I have written it with my Blut. You must bring it to life with yours.* Signed. Signed. Pardon. A mist. Mistiness. Hard to see."

The police chief holds out a handkerchief. Mayor Kunc speaks as I dab at my eyes:

"You see? Is command performance. In attendance wonderful gentleman President Bush. Also first President of Czech Republic, V. Havel. Not so wonderful."

"Gentlemen, I am touched. Please thank the Secretary of the States. And Director Volpe. Such an honor. Yet all of Iglau is my shire. Can I abandon it? Yes? No? How to decide?"

Suddenly the door flies open and the remainder of the Krupnick clan bursts into the street. Their father calls to them. "Tell him to take us to America!"

Arik: "We are your only family!"

Anat: "You are our only hope!"

Abdi: "We mutht thtick together!"

The rebbetzin leans toward me. Her mams, I see, have not diminished. "We only wish to practice our faith."

Her husband echoes her words: "In the Williamsburg section."

I turn once more to the telephone. "Hello? Director General

Volpe? I have relations. Cousins. On the Krupnick side. Satmar persuasion. Do you think it possible that—"

Again, Ambassador "Bill" takes the instrument from me. "We've already seen to that. Secretary Rice has arranged for all their visas."

Hearing this, the cousins rejoice.

"Hooray!"

"At latht!"

"We are going to America!"

Once more Mayor Kunc thrusts the parchment toward me. "Here is pen. Here is dokument. Please to make signature."

I take the pen, but pause. "Oh, my Hopfenfelder. How beautiful in the breezes of spring."

"Someone else wants to speak to you." That's the ambassador. He holds out once more his Bell-brand phone.

"Who is it?" I ask. "Not a Miss Williams, I suppose?"

"It's a Nobel Prize winner. Elie Wiesel."

Breathless, I begin to speak to the man across the sea. "O, my coreligionist. Oft have I wished we could thus parlay. Tell me! Tell me! I beg you! Did you know, while at—at that terrible place: Did you perhaps meet Herr Gaston Goldkorn? Medium-to-stocky type. Moustache. Perhaps with a Trabucco-brand cigar. Can you tell me his fate? And what of meine Schwester Yakhne? Did you on occasion note her, non-flirtatiously, through the wire? Athletic type, mit non-convex bosom. What did they do to her? How, sir? When, sir? Where? I want to know! Oh, Falma! My mother! Eine Brünette! Perhaps with a polka-dot dress. Hint of doubled chin. The sound of her voice, humming, singing. A Schlaflied to her babe! The smell of milk on her skin. Why, Wiesel? Why?"

For a moment I am overcome. No one speaks. Everyone has lowered his head. Shame of the nations. In a moment, or two moments, I recover. "When I arrive, sir, will you be so kind as to tell me what became of each of them, including the famed beauty, Minchke?"

Chief Broz interrupts: "Aha! *When I arrive.* So you are going? Out of our land? Rozloučení!"

The mayor: "At last you are signing?"

"Yes. I shall sign. Let me just unscrew the top of this pen—"

But before I write my name a last thought occurs. I ask Mr. Wiesel if he will once more put onto the phone Mr. Volpe. "Hello? Is that you, Giuseppe? I have a request. Is there not in the House of the Metropolitan Opera a special conductor's box? Ja? Parterre Number 1? Gut. I wish to ask a wee favor. Will you seat the reviewer of *The New York Times* within it? Yes, the famed half-Finn. Born, perhaps, in the town of Kauhajoki. Near Espoo. And is there yet a further seat? For one more guest? A little chap. An orphan boy. Ja! A handsome young señor. Name: Jaime Castillo. Please. I wish the pleasure of seeing him there. In a blue serge jacket. And brass buttons. With, if you can arrange it, a part in his hair. Dankeschön! My thanks to all!"

My next words are directed to the director of the opera and to all those standing about me. "Yes! I am coming! I give up my fortune! I shall live only for art!"

I see, to the east, that the first light of the dawn is making an appearance. L'Absolu. Rouge by Dior. I take the pen. I lean over the paper. I pause one last time.

"This is not a Waterman."

And then I sign, as indicated, on the dotted line. Farewell, Jihlava! A.k.a. Iglau! Farewell, Old Shatterhand! And Winnetou! Farewell, my youth! And Miss Crumsovatna too. I am returning to my home in the New World.

ACT TWO

ARBEIT

SCENE ONE

THE STURGEON KING

*Back home and flush with cash, Leib begins to
translate his father's opera into English.*

Good evening, Mr. and Mrs. North and South America,
ha-ha-ha, and all the ships at sea. Guess who's back in
town? That bon vivant and man of the world, Leib Korn-
gold, Graduate, after a triumphant trip to his boyhood
home. We used to run into him at "21" with the latest big
trouser-crease-eraser. Get me? Like that mischievous mermaid, Esther Williams. Yes, he's back. Still alive! Older than
Mrs. Astor! My sources tell me you can catch him most
mornings over at Barney Greengrass's whitefish palace. Welcome home, old-timer! We need good Americans like you.
Take a stroll down Amsterdam Avenue: you'll find him at
a front-room table, up against the wall. Down Eightieth.
Right on Amsterdam. Cross Eighty-sixth Street. Here we
are. Let's go to press!
                                    —*The Jew, W. Winchell*

YES, *back in town.* But the gay days of "21," also the "Stork"
Club, are over. Now I restrict myself to the six-block radius of
Number 138. And, yes, as noted, I sit with my back to the wall.

Prudent precaution, lest the S.S., the Sex Staatspolizei, approach unawares from the rear. *On the alert!* That is the watchword. Ah, but who is this that draws near? Only the majordomo.

"Greetings, my good man. Today I shall have the following delicacy: tongue, pastrami, and hard salami, on pumpernickel, mit cole slaw and Russian dressing. Hold the pickle."

The waiter, hands a-tremble, writes my order on a pad. Poor fellow: grizzled beard, the sparse hairs that cling to his head combed "over the top," eyelids drooping over rheum-filled eyes. Perhaps that is why he does not recognize his former colleague from the Steinway Restaurant, artiste on the Bechstein grand. But I know that beak of a nose and the two feet splayed outward: the descendant of Moses, surname Mosk.

"You got it, babe!" he exclaims, and moves off toward the zone of the kitchen.

Herr König! Herr König!
Wir grüssen untertänig!

These are first words written by my non-putative père on the parchment pages now spread before me. Let us, with my Bic-model pen, attempt an L. Goldkorn translation:

Mister King! O, Mister King!
Humble greetings we bring!

Hmmm. Not bad.

Amid the Lipton teacups and Lipton tea bags, I find room to continue:

Gott schenk dir langes Leben
—Gesundheit auch daneben!

A long life to you if it God please
And Gesundheit! at your every sneeze.

Observe how my penmanship, with its descending loops and semi-crossed *t*'s, resembles that of the progenitor. Naturally enough, certain thoughts follow: Have I inherited from that source, in addition to musicality, my hair-rich shoulders? My freethinking on the subject of religion? A taste for schnapps?

Where is Mr. Mosk? Sad to say, the service in this establishment has declined since, but a lad of fifty, I first breakfasted on nova heads and wings, side of scrambled, black coffee. In those days you'd hardly have the words "and a toasted bialy" out of your mouth before Barnard the First, the Sturgeon King himself, would appear, place the steaming platter before you, and complete the word puzzle that had a certain youth stumped: "Seven down? Six letters? 'Leggy star of *Footlight Serenade*'? G-R-A-B-L-E!" O King! O King! Gesundheit! Good health. Alas, in the year 1956, a goiter ball carried him off.

The King is dead! Long live the King! The heir, Marvin, a.k.a. Moe, was the first person in America to sauté the onions before mixing them into chopped liver. Perhaps the first in the world. Each of us has, under a bushel, his talent.

"Garçon! I forgot to order a Dr. Brown's!"

The elderly Lithuanian pokes his head through the rear door. "Somebody call me?"

L. Goldkorn: "Un Cel-ray tonic, s'il vous plaît."

The great wheel turns. Moe, with his belly-fat ring and card tricks, left this earth—it is now, hmmm, almost four years ago. The Dauphin now sits on the throne. Rather, he stands in the front, a sentry at the register for cash. Coins in all denominations jiggle, jangle, jiggle, in his right pants pocket.

See! But see! Do you note the look of scorn he casts upon

me? He desires that I depart this square of Formica, so that others might order the kippered salmon plate, with sable, and nova scotia. Thirty-nine dollars and fifty cents! Does he think I cannot pay? Ha! Ha-ha! One could say that I possess un embarras de richesses. Or, if you will excuse the pun, a King's ransom. In my own pocket: two Jacksons, a U.S. Grant, and a Franklin. And more secreted within the ice compartment of my Frigidaire. Why, I could order a caviar presentation, if I so wished, including the Supreme Sampler, one hundred forty-five dollars. In my opinion too salty.

Still, the Dauphin looks daggers. So what if I have been sitting here since ten in the morning? So what if yon sun is already descending over the glens of New Jersey, state insect the honeybee? In my homeland, and in all of Europe, is there not a long tradition of artistes who labor in cafés? Balzac, the coffee addict, for instance; or Monsieur Baudelaire; or, speaking of bees, Rimsky-Korsakov. So: about, my brains!

Ich danke Euch, meine lieben Untertanen
Ich will mich bemühen, euch immer weise und gnädig
  zu regieren.

Let me see. How to render this, the basso's first aria?

We give you, my people, our thanks
And promise to rule without any pranks.

No, no. The tone is too vulgar for such a great king:

We hereby pledge to each of our vassels
Mercy and wisdom in all of our castles.

Better, but no cigar. How difficult this work! More taxing than the arpeggios of *Il Segreto di Susanna*. Once more, dear friends, into the breach:

> *Our gratitude to you, good people*
> *In our reign thou shalt not be weepful.*

No, no, no! Tradutore! as the Italians say. Traditore!

> *You shall proclaim our goodness from every steeple.*

No wonder Balzac drank, each day, forty cups of coffee. *From every steeple!* This is Dummheit! Little wonder, too, that Baudelaire—mon semblable! mon frère!—took to absinthe. The cellars of the Sturgeon King have, for aperitifs, only such items as Rolling Rock and, at three-fifty, Miller Lite. So: we must try yet again:

> *My heart with your needs I shall keep full.*

"One Cel-Ray," says the woeful waiter. "One tongue and so forth. No pickle."

"Ah, so deep at my task was I, my good fellow, that I forgot I had ordered this repast."

"Ain't no room on the table. What's all that paper? You want I should clear the trash?"

"*Paper? Trash?* What you see here is the only opera by the great Gustav Mahler. Unless, as some scholars claim, you should thus classify *Das Lied von der Erde*."

"I don't go for that egghead stuff. Give me Irving Berlin. Hey, these platters don't weigh nothing. Make me some room."

"Let us push to one side for the nonce these Liptons. Voilà!

As for the difficulty of this opera, I can assure my dear friend it does not resemble the products of the non-Jews Webern, Berg, or P. A. Pisk. Their master, A. Schoenberg, went to Hollywood. Can you imagine? *Twelve Looney Tones!* Ha! Ha! Ha! Tremble, Uncle Al. What? No hint of a smile? What if I told you that his harmonies were examples of cacophony? Ha-ha! *Cacaphoney!* I see, Mr. Mosk, that it is difficult to get a laugh from a Lithuanian."

"Table two is waiting for a pickled lox. I got no time for highbrow music. It's way over my head."

"Not at all! Even a child could appreciate this opera. It is, like the masterpiece of Humperdinck, based on a fairy story."

"Humperdinck. Fairy story. Dear friend. What are you? Some kind of fruit?"

"But it *is* a fairy story. About the mountain spirit and the princess. Surely, in the days of your childhood, you heard this tale?"

"Is that the one about the girl who made gold out of flax? What a lot of hooey."

"No, no. In this tale the King's daughter is captured by Rübezahl and brought to his kingdom under the earth. Poor girl! Snatched from her home. From her loving family. And what of the King? Think of his loss!"

"How come you're crying? Too much onion? You want I take it back to the kitchen?"

The aged waiter—undoubtedly a centurian in his own right—is correct. The tears are spilling from the ducts of my eyes. But not because of the onion that lies on the pumpernickel slice. It is because I have remembered meine liebe Mutter, Falma, beside me on the Biedermeier: her hair up in two or perhaps three concentric rings, like the colored loops piled on my toy wooden dowel; behind her the curtain on the window blows inward, carrying the sweetness of the blossoming trees;

and her lips, full like those of all Krupnicks, moving, moving, moving. Her words! Can you hear her words?

Vor langer, langer Zeit, "Once upon a time, my little Lieb-chen, there was a beautiful Princess named Emma, who was seized by a monstrous mountain spirit named Rübezahl."

And so there comes back to me the tale of how the Princess was brought to the underground kingdom. There the ageless gnome tried to woo her with his magical turnips, Rüben, in the German tongue; with a touch of a wand they turned into all the people she had loved in her father's castle: her playmates and courtiers and her own dear sisters, Edelgard and—such a lilting name!—Irmentraut. What happiness, then! Such joy!

Alas! Just as turnips, plucked from the ground, wither and die, so too did all those from above the earth. Angrily, Emma confronted Rübezahl with the trick he had played on her. The gnome, still hoping to win her hand in marriage, went back to his fields and brought her a fresh batch. This time the clever girl was not to be fooled. She touched one of the turnips with her wand and turned it into a bumblebee:

Flieg, flieg Bienenkönigin klein
Fleig so schnell zum Prinzen mein

Leib Goldkorn translation:

Fly, fly swiftly little honeybee
To the Prince who belongs to me

Off went the little creature, only to be snatched out of the air by the beak of a hungry swallow. Undaunted, the Princess turned a second turnip into a cricket, eine Grille, and told him to hasten to her lover and tell him of her plight. Away hopped the messenger, only to be caught and gobbled up by a long-legged stork. Could the third time be the charm? The next turnip was turned into ein Falke, a falcon, who flew from tree to tree, until at last he came to the handsome Prince Ratibor, who sat sighing and pining for his lost Princess. "Emma, to-wit, to-woo!" sang the pretty bird. "To-wit, to-woo, Emma!"

Meanwhile, the Princess had thought of a plan to escape. She dressed herself in a wedding gown and sent her jailer to the fields to count the number of turnips needed for the bridesmaids and grooms at their ceremony. Off went the smitten spirit, counting and recounting and, fearing an error, counting yet again. Thus do we see how Fleischeslust can distract even the keenest of minds.

Emma had one fresh turnip left; she touched it with her wand, and behold: there stood a magnificent stallion, all girdled and bridled. With a laugh she leaped onto the stamping, snorting steed, and together they flew away.

By then the old gnome had finished his counting and returned to his palace. But where was his bride-to-be? Only the wedding gown, the wedding veil, and a sprig of myrtle lay on the ground. Up he flew, into the air, hurling thunderbolts and uprooting mountains. Too late. For as my dear mother Falma sweetly said one hundred years ago—

"All the furious Rübezahl could see was Princess Emma in the arms of Prince Ratibor, surrounded by the King and his courtiers and all the joyful members of his kingdom."

Finita, as the Italian people say, la commedia.

What's this? Sobbing? Weeping? Groans and sighs? I look up, to where the Lithuanian has pressed his white waiter's towel to his eyes.

"I can't help it," he declared, while dabbing his tears away. "I'm a sucker for a happy ending."

INTERLUDE

BELLES-LETTRES BALLET

*Leib writes letter after letter to the female star
of his opera—and at last hears back.*

> LEIB GOLDKORN
> AIRPORT PRAGUE-RUZNYĚ
> TERMINAL 1
>
> November 12, 2005

MISS RENÉE FLEMING
THE METROPOLITAN OPERA
LINCOLN CENTER
NEW YORK, N.Y. 10023

My dear Madam Fleming:

Greetings from old Prague! And from L. Goldkorn, Graduate, Akademie für Musik, Philosophie, und darstellende
Kunst. Also, onetime Glockenspieler of the Vienna State
Opera; flautist with the National Biscuit Company Symphonia, A. Toscanini conductor; and Bechstein artist in
the Steinway Quintet. Current status: widower. And you,
madam: If I am not in error, are you not a gay divorcee?
Loneliness we have in common. Also our art.

I have in these brief moments before boarding Flight 0050 time only to express with my Waterman how the prospect of hearing your voice in the role of Princess Emma fills an old heart—I dare not mention its numerical years!—with coltishness. Think of it, my dear! The premiere of Gustav Mahler's only opera. What a worldwide Phänomen! The Spaniard Domingo will sing the title role. And E. Wiesel is coming, too!

Ach! There go the three bells. Key of C, key of G, key, again, of G. Farewell, Iglau! Farewell, my youth! Farewell, the sweet smell of hops, the perfume of lindens. Entre nous, I have reason to believe I shall soon experience the uplifting aroma of Tommy Girl. Energetic floral notes, sandalwood, and heather. Ja! At ten thousand meters! And then, the myriad ordures of the big city, where I shall be, my lady, but a single zip code away from you.

Sincerely yours,

L. Goldkorn, Graduate
A.f.M.P.u.d.K.

Post Scriptum

You may write me at the Casa Blanca
138 West 80th Street
N.Y., N.Y. 10024
Suite Cinc-Derriere

LEIB GOLDKORN
THE PENTHOUSE
LA CASA BLANCA

November 20th, 2005

MISS RENÉE FLEMING
THE METROPOLITAN OPERA
LINCOLN CENTER
NEW YORK, N.Y. 10023

My Dear Madam Fleming:

It seems my letter to you has not yet crossed the storm-tossed seas. Or else it has been misplaced by the Togolanders, oft prone to such errors. Poor people, so far from their huts on the savanna. Another possibility: I did not, on the envelope, affix sufficient volleyballers (sport-heroes of the Czechists). If such is the case my missive will be arriving soon by steamship. Someday I hope to tell you persönlich, or tête-à-tête, as they say in La Belle France, the interesting tale of my relation to our composer, G. Mahler. A clue: Think of the Krupnick side of the family. Meanwhile, please be assured that I am each day working at the B. Greengrass establishment on the English translation of your role as Princess Emma. For instance, here is the moment when, after the abduction, you awake from your trance:

> *Wo bin ich? Ha. Ich fass' es kaum*
> *(erblickt Rübezahl)*
> *O weh mir!—Es ist kein Traum!*

> *Where am I? Where? It's all so queer.*
> *(spies Rübezahl)*
> *Ach! It's no dream! Oy veh ist mir!*

I need not explain to you, madam, that to translate the words of Herr Mahler—(Do you wish a further clue? Bueno. Fact one: The date of a certain person's birth is Nine November— Ha! Ha! Do not ask the year. Fact two: On February 24 of that same fateful annum the composer had a nuit d'amore with one Falma Goldkorn, née Krupnick. With fertilization. Do the math, Frau Fleming. Do the math—

To return hors de parenthèse: the translation of the words of G. Mahler is less important than the exploration of their deepest meaning. That is a task we must leave for future epistalations. Here is a third fact: In the City of New York there are 220 streets that run perpendicular to the East and H. Hudson Rivers. Fact four: Twenty such streets constitute one mile. Fact five, the finale: I am at West 80th Street. You are West 64th. Ergo, it is perhaps not a fantasia to believe I can detect the practice notes that rise from your "chest" zone, vibrate past the glottis and epiglottis, then fly in trills and tremolos into—dare I say it?—the air we urbanites breathe in common.

Au revoir,

"Leib" Goldkorn, Graduate

HIGH IN LA CASA BLANCA

November 29th, 2005

MISS RENÉE FLEMING
THE METROPOLITAN OPERA
LINCOLN CENTER
NEW YORK, N.Y. 10023

My dear Madam Fleming:

Still coy, my kitten? You make me feel like Prince Ratibor, though he is somewhat younger than truly yours. Younger even than Signor Pavarotti (this is not a spring chicken), who has agreed to play the role of that ardent lover. Poor Prince! Unhappy Graduate! Each knows that his beloved is near, very near—perhaps less than an American mile. Yet from her comes not a single word; of her white hands, mature torso, and the upturned nose of a blue-blood, not a single glimpse. How to escape these tormenting thoughts when all about him, par exemple, the sky glimpsed through a penthouse window, the fur on a feline, the porcelain of a Magic Chef oven—all remind him of the blue of his mistress's eyes, the strands of her chestnut hair, the creamy expanse of her noble brow? And other parts. Listen to the sighs of the pining Prince:

> *Und mag ich träumen oder wachen*
> *mir klinget immer ihr silbern Lachen!*

> *Whether I dream or whether I wake*
> *Her silvery laugh doth take the cake.*

Can there be the least doubt, madam, that the lament of Ratibor is the sad song within the composer's own heart?

There Herr Mahler was in Vienna, dreaming of the woman he had left behind in—very well, I shall say it—Iglau, a town which lay but a short train ride away, but which might as well have been in ice-locked Antarctica or in the underground kingdom of the jealous gnome—so high were the borders of decorum that kept him from embracing his beloved and holding high with a cry of delight his newborn son. Button nose. Notable ears. Baldish. Who, my dear, could this little chap be? That shall remain our secret.

Basta! Addio!

Your "Leibie"

Post Scriptum

Please send signed photo, medium décolletage, to the address above.

RENÉE FLEMING APPRECIATION SOCIETY
9782 DR. MARTIN LUTHER KING, JR., BLVD.
BRONX, N.Y. 14587

December 2, 2005

MR. LEIB GOLDKORNS
138 WEST 80TH STREET
NEW YORK, N.Y. 10024

Dear Mr. Goldkorns,

Thank you for your interest in Renée Fleming. I regret to inform you that we cannot provide signed pictures of Miss Fleming unless your request is accompanied by a check for twenty-five dollars made out to the R.F.A.S., Inc. However, we are pleased to enclose this schedule of Miss Fleming's upcoming 2006 season and tour, featuring performances in *Eugene Onegin, La Traviata,* and her signature appearance in the title role of Antonin Dvorak's wonderful fairy-tale opera, *Rusalka.* We are also enclosing a discount coupon for the purchase of her new album, *Love Sublime.*

Thank you once again for contacting the Renée Fleming Appreciation Society and for your interest in this great star.

Sincerely,

E. E. Zinggieser,
Secretary
R.F.A.S.

LEIB GOLDKORN
LA CASA BLANCA
ISLE OF MANHATTAN

December 4, 2005

MR. JOSEPH VOLPE
GESCHÄFTSFÜHRER,
THE METROPOLITAN OPERA,
LINCOLN CENTER
NEW YORK, N.Y. 10023

Caro Giuseppe,

Remove R. Fleming from role of Emma in world premiere *Rübezahl.* Stop. Cause: Aufmüpfigkeit. Stop. Also violation of Kommunikationsprotokoll. Stop. Engage at once Anna Netrebko. Stop. Provide signed photo of same. Stop. Invite V. Putin World Premiere. Stop. Inform winner of Russian

Federation State Prize that L. Goldkorn, Graduate, kisses her hand.

Cordiali saluti,

Leib Goldkorn, Regisseur

RENÉE FLEMING
9 THISTLE ROAD
ESSEX FALLS, N.J. 07021

December 7, 2005

MR. LEIB GOLDKORN
LA CASA BLANCA
138 W. 80TH STREET
NEW YORK, N.Y. 10024

Dear Leib Goldkorn!

How embarrassed I am! How can I apologize? It is all a terrible mistake. Your letters—your kind, warm, and intriguing letters—all arrived at the opera house and only this very morning reached my home on Thistle Road. There is so much to digest and think over that I am eager to read everything again. But I wanted to write you at once to let you know that the part of Emma seems perfect for me. Already I imagine myself waking from the magic trance and seeing before me the hideous and all-powerful Rübezahl.

Did you know that in the role of Rusalka I am also put under a spell, though this time it is to leave the world of spirits and join the world of men? Sometimes I feel that I have been sleeping my whole life and that one day I shall wake to see before me—well, instead of a "wart-covered gnome," a gentleman of taste and musicianship and genuine erudition. We can dream!

Mr. Goldkorn, I have to tell you that I am already under the spell of your old-world charm. How is it that you are able to understand me so completely? And we haven't even met! Is it because we both have had our share of loneliness? Permit me to express my sorrow at the passing of your wife. She must have been a very special person. And, yes, it is true: art we share as well. At least I do my best each day with those "trills and tremolos" to improve my modest skills.

Of course, there is one more thing we have in common: our secret! Yes, Leib Goldkorn, I have solved the riddle of that little boy, that fatherless boy, in the little town of Iglau. On the banks of the sparkling Iglawa. With the smell of cheroots from the tobacco monopoly in the air. You see, my maître, that I am a hard worker. I have done my research. Shall I write here what I have learned? The thrilling news? I promise to tell no one that the man whose vision I shall be striving to realize; the man I shall sing for; the man whom I am hoping soon to meet and work with each day and each night—that this man has in his veins the blood of the greatest composer since Beethoven and Wagner. You see how clever I am? From just your few clues I have deduced that the infant of Iglau was not only the master's own little boy—but also Mister Leib Goldkorn's very own grandfather. The secret? *You are the great-grandson of Gustav Mahler!*

But hush. Hush. Not a word.

> With my respect, my admiration,
> and warmest good wishes,
>
> *Renée Fleming*

LEIB GOLDKORN
LA CASA BLANCA
ISLE DE MANHATTAN

December 9th, 2005

MR. JOSEPH VOLPE
GESCHÄFTSFÜHRER
THE METROPOLITAN OPERA,
LINCOLN CENTER
NEW YORK, N.Y. 10023

Caro Giuseppe,

Cancel appointment A. Netrebko. Stop. Retain Fleming role of Emma. Stop. We must forgive petty misunderstandings. Stop. Send signed photo Netrebko nevertheless.

Ciao à tutti,

Leib Goldkorn, Regisseur

SCENE TWO

WILLIAMSBURG BRIDGE

*Leib and his cousins cross the East River
in a Lincoln Continental. He tries to teach them
American history and to discover for himself
the hidden meaning of* Rübezahl.

A NEW YEAR: 2006. Thus far a cold one. Shall we have a
little nip? No, no: not you, dear readers. I am addressing
ma famille, with whom I am enclosed within this Lincoln-type
limousine: leatherette cushions, one-way windows, and, with
all varieties of schnapps, a non-minibar. Absinthe to, alphabeti-
cally speaking, Yukon Jack.

No more does this centurian, in order to signal a cabriolet, have to step off the curb into a snowbank. No longer does
he have to stretch out his arm, the way his fellow Viennese
greeted their liberator. That was—hmmm, the one hops two
zeros—sixty-eight years ago: 4/3/38. A day of humiliation for
that town's Israelites. I was then employed at the State Opera.
During the performance of *Die Zauberflöte*, the glockenspiel
artist—a.k.a., truly yours—picked up his rubber mallet:

> *Das klinget so herrlich
> das klinget so schön!*

> *How pretty this chiming
> How clever my rhyming!*

The next thing I knew, I was, with a kick to my swallowtails, thrown out the doors of the Staatsoper and into the Schneeverwehungen, the drifts of spring snow that lined the Ringstrasse. There had been, in that audience, the most astute of critics:

> *At this Jew's music the folk are snoring.*
> *Out with him!*
> —FELDMARSCHALL GÖRING

Taxi! Does one not *heil* a taxi? Ha-ha. Multilingual pun. But now, friends, in this Lincoln-model, all is first-class.

Did someone say Yukon Jack? One hundred proof. With a hint of honey. Personal favorite, the Crystal Virgin:

> *1 oz. Yukon Jack, "The Black Sheep of Canadian Liquors"*
> *3/4 oz. Amaretto*
> *2 1/4 oz. cranberry juice*

> Chill with ice the ingredients above
> Strain into "shot" glasses until all is spent

> Guaranteed to make you fall in love
> Alcohol content: seventeen percent

Or should I, in honor of Hymena, curled up asleep on our "jump" seat, concoct instead a Canadian Pussy:

> *1 oz. Yukon Jack, "The Black Sheep of Canadian Liquors"*
> *1 oz. peach schnapps*
> *1 oz. orange juice*

> Mix together in a shaker with ice
> Into shot glasses steadily pour

> You can't beat this treat at any price
> Alcohol percentage: twenty-four

At sixty miles per hour, and in the middle lane of the Williamsburg Bridge, it might be wiser to manufacture a simple Snakebite. "Hola, friends! May I invite you to partake in this refreshment?"

2 oz. Yukon Jack, "The Black Sheep of Canadian Liquors"
1 dash lime juice

> Decant the whiskey o'er these frozen cubes
> It's just as kosher as Passover wine

> What? No takers? What a bunch of rubes—

Ach! Who would have thought these Satmars were such teetotalers? Lucky for Leib Goldkorn he's a non-religious. "Rabbi! Rebbetzin! Dear relations! Mud into your eye!"

> Percentage of alcohol—a robust forty-nine!

The abstemious Krupnicks are twisted about, staring through our tinted windows. Who can blame them for wanting to examine this sight? At one time the longest suspenseful bridge in the world. *Click-click-click*: What shutterbugs! Even the rebbetzin possesses a Polaroid-style, which she now points upward toward the westernmost tower.

"Madam, this structure is three hundred thirty-five feet in height, measured from the high-water mark of the river below us."

Click!

"This fact I learned when preparing for my naturalization exam before his Honor Solomon Gitlitz some, hmmm, sixty-three years ago. Is this not a feat of memorization? Ha-ha! No hint here"—a knock with knuckles on the side of my cranium—"of Uncle Al."

Out of her machine comes the paper that, unlike her mammary, is not fully developed. Now she aims her instrument again.

"A further fact: at one time there existed rails for trolleys, to wit, the Nostrand Avenue Line."

Click!

"Ho-ho. How high we are! I feel a touch of the vertigo. Rabbi, would you object if I had another wee drop?"

> *A long time ago, way back in history*
> *With nothin' to drink but mere cups o' tea*
>
> *Along came a man by the name of Tim Farley*
> *Who made many fine things out o' plain barley*

Rabbi Yitzhak, son of Kaspar, looks up from his Kodak-brand. "Cousin Goldkorn, what may I ask is that train I see from this window?"

I down my dram and lean forward, toward the portside glass. There, running in tandem with our "stretch" limousine, are the linked cars of the Brooklyn-Manhattan Transit Corporation, known to sophisticates as the BMT.

"That? That, Rabbi, is the J train, on its appointed rounds to Myrtle Avenue and the world beyond."

"Interesting. And what is the schedule of this railway?"

"Hmmm. Hmmm. Je pense. The J runs each day at all times, but its companion, the Z train, operates only at rush hours and only in the peak direction. Added fact: these tracks were first known as—"

The Satmar raises his hand. "And when are these so-called rush hours?"

"Oh, to Manhattan mayhaps eight to ten, ante meridiem; and to Brooklyn, which we now approach, maybe four to six, post meridiem."

"And how many passengers are thus transported?"

"I once heard, on our Philco-brand, this same question. On a challenging *Quiz Kids* show. Answer: each year, five million."

"No, No, Leib ben Gaston. I mean how many Jews on this train at that hour?"

"You have made a common error: *J* is not for Jews. Nor is Z for Zion. But let us deduce the answer to your question. If at, ha-ha, *crush* hour each person occupies a single square foot, and that each car is, rounding off, fifty feet in length and ten in width, we might say that each wagon carries five hundred souls. If the train has nine cars, that would mean, hmmm, hmmm; let us instead suppose there are ten cars. Ergo, any such train might carry a maximum of five thousand travelers, based on the assumption of girth and that they are non-Nipponese."

Here Rabbi Yitzhak snaps his fingers. In response, all three of my young cousins—do you remember their names? Arik, Anat, and the dubious Abdi—rush to the inward portals of the limousine and begin to take snapshots of the new attraction. How touching, these greenhorns! Their touristics in New York City began the very moment our flight touched down at airport "Jack" Kennedy, and I turned to address them:

"My dear Kopitshinetsers. How happy I am that we are all here gathered together. Allow me, on behalf of our President, George "W." Busch, to welcome you to this land. A great task lies before you. Hard study. Much toil. For example, you must learn the capital of each state, including newcomers Alaska and Hawaii. Also, date of the Louisiana Purchase. But at the end of this difficult journey—*bicameral*, do you know this word?— at the end of this journey there awaits a great reward: Amerikanische Staatsbügerschaft."

Anat, the endomorph: "I want something to eat."

"Take us," said the rebbetzin, "to Statue of Liberty. We want to take pictures."

"And Empire Thtate Building," said Abdi.

Arik: "The United Nations."

That was when Rabbi Yitzhak ben Kaspar, the paterfamilias, threw wide his Kodak-full arms: "G-d project, and G-d bless America, our new home!"

"Driver! Achtung! Driver! Why are you slowing down? Why have you stopped?" The answer is all too clear. A van for the moving of pianos is in front of us. A yellow cabriolet is just behind. And alongside, painted black, with black curtains, a limousine. Squint: bernard korn funeral home. Heavens, a hearse! For the nonce, all is as still as the poor fellow—could it be, at long last, Lester Lanin?—who lies inside it.

A non-Bulova moment goes by. A moment more. Nothing budges. Anat wipes one plump cheek with a handkerchief; Abdi looks musingly down at his sabots. Under his breath Arik hums and re-hums a Hebrew melody. Squint: the Korn-mobile is still beside us. Who lies within? A captain of industry? A concertmaster? *Imperious Caesar, dead and turn'd to clay?* Even he must take the Brooklyn-Queens Expressway, I-278, to Hachilah Hill. Dire thought: Is this curtained chariot a portent of my own fate as well?

Still the livery lingers. As does the van in front. And what does *it* carry? A Steinway? A Bechstein? An American Chickering? Or—a catch in throat here—a Vopaterny, stand-up or grand? Odd: the humming sound continues, even though Arik is now drinking a Nesbitt's through a straw. Sudden comprehension: it is the *bridge* that is humming; the wind blows through its cables as if they were the strings of a harp.

L. Goldkorn: "Snap Quiz! Number seventy-two! Who was fourteenth president? Eh? Eh? You, Anat."

"Why do I always have to Beat the Clock? Ask someone else."

"Very well. Cousin Abdi."

The mesomorph nods. Nods again. I see how the thoughts, in the form of muscles, move over his brow. What a powerful youth. A torso like that of Breitbart, the Strongman of Lodz. The eyes, in concentration, close. The tongue comes out.

Arik: "Why ask him this? Why ask anyone? We will not be Americans. You must wait five years."

"Exactement. I came to this land in 1938. I have been a citizen since 1943. Did I not in those years study my new nation's history with the same devotion that you yourselves study the Torah? Result: flying colors! Gold Star!"

Anat: "Who cares what you did? You'll be dead in 2011."

The KORN Car! The B.Q.E.! "Of such things we cannot be certain. Like America, constitution is sound."

Arik: "We never asked to be citizens. It's your idea."

A sudden blur, a sudden concatenation. The rebbetzin has struck her son on the side of his head with the classified section of the *New York Post*. "Do not say this. We want to be real Americans. Like everyone else."

"Wait. I think I have it." That is Abdi, who, with his chipped incisors, breaks into a smile. "Franklin Pierth! Ith that Gold Thtar?"

"Bravo! Bravo! F. Pierce. Non-Jew. You have won the Speed Queen washer!"

Outside our vehicle, several automobiles sound their horns, as if joining in the applause. Inside, the Graduate raises a Snakebite "shot":

"Let us drink, friends! To Cousin Abdi. As they say in Lithuania, I sveikatą!"

WHY, THE WHOLE WORLD wishes to know, were we wending our way to Williamsburg? (Whew!) The answer is easily given: I sought to discover, from the greatest of all rabbinical sources, the true meaning of the only opera by my non-putative père, together with the secret of the last words that, as a lad of five, I had heard from his lips.

HERE IS MY LIFE. HERE IS YOUR LIFE.
HERE IS THE LIFE OF OUR PEOPLE.

Why, in brief, did this composer, the equal of Mendelssohn and Meyerbeer, choose such a simple fairy tale, fare for Silesian tykes, to reveal the destiny of the Israelites?

Before embarking on this journey to the King of the Satmars, I attempted to solve the mystery on my own at the King of the Sturgeons'. Surrounded by homemade whitefish salads or the occasional roast beef, chicken fat and liver, turkey, coleslaw, Russian dressing, $11.25, I sat day after day and then week after week, reasoning thus:

Rübezahl, in the German, means counter of turnips, and undoubtedly refers to the underground gnome who must add up the root vegetables in his garden before Emma will consent to be his bride. As many have remarked, the turnip, genus *Brassica*, resembles in shape the male member of a Turk.

Note, in addition, that in the G. Mahler libretto, Emma repeatedly strokes this root with a magic wand. A hint of Selbstbefriedigung here. The observer need not comment at length on the fact that after each of these rub-a-dub-dubbings the turnip withers and dies. During the phase of Schwellung, however, it is transformed: first into innocent playmates and sisters; next into a bee, with its little stinger; then a falcon, with its sharp beak; and finally into a prancing white stallion:

Fliege, Rösslein, fliege fort,
Entführe mich dem bösen Ort!

Noble steed, let's flee a land that is heinous,
Off we go! Goodness, the size of that penis!

But what do such innuendos have to do with the fate of the Jewish people? We return to the name *Rübezahl*, turnip counter. Turnip, in German, is *Rübe*; and the plural, turnips, is *Rüben*, or, alternatively, Reuben. Aha! Reuben! Firstborn of Jacob! Progenitor of all twelve tribes!

"Mr. Mosk! Mr. Mosk! Eureka! I have found it! Turnips equals Reuben, with lack of umlaut!"

"What's that?" asked the Lithuanian waiter. "You want a omelet? With lox?"

"Ah, our native of Vilna. Tell me this: In the history of our people, what was the role of Reuben?"

"We got no Reubens. Not on a roll. And not on pumpernickel either."

Foolish fellow. I dismissed him, even as bits and pieces of ancient lessons swam upward to consciousness. Was not this firstborn son of Jacob deprived of his birthright? Did not his father, while on his deathbed, deliver instead of a blessing a curse?

Unstable as water, thou shalt not excel; because thou
wentest up to thy father's bed; then defiledst thou it.

But why? What was his crime? Goldiamond! S. T. Goldiamond! Help your bar-mitzvah boy! Of a sudden the archenemy, Uncle Al, loosened his grip. *Up to thy father's bed! Defiledst!* Did not Reuben, with his lusty mandrake root—yet another troublesome tuber—slip into the bedchamber of Jacob's Rubenesque concubine? That is to say, did he and his father not engage in congressionals with *the very same woman*? En court: a ménage à trois, a triangle, a Reuben's cube. With a hint of Inzesttabu, to boot.

At first the terrible curse of Jacob had little effect. Reuben, his firstborn, became in his turn the father of four sons, who themselves begat lads and lassies, who ditto, until at the time of the Exodus from Egypt their number had reached forty-six thousand five hundred—and those were just the males over the age of twenty. What multipliers! Like Hasen! Not to mention that in those days of yore the Jews lived longer than Bernard Baruch.

But in the course of time Jacob's words—*thou shall not excel*—fell upon Israel. The progeny of Reuben were overrun by Shalmaneser V and all those uncountable thousands were spread to wander and to suffer at the four corners of the earth. And where are they now? Who can say? The Ethiopes, the Persians, the Igbo of Nigeria—all claim that because of custom or ancient memory they are the members of that lost tribe. Not to mention the Irish with their gay jigs:

> *Musha ringum duram da*
> *Whack fol the daddy-o*
> *There's whiskey in the jar*

Also the American Indians and the excellent Mormons, the peace-loving Pashtuns, and even—think of the cry, *Tora! Tora! Tora!*—our former foes, the Nipponese.

Capital work, Holmes. By jingo, you've solved the riddle of Rübezahl. If only that were the case. True, I had made the crucial connection between the opera and the Torah, Rübezahl and Reuben, and discovered what my echt Vater meant when he said that his work would reveal the "life of our people." But did he not also say, *Here is my life. Here is your life*? What was that other connection—the one between his life and mine? And what had our two lives to do with the work I was translating and the fate of the Israelites? Here I put, on this bald head, the skullcap of thinking.

G. Mahler had, of course, his own mandrake root, a magic wand. With that baton he seduced all of Vienna. And his son had a magic flute, eine Zauberflöte, that similarly charmed the same Viennese. Yea, and both of us, like the descendants of Reuben, were sent into exile—not by Shalmaneser V but by the youth in salt-and-pepper when, all grown up, he covered himself in brown.

Both Gustav and the Graduate ended in America and—see how the apple tumbles in proximity to the tree—both at the Metropolitan Opera, where the work of the father would be conducted by the son. That work. *Rübezahl.* What did its composer mean to say at its conclusion? What did he want me to understand? There, at the end, the evil gnome—no longer the harmless figure in a fairy tale but the embodiment of all those demons from Shalmaneser to Haman to the popes of Rome and the tsars of Russia, and indeed those who have carried out the curse upon the Jews down to the present day: there that gnome is defeated and in his pain and misery cries out for the world to hear:

Ich will im Geisterreich genesen
Von der Wunde—die mich quält—der bösen
Lebt wohl, ihr Menschen, in Ewigkeit!

Back in my underground world I shall dwell
Without the comfort of a single tuber

People of flesh, I bid thee farewell!
   —Yours truly, A. Schicklgruber

At last I had before me the question of questions. What is the name of that Prince who will restore the Princess to her King and her kingdom? Who is that hero who will gather back to our homeland the far-flung tribes of the Jews? The answer: it was coming to me. It was drawing near. "Yes, yes. I have it! It is on the tip of my tongue!"

"Tongue?" There, splay-footed, stood Mr. Mosk. The waiter. "You want that on the triple-decker? With mustard and Swiss? How about some dessert—maybe a black-and-white cookie?"

A curse on all Lithuanians! All my ruminations were ruined. I rose from the table. I marched to the door. Already a new plan had formed in my mind. Had I not, at 138 West Eightieth Street, greater resources than existed in my own aged head? Or in the teaching of Samuel Taylor Goldiamond? My very own relations! Were they not students of Torah? Disciples of the Wizard of Williamsburg? Surely they, in their wisdom and their learning, could answer that most profound of all spiritual questions: Who would defeat Rübezahl, ruler of the nether kingdom? Who is it that will send the reawakened Golem back to the land of the dead? Who will bring back to their homeland the long-lost Jews?

FOR A MAN at the age of one hundred and four, five flights of steps are not a cake waltz. Thus the sun had almost descended by the time I reached the fifth floor and turned not toward my own abode at Number 5-D, but toward the door of the former dwelling of Madam Schnabel, contralto, at 5-C. What was that sound that came from within? Of course! Rabbi Yitzhak ben Kaspar and his devotees were undoubtedly facing east, in other words toward the Williamsburg section, and, as was their wont each day at sundown, percussing their heads against the floor. Just the type of folks I needed!

I waited, both to catch my breath and to allow the sound of prayers to diminish; then, lightheartedly, to disguise my eagerness, I called out to the Krupnick clan:

"Knock, knock!"

"Who's there?" responded a voice from within.

"Doris."

"Doris who?"

"Door is closed. Ha. Ha. Ha. That's why I knocked."

At once Reb Yitzhak himself, eyes blazing, beard trembling, flung open the portal. "What do you want, Cousin Goldkorn? Why do you interrupt our evening prayers?"

"I have a question. An important one. One that will change all our lives."

Before the rabbi could answer, one of his sons pushed into the doorway. "I know!" cried Abdi. "Wethtern meadowlark. Thtate bird of North Dakota."

"No, no. This is not a snap quiz."

"No Gold Thtar?"

"My question is about the destiny of the Jewish people. I want to know who will save them. I want to know who, for all these thousands of years, they have been waiting for. And when will he come?"

The other sons crowded into the doorframe. "What's he want?" asked Anat.

Arik: "The name of the savior."

"What? The Methiah?"

"And when he will come."

Reb Yitzhak spread wide his hands. "No one knows the name of Moshiach. Perhaps not even G-d Himself."

"But what about Rebbe Teitelbaum? Don't you study with him? Isn't he your master? The wisest man on earth?"

"True, if any man possesses such knowledge, it is the Rov, may he indeed live to greet Messiah."

"Then take me with you! To Williamsburg! I shall call J. Volpe! He'll arrange it! First class! Prima! With maxi-bar! All the way by limousine!"

WHICH IS WHY, friends, we now find ourselves surrounded by a van for pianofortes and a van for corpses, high above the roiling waters of the East River. Traffic jam.

INTERLUDE

PAS DE BILLETS-DOUX

A friendship blossoms.

RENÉE FLEMING
9 THISTLE ROAD
ESSEX FALLS, N.J. 07021

December 15, 2005

MR. LEIB GOLDKORN
LA CASA BLANCA
138 W. 80TH STREET
NEW YORK, N.Y. 10024

Caro Maestro (if I may be so bold!):

I am so happy to hear from you again! I was worried that
you would not accept my heartfelt apology. And thank you
so very much for Emma's defiant aria when she snatches
the magic wand from her oppressor. There are mysteries in
her words that I hope to explore with you in person. For
instance:

> *Oh, here comes old Rübezahl, that hideous lout*
> *With his magic stick: there's nobody meaner.*

Can it truly create dear sister Irmentraut
From a turnip the shape of a sultan's wiener?

Perhaps we could discuss this together? I wonder if you could drive up to Essex Falls for cocktails. May I suggest December 24th, Christmas Eve? It would give me such pleasure to have you on Thistle Road when the children open their little gifts. Wait till I tell them who's coming! The great-grandson of Gustav Mahler! I eagerly await your reply. In Emma's own words to her handsome Prince:

O Komm!

In anticipation, and with warmest holiday wishes,

Renée Fleming

LEIB GOLDKORN
LA CASA BLANCA
CINQUIÈME ÉTAGE
ISLE DE MANHATTAN

December 19, 2005

MISS RENÉE FLEMING
9 THISTLE ROAD
ESSEX FALLS, N.J. 07021

My Dear Miss:

I note that you have left out the remainder of the Princess's line. To wit:

O Komm! Willst du dich neben mich nicht betten?

Oh, come! Lie with me on this bed of petals.

Undoubtedly you felt in your maidenish way that this was a bit salty.

Did you say the 24th? Alack! You must remember Emma's next line:

> *Ach! Hab' Acht!—Geliebter—Hier sind Nesseln*
>
> *Ach! Take care, beloved. Here are some nettles.*

The petals, my dear, are the thought of our coming rendezvous. The nettles are that thank you very much, but I cannot accept due to an important business engagement.

Yours truly,

"Leib" Goldkorn

RENÉE FLEMING
9 THISTLE ROAD
ESSEX FALLS, N.J. 07021

December 25, 2005

MR. LEIB GOLDKORN
LA CASA BLANCA
138 W. 80TH STREET
NEW YORK, N.Y. 10024

Caro Maestro,

I sincerely hope my invitation did not offend you. I should have realized that you could not partake of our Christmas celebrations. It was very thoughtless of me to put you in such an awkward position. I know that even though your great-grandfather converted to the Catholic Church, he did so only for practical reasons, and that he remained in his heart and in his work a proud Jew. As, Maestro, are you.

Perhaps the Princess could meet her Prince in a place less "nettlesome"? (It occurs to me that perhaps you were referring to mistletoe. Poor Renée! She has no one to stand in the doorway with her this Christmas morning.)

Forgive me!

Renée Fleming

P.S. Could we meet instead in New York? Shall we say next Thursday, the 29th? Oh, let's make it Wednesday! The 28th! In my private room at the Met. I am eager to meet you and shake your hand.

Renée

LEIB GOLDKORN
LA CASA BLANCA
RÉSIDENCE PRIVÉE
ISLE DE MANHATTAN

December 27th

MISS RENÉE FLEMING
9 THISTLE ROAD
ESSEX FALLS, N.J. 07021

My Sweet Miss,

Offended? Pas du tout! Happy Chanukah! If I had been able to attend your holiday celebration I would, on my knees with your two Fräulein—you see? I too have done scholarly researches—spin our little top:

Draidel, Draidel, Draidel: I made you out of clay.
Here's a chocolate dollar: ha, ha, that ain't hay!

I am aware of the mistletoe, *Phoradendron serotinum*. Is it not a Yankee custom to stand beneath it so that a gentleman may fondle a lady? But Ach! Hab' Acht! This shrub may cause distresses, with spews from the bowels. How oft in life do we thus find pleasure mingled with pain, beauty with ugliness, innocence with sodomistics. Is not the thorn, madam, close to the rose? Does the doorway to amours not abut the exit of the excrementas?

It is after the midnight hour. In the forest the owl stares with his yellow eyes. The opossum crawls from his den. The bat, my dear, is on the wing. Time for the Prince to say good night to his Princess.

I do not shake your hand.

I kiss it.

"Leib" Goldkorn

RENÉE FLEMING
9 THISTLE ROAD
ESSEX FALLS, N.J. 07021

December 29, 2005

MR. LEIB GOLDKORN
LA CASA BLANCA
138 W. 80TH STREET
NEW YORK, N.Y. 10024

Caro Maestro,

I really should be angry with you. Do you know that I waited and waited? I don't mind telling you that my heart was beating; it's not every day that you meet a genius. But you stood me up. Has that ever happened to you? What a terrible feeling. Like the blade of a knife. Oh, Maestro! Dear Leib! Is anything wrong? Has something awful happened? I laugh at my own fears. After all, a man in his prime: What could befall you? An opera singer spends her life surrounded by calamity and suffering—Tosca! Violetta! Desdemona! Povera Butterfly! Perhaps that is why I can't help imagining the worst. So, please, Cher Maître, drop me a note. Tell me you are in good health. Tell me that I need not worry.

Isn't it strange? I've never laid eyes on you, but I miss you. I wish you would visit me. Will you, my dear man? Soon? Say *Yes!*

I wish you a wonderful 2006, a year in which we shall strive together to bring the vision of Gustav Mahler to all the world. Perhaps our friendship, like the work we shall stage, will have a happy ending!

Your own Renée

LEIB GOLDKORN
LA CASA BLANCA
ESPACE PRIVILÉGIÉE
ISLE DE MANHATTAN

January 3, 2006

MISS RENÉE FLEMING
9 THISTLE ROAD
ESSEX FALLS, N.J. 07021

Dear Madam Fleming:

In regard to your letter of December 29, I can tell you that my health is in the top drawer. I am feeling oats. Please convey to your family my wishes for a fruitful new year.

I am remaining
Sincerely yours,

Leib Goldkorn, Graduate

Oh, Leib! My Leibie!

How could you send me such a cold and heartless letter? Don't pretend there is nothing wrong. *Feeling your oats!* I know what you're feeling! And I know her name. Anna Netrebko! Thought you could fool me, didn't you? Joe told me all about it. You wanted to replace me, *me!*, with that skinny Russian tramp! And you wanted her photo, too! With those horse-teeth! If I didn't know better I'd think you were some dirty old man!

Leib Goldkorn, you can't hide from me any longer. If you won't come to see me—Monday, the 9th, six p.m. I'll have them bring in a light supper. What do you like, darling?

Some canapes? A little grilled fish? Or if you prefer, a real he-man steak! But watch out, Mister G! If Mohammed won't come to the mountain . . . That's right, *I am coming to you.* Sixteen! Sixteen blocks away! I could be at your side in ten minutes! Oh, I'll fly there in five! So near, my heart—and yet so far!

Always!

Your Renée

P.S. Find enclosed a photograph of a different soprano. Yes, there is her head, though I fear she is losing it.

LEIB GOLDKORN
LA CASA BLANCA
CINQ DELUXE
ISLE DE MANHATTAN

January 9, 2006

MISS RENÉE FLEMING
9 THISTLE ROAD
ESSEX FALLS, N.J. 07021

Mein Schnuckiputzi,

No! No, no, no. Do not come to La Casa Blanca. All is under constructions. Self-flushing not available. Also, in residence are cousins on maternal side, of the Satmarian persuasion. They must not know of our dalliance. Should they read these billets-doux or discover that I have in my life an inamorata, there would be a family crisis. Not to mention a possible violation of an Order in the Court.

"Heartless," you say? and *"cold"*? I confess, my last billet-doux was not so sweet. On purpose, my buttercup. Such are the obstacles to our romance—the sharp sword of King Mark lies between Tristan and his Isolde!—that I thought it best to end matters before they could accomplish a fecundation.

But I failed! How could I resist you? Not when I hold your foto replication in my hand. Danke! Dankeschön! Such charms! Mascaras. Pendants from lobes of ears. We speak poetically of ruby lips. "Kyoto Red" by Tabu? "Naked Kiss"? And the little apple of the chinny-chin. I remove my eyes from lower temptations. Please give no thought to the Russian. There is in her case a palpable absence of cleavage. Madam: no contest.

Gaze on, former flautist! The eyes: hazelnut. The cheeks: rouged. Behind the flash of dentals, is that not a tongue-tip? A tongue-tip, dear Jesus! I wish that I— What's that? A Niagara! A cousin has completed, upon the W.C., his business. A quick farewell. A brief caress. A Gutenachtkuss

From your own Liebchen,

"Leib" Goldkorn

January 12, 2006

Dearest Liebchen,

I understand. I shall not pursue you to your lair. But soon, soon, soon, we shall be working together. Luciano arrives at the end of the month. Next month you will guide us in our duet and in all of our efforts. Until then, will you do for me what I have done for you? A photo! Send it! Something I can hold in my hand as you hold me in yours. You must do that for your

> Povera Butter . . . cup!
>
> *R.*

> LEIB GOLDKORN
> LA CASA BLANCA
> SUITE PERSONNEL
> ISLE DE MANHATTAN
>
> January 15, 2006

Meine Zaubermaus,

Here is a small candid-type. I have hesitations. The hairless-ness. Also the ears. Woodwinder's lips. But such has God made me, and such I am. Do not laugh, madam. Could this be farewell?

> Dein ist mein Herz.
>
> *"Leib"*

Post Scriptum: Luciano? You are with this tenor on a first-name basis?

> January 15, 2006

Dearest,

Laugh? Yes, I laugh. With joy! You silly mouse! Don't you know that baldness is a sign of manhood? And I love your dear ears! Why do they stick out that way? Because all the pretty girls have been pulling them? When in your arms? I'll try not to think about that. I prefer to see in them a sign of musicianship, extended, as a snail does its antennae, or a beetle its feelers, to catch any stray note in nature, any tone, the least semi-demi-hemi-quaver. True, the lips are large. Oh, my cavalier! May they soon be pressed to mine! And what taste in clothes. That jacket! Those pants! They used to call them "zoot suits," I believe; and yes, they are just now coming back in style.

Isn't this a photograph taken from one of those automatic machines? Dear man! Did you run out in the cold just to please your Schnuckiputzi? But where did you find the booth? I doubt there is a single one left in all of New York. It is so cute and adorable that you would be jealous of Luciano. A great artist, yes. But do you know when he was born? 1935! La! That's too old for me! But I wonder, with a beating heart: Am I perhaps too old for the dashing youth whose likeness I hold in my hand?

Now it's my turn to be jealous. This photo has been torn in two. Who was in the other half? That Communist? Netrebko? I thought you did not care for flat-chested types. Beware, sir! I have had much practice in revenge. *Muori, dannato! Muori! Muori!* Who is she? One of those "cousins"? *Maledetto!*

Oh, the light on your scalp. How it shines. And have you—I tremble to ask—large-sized shoes?

What does my Prince say in our love duet?

> *Ich halte dich in meinen Armen.*

Perhaps Leib Goldkorn will translate those words into flesh, into blood.

Yours forever,

R.

Mein Schneckchengehäuse,

> *In these arms my love now safely lands.*

To which my Princess replies:

> *An meine Brüste dich erwärmen.*
>
> *Warm yourself on my mammary glands.*

Thus do we venture, for an American audience, into the risqué. You ask about the missing portion of the rotogravure. I am experiencing here a déjà vu, for only recently did I come across another pictorial of a man and—yes, you guessed it—a missing woman. In that case the man was my late Vater and the woman was Falma, meine Mutter. Only the double-dots of her dirndl remained in view. Now I must speak the painful truth: the woman once shown in this reproduction was—was— Give me a moment. Clara Goldkorn, née Litwack. Wife! Helpmate! Spouse! Gone! Gone! Widower Goldkorn is now alone. Forgive this fulmination. Now you know why the imago is torn. I could not, I cannot, bear to see it.

You are correct, my Liebling, my little snail-shell: the camera that "snapped" this picture was indeed inside an automat-style machine. You can find these still upon the Boardwalk at Coney Island, where I venture to take part in Polar Bear aquatics and to view the Mermaid Parade. Perhaps you would like to join me for a non-skinny-dip? Alas, you have missed our annual plunge upon New Year's day. But you may partake in other immersions. Bring a one-piece suit. It is such exertions, along with physical jerks, that have kept me through the years in such fine fiddle.

My heart, too, has been ripped in pieces. Will it soon be healed?

I give you ein Knutschfleck.

Your Liebe "Leib"

Post Scriptum: Thom McAn size 5. Why do you ask?

Maestro Mio,

Oh the pain I must have caused you. Your Clara. Your dear wife. I should have known. Never again will I doubt you. Two lonely souls, it seems, have found each other. I long to hold your dear head, so smooth and shining, so full of musical ideas, to my breasts. My Polar Bear: Are you getting warm? Dearest, how this has happened I do not know. A mystery. A miracle. But I can fight it no longer. Leib Gold-korn, Graduate: Renée has fallen in love.

I am overcome with sudden shyness.

R.

LEIB GOLDKORN
138 WEST 80TH STREET
APT. 5-D
NEW YORK, N.Y. 10024

January 28, 2006

THE NAME NOT FIT TO PRINT
THE NEW YORK TIMES
TIMES SQUARE
NEW YORK, N.Y.

My dear FINN [Former Inamorata Not Named]:

How are you? I am fine. Before going further let me make an inquiry. Have you ever in your life been left "standing up"? What a terrible feeling that is. Like the stabs of a knife blade. Cast your mind back to August of 1997. August 31st, to be precise. Need I say the words "Court of Palms"? Or "Hotel Plaza"? Surely you remember the scene of humiliation.

The bill for schnapps and for condiment carousels was one hundred and twenty dollars: stab number one. The shame of a mistaken identity, during which I asked a blond woman with heft if by any chance she wished with me to "faire l'amour." Stab number two. Number three? The many hours that I spent in the effort to master your native tongue: *Onniteluni, rouva, charmikkaasta ja ilahduttavasta hatustasi.* "My compliments, Madam, upon your charming and delightful hat."

You are no doubt aware that in writing this missive I am entering a zone of extreme danger. Wait! Observe that I have not once mentioned your name, not even in the Esquimaux version. S. A. Lubowitz, note you that. Innocent, Your Honor! Still, with the mere expression of these words

I am putting myself at risk of incarcerations or—leeches, madam!—even worse. Nonetheless, as a grandee I felt I must give you news that I fear will itself "stab" your heart. I advise you that if you are not already doing so, please sit on a chair. Very well: no more beating the bush. Madam, I have found another. True, with her there shall be no saunaistics. She will in all probability neither beat me nor walk upon my back. But she has definite mams, and is, in her pedigree, American: one hundred percent. And so, farewell!

With no hard feelings,

Leib Goldkorn, Graduate
Akademie für Musik,
Philosophie und darstellende Kunst

SCENE THREE

SATMARIA

Leib takes some important steps and then,
with a Rhode Island Red, confesses his sins.

Ich bin a kleyner Draidel, gemakht bin ikh fun blay

Ho! Ho! Ha! I'm spinning! Oh what fun to play!

How dark it is. Only blackness before me. They have pulled my hat over my eyes the way Falma used to draw the night shade over Falco and Fieke.

"Tweet! Tweet! Hee, hee, hee. Fellows! Where are we going? Everything is turning around, like ein Karussell. Is it possible that I, a non-teetotaler, have had a drop too much to drink?"

Nun! Gimel! Shin! Hei!

Let's raise a glass of Yukon J!

Rabbi Yitzhak ben Kaspar: "Quiet, fool! The Jews are looking!"

"They can see me! Ho! Ho! Ho! But I can't see them! This is a problem of metaphysics. Where are we? On Rodney Street? On Rutledge? Friends, this chapeau is stuck."

————

A BRIEF WORD, my dears, by way of explanation. As in the days when the former Clara Litwack poured salts of Drāno down the kitchen pipe, creating a small sensation, so at last did the traffic on the Williamsburg Bridge begin under the influence of the setting sun's rays to loosen its impedimenta. The van with the pianolas rolled forward. The curtained KORN— Who was inside? The last of the Andrews Sisters? A Dionne quintuplet?—began also to move. Our driver, swarthy in complexion, stepped on the gas. Would there be time for a last little nip? Perhaps a Harbor Lights?

1/2 "shot" butterscotch schnapps
1/2 "shot" Baileys® Irish Cream
1 splash Yukon Jack, the "Black Sheep of Canadian Liquors"

> Mix the Baileys® and butterscotch, put the
> liqueur on top
> Ignite the "Jack" and make it go poof!

Arik, the ectomorph:

> "Abdoul! This is our exit! You've got
> to stop!"

> So sweet! So tasty! And just 38 proof

"Driver! Abdoul! Broadway West! Move to the right! To our exit." Now the speaker was plump Anat. The Continental— there is a song by that name—swerved into the adjoining lane, causing truly yours to spill half of my pick-me-up. I managed, nonetheless, to follow the recipe instructions.

"Yeeee!" That was the rebbetzin, emitting a scream.

"What are you doing?" demanded her spouse. "Put down that match!"

Poof!

"Help!" shouted Arik. "We are going to die!"

The limousine swerved even more sharply, onto the Broadway West ramp. The flames of the Harbor Lights shot into the air.

"An la illaha illa Allah!" cried the driver, or words to that effect.

"Ha! Ha! I am not a member of the Roumanian Circus. I cannot swallow a drink when it is on fire."

The mesomorph made a circle with his lips and blew out the conflagration.

"Excellent. Well, friends, as they say: Na zidovima!"

> *It's something daring, the Continental,*
> *A way of dancing that's really "entre nous"*

"Cousins, can any of you tell me—Miss Ginger Rogers: Alive? Or not-alive?"

No one responded. Instead, all of the passengers were digging into a kind of cloth-covered valise and removing a half dozen fur-bearing hats.

Meee-too?

"Ha, ha! Not *cats*, my honey-bear. *Hats!*"

Yes, of the type that Jews from Poland used to wear on the Sabbath, and sometimes on weekdays too. One after the other my mekhutonim put on this haberdashery.

"I like them, chums. Stylish. And suave."

The rabbi pulled out the last such item. "Here. It is for you."

"No, no. Danke. I am a non-religious. This is, for the masses, an opium."

The Lincoln, meanwhile, had left the Broadway West exit and turned southward onto what, with maneuvers, became Lee Avenue.

Mee-wow, wow! Hence Hymena, with her pink nose and

half whiskers pressed to the window glass. Who could blame her? It looked as if the whole world at that twilight hour was walking about with herbivores on their heads. Then it dawned on me: the men in beards and long black coats, the women in head scarves, the shops with Yiddish-type script—we had arrived in Satmaria.

Once more the rabbi held out, toward his elder kinsman, the headgear. "Put it on, Leib Goldkorn. At once."

"Ha, ha. Not this non-believer. I am a man of the world."

It's very subtle, the Continental
Because it does what you want it to do.

Suddenly the three brothers seized my arms, while their sire leaned forward and thrust the hat not only over my head but also my eyes and, no mean feat, my ears.

"Wait, lads! An error. This is not a size six."

Eeeee. Was that my pretty pet? Protesting such rudeness to her patron? No, it was the brakes of our automobile as, with a thump, we came to rest against the curb. Someone pushed from behind. Someone else pulled in the front. The next thing I knew I was standing on the avenue. In my confusion, my dizziness, I began to spin this way and that, like a top. Thus we have arrived at the answer to the aforementioned question: Ja! I have had a bisel too much to drink.

IN TOTAL DARKNESS, save for the comets and meteors that now begin to whiz about in the cavern of my Satmarian streimel, I feel myself drawn several blocks in one direction, after which our assembly makes a rightward turn and then a contrary turn to the left. "I know! I have guessed it! We are on a treasure hunt!"

"Yes." I recognize—they say that the loss of one sense increases the acuteness of the others—the voice of Anat. "The treasure of our rebbe, may his name endure forever."

Ah! The Rov. The Teitelbaum. "Cousin Yitzhak: Was this not your teacher in the land of Israel?"

Ptui. Ptui. I need not explain these spittoons.

Arik responded. "Not Reb Yoel, our great King, but his nephew, Moshe."

"And he is the one who will answer all my questions? About the tribe of Reuben? The savior of the Jews?"

"Quiet! We have arrived at the residence."

"What's that? Do I smell blintzes?"

"Shah! We must climb the stairs."

Someone in our party pulls open—what rusty hinges!—a door and we all push inside. Then, step by step, we make our way up the staircase. A minute of such exertions goes by. Then another. I begin to hear Anat, of avoirdupois, pant-panting. From the rebbetzin, a gasp. From Arik, a groan. At last, a landing. Huzzah! But without pause we turn and continue our upward migration.

"Tell me, is it the custom among the Satmarians to serve their guests a thimble of schnapps? Par exemple, a Buffalo Sweat?"

1 tsp. Tabasco® sauce
7 tsp. Yuk—

A harsh blow descends on the crown of my beaver-fur topper. An elbow, a sharp one, drives the air from my lungs. In silence we continue—on this Everest one needs a sherpa!—our not so bon voyage.

"How high we are climbing, friends! I wanted to ask questions about the nature of God, not have dinner with him. Ha—"

All of a sudden we bump up against each other and come to

a halt. In short, arrival. Rabbi Yitzhak ben Kaspar, I assume it is he, knocks on the wood of the door. Count to ten. The endomorph seems to have caught his breath, for it is his voice that now addresses his father: "Knock again. Harder. The rebbe—his hearing is bad."

Knock. Knock.

"Who's there?" say I, in a reflex. "Abbott?"

"Abbott who?"

"Abbott time you opened this door."

But no one opens. Again Reb Yitzhak pounds, this time with force. From the other side a faint, frail, wavering voice says, in English, not Yiddish, "Come in."

Within my gabardines I feel some ado. A hand has entered the pocket. *Oh, ho!* think I. "Is this Zipporah once more at the zipper?" Indeed, it is the voice of the rebbetzin I hear next:

"I must leave you, my Leib. Women not allowed. This for you—for all of us—will be a great moment. You must follow all of the steps."

"What? Haven't there been enough of them already? My head, from such thin air, is spinning."

"Only twelve more. Number one: *Admit your affliction and that you are powerless before it.*" Here, with with several fingers, she creates a refreshment amidst the lint. "Adorable. That's what you are in that hat." Then she is gone, a will-o'-the-wisp, and we menfolk in a phalanx crowd through the door.

The room—I sense this, as a bat does the contours of his cave—is a large one, dimly lit. I hear soft greetings and the sound of hand kisses. With a firm grip I attempt to remove my hat. Difficult task. I push with all my strength against the brim. Ach! The lobes of these ears! Now two humans clasp my elbows. I hear Reb Yitzhak say, "This way. Over here. You must meet the Rov."

I am guided across the room and halt before a personage;

I cannot see him, but I can smell him: "Youth Dew" by Estée Lauder, though I might be mistaken since the plush of the beaver is partway up my nose. I feel a touch, chest-high. "The hand of the Rov," says Arik.

"Kith it," says Abdi.

I seize le main du monsigneur. Light, soft, full of bones, to be compared to a herring. I kiss it.

"Shalom aleichem."

"Aleichem shalom, as they say in France."

"You have, dear friend, very large lips."

"A woodwinder's, Majesty. Because of the pursing."

"The sign, good Goldkorns, of a sensitive spirit."

A general sigh from those nearby.

Anat: "He approves."

Arik: "He sees into the soul."

Abdi: "He likth you."

"I'm a little light-headed, Your Excellency. You wouldn't have by chance a slivovitz? You get the idea, ha-ha. The hair of the dog."

Fitz! Footz!

"Hush, my Honigbienchen. This is a folkish expression."

"I hope the Rebbe will forgive our cousin—" and here Reb Yitzhak gives me a painful pinch. "It is his habit to make such jests. He knows we regard alcohol as the work of Satan."

The Rov, addressing truly yours: "Is this a fact? You do not indulge?"

"Is that what I'm supposed to admit? Is it step one? Okie-dokie. I confess that on special occasions—let us say a wedding night, with confirmed penetration—I might take a wee glass. You know, Mission Bell."

"You misunderstand. That is not why you have come to us."

"True, Your Grace. I seek instruction from a learned rabbi about, and I quote, *the life of the Jewish people.*"

"A problem exists. A difficulty. You are not—I should say *not yet*, for who can determine what lies before us? We are all in the hands of HaShem—"

"Gesundheit!"

"—You are not yet a Satmarer, or a member of Bnai Ya Yoel?"

"No, only the Steinway Quintet, now defunct."

"Give me, good Goldkorns, your hand."

I hold it out. He takes it, rubs it, kneads it. A terrible notion: I am ashamed to repeat it. I won't repeat it. Oh, very well: those priests, you know, those bishops, and the little boys. Perish the thought!

"No," the great Moshe continues. "He is not a Satmarer. And I fear he has never seen in person or read the works of my uncle, our beloved Grand Rebbe Yoel, may his merit protect us."

"No, but I once knew a Moe who inherited the throne of a king. The Sturgeon King, ha, ha!"

In response the Rov squeezes my fingers, then turns up my palm, like a Gypsy telling a fortune. "Nor does he say the prayers. Neither the Shacharit, the Mincha, nor the Arvit. He does not wear tefillin."

"Don't worry, Your Serenity. These Kopitshinetzers pray enough for all of us."

"Is it possible? Is he not even a bar mitzvah?"

"No, no. *Hayon Leib ben Gaston, Ata Bar mitzvah.* The words of Rabbi Goldiamond. I remember them like yesterday. Goodbye, good luck, Uncle Al!"

"You see?" This is the voice of Yitzhak ben Kaspar: "We would not bring before the rebbe a heathen."

"I had a little trouble with Genesis 38. Judah sends his second son, Onan, so that he would 'know,' hee-hee-hee, Tamar and give her children. But he did not accomplish an infusion. A clear case of self-befriendingness."

The one Rebbe, Teitelbaum, to the other, ben Kaspar:

"True, I am able to see in this hand"—*still with the hand, eh, Padre?*—"the presence of a true Jew."

"Take a good look. They say that this—you know, what Onan did—causes hair to grow on your palms. Ha! Ha! Ha! An obvious canard. Or hair to fall off your head. Uh-oh."

Anat: "Enough words!"

Arik: "He must admit his addiction."

Abdi: "He must take the firtht thtep."

Now Reb Teitelbaum, the head of the Satmars, in his aged voice, intones:

"It is time, my son."

Strange, the sensation that arises within me. It is as if someone else, some force, some destiny, were moving the tongue in my mouth. Blind, at full attention, I hear my own voice:

"Hello! My name is Leib G., and I am a roué."

The assemblage breaks into applause. My cousins slap me on the dorsals. The nephew of the legendary Yoel squeezes even more tightly my hand in his own.

Abdi: "Thtep two!"

Rabbi Yitzhak: "*You must come to believe that a higher power than yourself will restore you to righteousness.*"

"A higher power: that's easy. Judge Solomon Gitlitz, for example. Or Wendell Willkie. Or the excellent Thomas E. Dewey. Are we not all Republicans here? But perhaps you mean a greater power than any one man? Once an Afrikaner stole from me on the Avenue Amsterdam my Rudall & Rose–model flute, and then after many years restored it to me. What power was it that moved the Moor? Can you tell me that? Thus we see that even the simplest folk are touched by this force: maybe even the idiot of Iglau. But we have not yet spoken of the power of art. The murals, by Feiner, at the Steinway Restaurant, for instance. Und Musik! Once, at that same establishment, we quintet members each experienced a certain sensation, Zusammengehörigkeit, we call it, yes, *connectedness*: to one another, to musicians of the past, and even to the divine music of the spheres—all while playing 'The Indian Love Call.'"

Arik: "Perhaps we should move on to step three."

"Three?"

"Yeth. *You muth turn your life over to the care of G-d.*"

"*G-d?* Now you're talking. That's what I'm here for. Rabbi! Reb T.! You are a learned man. Here is the question of questions: *Who is it that will save the Jewish people?*"

Before I hear the reply something falls on my hand. Something wet. A drop. Another drop. Is the roof leaking?

Consternation among the Krupnicks.

"Perhaps the Rebbe is disturbed?"

"Ith he thad?"

"Why does he weep?"

"Why?" echoes the Satmar Rebbe. "Because I am, in years, ninety-one."

"Ha, ha, barely a senior citizen!" That is my response. From the others:

"Thanks to G-d!"

"May each year be multiplied!"

"May the Rebbe live to a hundred and twenty!"

"A hundred and twenty? I shall not live to ninety-two."

Gasps from the assemblage. But from the centurian:

"Moe, you shouldn't be pessimistic. Look at truly yours. Four months ago I wanted to put my head in the Magic Chef oven. And now? I can order the caviar sampler. I am conducting a world premiere."

Another tear. Yet another. They are pouring into the cup of my hand.

"Listen, Holiness, here's a tip from Goloshes, M.D.: *A paroxysm each year / Or the doctor comes near.*"

"No, no. My time has come. I shall not see the completion

of the year 5766. You wished to die four months in the past. I shall not be alive four months in the future."

Here my relations begin to sniffle, to groan.

"Foolish mortal! In my vanity, my white robes, my jewels, I told myself that I would be privileged to see Moshiach."

All: "The Messiah!"

"Now I know I was mistaken. True, I shall mount the heavenly steed that will take me to another world; but I shall never see the light that shines from that face."

At that, all fall into a sorrowful silence.

"Steed?" I say, hoping to lighten the mood. "We got one of those in my father's opera:

> *Off, great stallion, o'er field and forest far flung,*
> *Fly high, fly far, let the world see how you're hung."*

"Ah, yes," says the Teitelbaum. "No sooner did the Kopitshinetzer rabbi speak of this *Rübezahl* than I knew that your ancestor, though he was an apostate, and Viennese, had experienced a divine revelation. He had seen how our poor Jews, scattered like the children of Reuben, would make their return. Not to the State of Israel—"

Ptui!

"But to the land that Moshiach shall set free."

From my own lips there comes the anguished cry: "And where is he? Who can he be?"

"Leib Goldkorns—"

"Present, Your Exalted."

"If I assist you in answering this question, will you in turn assist me?"

"At your service, Reverend Father."

"In my opinion, it is no accident that your opera shall take place at Pessach. I may not live to see it, just as, like that other

Moshe, I shall not live to see the promised land. Never mind these tears. They are not only of sorrow but also joy. For if I cannot enter, my people will. Here is the favor I ask: I want my sons to take part in your production, so that my voice might be heard through them, even after it has been silenced forever. Will you do this for me?"

"Pas de problème. We'll stick the wee lads in the chorus."

"You misunderstand. I do not mean the children of my loins. To me they are a burden. Unworthy, they only wish to inherit my throne—"

"Maybe they feel *entitlebaumed*, ha, ha, ha."

"No, I refer to my true children. These Satmars who have come from afar to join me. Look at them. Your own cousins. My true sons."

"Actually, I can't see a thing. This hat is at least size eight."

Now, with both hands I push once more against the fur. The beaver doesn't budge. I yank. I jerk. If anything, the crown drops even lower. Am I doomed, like the planet Pluto, to exist in perpetual darkness? "Help, Jews! It's going into my nose. I can't breathe. I'm totally blind!"

Anat: "It is hopeless. Do not attempt to remove your hat."

Arik: "Even if you should succeed, you would remain in the dark."

"How could that be? Is there, in this room, no Sylvania?"

"Do you not grasp your condition?" that is the voice of Rabbi Yitzhak. "You are in a state of spiritual blindness. Enlightenment comes only after you have completed the remaining steps."

"We were on number four: *Make a thearching and fearleth inventory of yourthelf.*"

"Inventory?"

"Then comes number five, says Rabbi Yitzhak. *Admit the exact nature of your wrongs.*"

"Wrongs?"

"Be ready to have G-d remove all these defects of character. That is step six."

"Defects. Do you mean these woodwinder's lips? Or mayhaps—though they are covered now—les oreilles? Don't ask about the shoulders! And they say the woolly mammoth is extinct! Exaggeration for comic effect. As for schnapps—"

"No, no, no. we are talking about your one great sin. The thing that has marked your entire life. It is difficult to speak of it aloud. Would the Rebbe allow us to say the word?"

"If one wishes to purify a soul it is permitted."

Arik: "Anat, you say it."

Anat: "Father, you do so."

Yitzhak ben Kaspar: "It is not fitting for a rabbi to utter such a sound."

A pause ensues. I sense that everyone has turned to Abdi. I hear him swallow once. Then twice. Then he speaks:

"Lutht."

"*Lutht?* Do you mean the German word *Lust?*"

"Yeth."

"Ho. Ho. Now I get you. Very well. Have you considered the anatomy of a violoncello? The small curvaceous at the top? The larger convexity at the bottom? Is this shapeliness not akin to the image of the Earth Mother? With emphasis on the flanken? Hence my confession: more than one time did I think with envy of Mr. A. Baer and Dr. Julius Dick, who played respectively this instrument and the bass viol in the Steinway Quintet. Oh, how their arms embrace the doubled dilations! With what perfection do their knees fit into the indentures! And then to give the old gal a good bowing, eh? A good bowing! In F-sharp minor! Worse, cousins—and this must not leave the room: I have on one occasion, or two occasions, allowed a certain thought to enter my mind. What must it feel like *to be a violoncello?* To be ravished in a muscular lap? Enough! Enough! That is my confession."

The Rebbe, M. Teitelbaum: "What is he saying? I'm a little hard of hearing."

Yitzhak ben Kaspar: "Nothing. Only rubbish. Cousin Leib Goldkorn: Did you not marry when you came to America? Did not the evil inclination burn when you thought of your wife?"

"Clara? My beloved Miss Litwack? Sure! I took pleasure at seeing the twinkle of light on her garter trolleys. Mein Gott! The elastic! The nippers! The corselets!"

I cannot see, but I can feel how the congregation draws near. And I hear the eagerness with which the endomorph inquires, "Really? And what else?"

His ectomorphic brother: "Do tell us more."

"Well, I took no less pleasure, as who would not, at blowing on her fingernail polish. You know, to help it dry. Those were always moments of Kameradschaft. On one memorable occasion I was allowed, with the little brush, to apply the lacquer myself."

If I sensed eagerness and anticipation before, I cannot help but pick up the tone of indignation now.

"What? He touched her hand?"

"And he calls himself a Jew!"

"What if she were in niddah?"

"Then he thoudn't even be in the thame room!"

"And he performed these acts in daylight!"

"Are not garter trolleys in proximity to 'that place'?"

"Did he first insert a testing rag?"

"And what if he had just returned from the privy? And the privy-demon had not departed?"

"Maybe he ith a thailor. Thailorth are away tho long."

I hear the nephew of the great Yoel clear the frog from his

throat. "If I am not in error, our friend Leib Goldkorns does not seem to understand that it is not allowed even to shake the hand of a woman, whether she is in niddah or not. Perhaps he is not a bar mitzvah after all."

"Would the Rebbe agree that one is allowed to take the hand if the woman offers it first? To spare her the embarrassment of rejection?"

"Ethpecially if it ith a buthineth deal."

"Further exceptions: *If while doing so he looks over her shoulder at a bird.*"

The Rebbe: "On these matters the Litvaks are lenient. One may grasp the woman's hand if she is drowning."

"But not if she is wearing socks."

"Also: a man may take the pulse of his wife."

"Unless she is in niddah."

"But the man himself may be impure—if, for example, he has touched himself when passing water."

"Excuse me, but a married may support his organ from below."

"Would the Rebbe care to make a clarification?"

The Rebbe: "I have been considering whether one may shake hands in an elevator. For it is neither in earth nor in heaven."

"Unless the elevator is stuck."

"What if she is eating a coconut?"

"Lithen! what if a man, he can't help it, likth another man? Can they thake handth with each other?"

"We must bring this discussion to an end." So says the firm voice of Rabbi Yitzhak. "Let us move on to step seven. *Are you willing to ask G-d to remove your shortcomings?*"

"Number seven? Ha! Ha! More than halfway done. Sure. *Dear God, please remove my shortcomings.* There! I feel better already."

"Don't believe him!'

"It's a trick!"

"It's not as easy as that!"

"A tetht! We have to put him to a tetht!"

At that moment I hear, from some distance away, a familiar voice:

"Meu tio Leibie. Meu namorado."

The Bombshell! Impossible! When last seen she was pouting in Prague.

"Big poppa!"

"This is an illusion, friends. No women allowed. Not even the rebbetzin."

Yet through the beaver bristles I can make out the scent of oak. Of moss. "Jicky"! By Guerlain!

"Oh! Oh! Meu macho potente!"

It is no dream. She is here. Not only here: drawing closer. And still closer. Ho, ho! It is like our first encounter: my own flesh! My own blood! Abdominal to abdominal. Ham to ham. Haunches too.

"Meu querido. Where have you been?"

At these words there is a perturbation in Patagonia. No, no! Heaven forfend! Not in the presence of the Rov!

The Rov himself speaks: "What abomination is this?"

"Oh, my G-d! What a horror!"

"He's sinning in the daytime!"

"And thtanding up!"

"Ha, ha. Sorry, fellows. It's a reflex."

Cock-a-doodle-doo!

"Beg pardon?"

"Leib Goldkorn!" Could it be? Are they letting women in now? For that, without doubt, is the voice of the rebbetzin. "You must atone!"

"Atone!" everyone cries.

"Transfer your sins!"

The next thing I know, someone is putting into my hand what seems to be a chicken or a rooster, and someone else is lifting my arm over my head, and then all sorts of people start to turn me around, even faster than on Lee Avenue. *"Ich bin a kleyner Dredyl.* Haven't we already played that game?"

From afar, the high-pitched voice of Reb Moshe Teitelbaum: "This is no game. This is the ceremony of Kapporat. You must atone for each of your sins."

Rabbi Yitzhak: "Your uncleanliness."

"Your lutht."

"Wait! Wait a moment!" Even though the hat, of the Schwarzenberg type, is pulled all the way down to my button nose, I suddenly begin to see. The scales, as they say, are falling from my eyes. "The twelve steps. The rules about pollination. The ceremony of Kapporat. Are you acting on the Court Order of S. A. Lubowitz? Is this the love addiction seminar?"

"Turn! Turn! Wave the beast! It must take on your wrongdoings."

"And pluck, pluck, pluck! With each feather confess a sin."

"Help! Help me, Jesus! It's the Sex Staatspolizei!"

Now the hands are spinning me even faster.

"Pluck a feather!"

"Confeth a thin!"

"All right! I'll do it! I'll confess every one. But I am begging you. No leeches!"

The congregation begins to clap its hands and, in rhythm, stomp their feet. The two women utter their ululations. Hymena hisses. The poor rooster crows. I reach up and pluck a feather.

"Minchke!" I cry.

Cock-a-doodle-dooo!

"The Stutchkoff!"

Cock-a-doodle-doooo!

"Miss Litwack! A definite penetration."

Cock-a-doodle-dooooo!

"Isn't that enough? Three women: that's plenty for lots of chaps."

But the clapping grows louder. So does the stamping, the crying, the ululations.

"Frau Henie! Queen of the ice."

Cock-a-doodle-doooooo! From above comes the sound of frantic flapping. The fowl is attempting to fly away. Would that he were able. And to carry Leib Goldkorn, with all his transgressions, off into the atmosphere.

"Madam Miranda!"

Now the feathers, not just those I have plucked, but those torn loose in the turbulent air above me, come floating down, tickling my cheek and my chin and piling up on my shoulders.

"Miss Williams! My Esther. Four fingers and thumb."

Cock-a-doodle-dooooooooo!

"The half-Finn! Ha! Ha! Ha! The She-Who. Miss NOH: Name Obliterated Here. Do you see? It's endless. Endless. I confess. I confess to everything. I am a man of the world!"

"Evil! Evil!"

"Here is the devil!"

"The ha-satan!"

Cock-a-doo—

Fitz! Futz! Footz!

"Even more. Miss Fleming! She sent me a photo. With a little knob of a chin."

"Stone him! Stone him!"

"He is not fit to live!"

"What a cleavage."

"Death! Death! Death!"

My head goes back. I take in a breath. "*Ah! Ah! Ah! Ah!*"

I halt my rotations. My arm drops down; the Rhode Island Red, struck dead by the accumulation of all my sins, lies limp in my hand. Yet his feathers fly about me, tickling my nub of a nose.

"*CHOOOO!*"

At that sneeze, and with the sound of a cork leaving a bottle of Mission Bell—*POP!*—my hat flies from the top of my head.

I blink in the light of day. Through the floating flakes of feathers I see my cousins: Anat, Arik, Abdi, the Rabbi of Kopitshenets. Yes, and the two forbidden females, the Bombshell from Brazil and Zipporah, the rebbetzin. All of these have dark scowls on their faces, and the faces themselves are as red as stop signs along the road. They are advancing upon me, their fists held high. Do they have stones? Is this the end of Leib Goldkorn? Farewell, life! Farewell good-looking women! "SH'MA YIS—"

"Halt, Jews! Jewesses, halt as well!"

The crowd obeys. They part, looking around. I look too.

There, on a sort of high chair, sits a figure wearing a white robe and a hat like a flying saucer. The skin: tanned. From the chin the threads of a beard hang down exactly like the strings of a mop. The Rebbe! Grand Rebbe of Satmaria! But if Leib Goldkorn sees Moshe Teitelbuam, can it be no less true that Moshe Teitelbaum sees Leib Goldkorn?

"How do you do?" I say.

No answer. Instead I watch as the mouth drops open and the Brazil nuts of the eyes grow wider and wider. Then the color in the cheeks drains away, leaving only what I might fancifully say is the pale porcelain of the tub. The Rebbe is going to faint!

"Watch out!" I cry. "He's got a charley horse!"

Everyone rushes to the stricken man. But he puts up two trembling hands, then half rises to his feet. All fall back. The Rebbe, he's trembling all over. His open mouth closes. Then it opens again. Teeth an off-white. Carmine-colored tongue. Up fly his arms even as, with an audible thump, his knees hit the ground.

Who is he staring at? At truly yours—at least he is until his eyes roll upward in his head and he cries out for the entire borough of Brooklyn to hear:

"The question has been answered. Mossiach has come! It is he! Leib Goldkorns! The King of the Jews!"

ACT THREE

TOD

SCENE ONE

REHEARSAL

Time for Leib to rehearse his opera at the Met. But how can he stop Renée from learning the terrible truth?

Chor der Landleute und Hochzeitsgäste:

Glück auf! Glück auf! Zum Hochzeitsreih'n
Viel Glück und Segen Bringe!

Gar so stillen Muths wir zogen aus
Mit Hochzeitsklage wir zieh'n nach Haus Glück auf!

THOSE ARE THE very last words of my father's opera. The Prince and Princess are married. The crowd shouts their huzzahs. Now, sitting at my isle of Formica, I take up my pen to produce a Leib Goldkorn translation.

Chorus of Rustics and Wedding Guests:

Good luck! On this day that you are wed
Blessings on this marriage bed!

With a song we march off to our houses
Where women do the trick that arouses!

Good luck! Good luck! Good luck!
*Now we dance and sing and ****!*

There! *Finis*. Tears of joy fill my eyes. Father! Dear Father! Your son has completed his task. But hark: here comes the Lithuanian, late as ever with my Dr. Brown's. Hush. Let us hear him speak:

"Here you go, young fella. One cream soda. With a straw." Hee. Hee. Hee. *Young fella!* "Thank you, my good man. Here for your trouble is a handsome pourboire."

Amusing to see the aged jaw drop wide: Is it because he is in a state of stupefaction at the size of his gratuity, a bright and shiny American "nickel"? Or is it because the youthful client he sees before him has just spoken with the venerable voice of the Graduate? Who can blame him for being surprised? For the fact is that the customer at the table, with paper and ink pushed one way and his breakfast omelet with side of sable pushed to the other, is a figure that neither you nor Mr. Mosk has ever seen before. Let us describe him:

On both cheek and chin, a black beard, cut in the style of Rutherford B. Hayes. Atop the head, a jet-black coiffure slicked back with Brylcreem—*A little dab will do ya*—creating the appearance of a Hungarian count.

The gals will all pursue ya.

Think R. Valentino.

You'll look so debonair.

I rise to my full height—a confession: I have, into my McAns, inserted lifts—so that the waiter can assess my attire. Lumberman: long gone, replaced by a "sports" jacket with padded shoulders and wide lapels that hangs, Satmar-style, to the knees; trousers that are belted just beneath the male papillae and that, after loosely falling, are gathered at the ankles. Color coordination: plum-purple coat, pants mustard-yellow, mit Nadelstreifen. Finishing touch: pocket square and watch chain to the calf.

"You don't," mutters Mosk, "see these anymore."

"Would you, good garçon, care to hazard a guess as to the age of your patron?"

"That's you? Okay. Black hair. Black beard. Swell suit. Maybe forty-five. No glasses. No cane. Maybe forty-three."

"Forty-three!"

"Tops."

They'll love to run their fingers
through your hair.

Honk! Honkety! Honk!

That is the call of the Continental. Abdoul, chauffeur. What is the expression—*to walk on the air*? I experience such pneumatics as I float toward the waiting limousine. Forty-three! Ha! Ha! Ha! Forty-three! Leib Goldkorn is incognito!

Honk! Honnnnnnk! Coming, Abdoul. Coming. Farewell, melancholy Mosk. Adieu to the Sturgeon King!

ROUTE: up Eighty-sixth Street and then, after right-hand turn, down Avenue Christopher Columbus. Genoese Jew. Downtown. Always downtown. Eighty-fifth. Eighty-fourth. Eighty-third.

There occurs, at this spot on our journey, one small incidental. We stop at a "red" light. The better to see the world around me, I roll down the smoked-glass window. Between our vehicle and the Teriyaki Boy establishment sits a green roadster with,

222 • LESLIE EPSTEIN

at the wheel, an undoubted doxy. Blond, but black at the roots. Glasses for sun. Brünnhilde bosom. I lean from the limousine. I doff—this is the last item in my garmenture—my feathered felt. "Excuse me," I say, in an Oxford intonation. "Might I inquire if you have the correct time?"

The ultimate test. For a heart-stopping moment nothing occurs. I lean farther. "I have left my Bulova at Chez Casa Blanca."

Down goes her window.

"What?"

Lipstick by Chanel. Number 33, if I am not mistaken. "Allure." With those coated lips, smooth and satiny, she makes a decided moue. Tongue tip! "Were you talking to me?"

"Ja! Shall we have a coition?"

Those words are scarcely out of my mouth when the light changes, and the relentless tide of traffic carries us off to our differing fates. But I have, in her neighborliness, all the evidence I require. Transformation complete. A youth! A youth! A youth of forty-three!

Eightieth. Seventy-seventh. And now Seventy-sixth, the boundary of the 10023 zip code itself. Seventy-fourth. Sixty-eighth. There are the towers, like huge blocks of unsinkable Ivory-brand soap, of the Abraham Lincoln Center. We cross the Boulevard of Broadway. Our vehicle slows and comes to a halt opposite the opera arches. A person stands in the plaza, a person whose voice rings out:

"Lee-ho! Lee-Leib!"

"Step on it, Abdoul! Allez!"

Meee-ow! Our G-force acceleration, the barking of orders, has awakened Hymena in her hamper.

"To what destination, sayyid?"

"Turn! Turn here! To the right. Rechts!"

With a protest from rubber tires, we flee onto Sixty-second Street. "Another right, if you please. Now you may slow. Stop there, at the Avenue Amsterdam entrance."

May I explain? I had recognized at once the female who was standing near the spurting Fontana: heart-shaped face; chinny chin; hourglass figure, with more sand in the top. It was the Fleming! Beneath her nose, a nosegay, a bouquet of—were they marsh marigolds? Morning glories? Up they rose, at the end of an arm. She had seen the Continental and its passenger. Incontestablement, she was waving those flowers at me. But who was I? The echt Leib, born in November of 1901? Or the caballero with the key chain? Age forty-three. At this crucial moment, I lacked the courage to find out.

Now, at the stage door, someone else is waiting. Tall, with aviation-type glasses and three-part beardelet.

"Giuseppe! Signor Volpe! Here is the natural son of G. Mahler. In disguise!"

Like the Lithuanian's, the intendant's mouth drops open in surprise. Excellent dental work. Before he can close it, I pull down, on my chin whiskers, the elasticized straps. "L. Goldkorn. Graduate. Greetings."

"Maestro! We have been waiting all morning. Where have you been?"

"Where the Grass is Greener, ha, ha, ha! I am happy to announce that the translation of *Rübezahl* is now complete."

"Glad to hear it. But we're hours behind schedule. We're about to begin the rehearsal for the love scene. Between the Princess and the Prince. Let's hurry backstage."

"Lead on, Macduff!" So saying, I leave the limousine and, with Hymena at heel, enter the rear of the Metropolitan Opera.

No glamour here. Neither crystal chandelier nor diamond horseshoe. Velvet plush nil. What I see before me resembles the

interior of the naval vessels we used to see in Pathé films: cor-
ridors and staircases, a warren of storerooms and coiled rope,
all dimly lit and painted battleship-gray. From everywhere
and nowhere the sound of pounding and the whine of multiple
machines. I follow my guide into a small Otis-brand and after
a short journey emerge into a mist created by a multitude of
atomizers pumping in unison. About me are the tremolos of
soprano and mezzo-soprano and contralto voices. Oh, and the
boom of a basso and a bass baritone.

Now, dimly, I see a figure in the distance. "Lee-ho-lee-ho-
lee-Leib!" cries this Valkyrie of the vapors. Through the driz-
zle, arms out, races the diva. "Lee-ho-lee-ho! Lee-Leib!"

In a flash I dart through the nearest closed door and slam it
behind me. There is a bolt. I slam it too. I am, I see, in a W.C.
The crucial question: Damen? Or Herren?

Inna these arms . . .

What? The words of Prince Ratibor. I whirl around. At the
bottom of a stall, the kind for doing business, a pair of wingtips. Again, sotto voce:

Inna these arms . . .
Inna these arms . . .

Could it be? Is this our tenor? Out of retirement? I move to
the adjoining booth and haul myself upward. As I do so the
Prince, a cappella, continues:

. . . my love-a now safely lands.

I peek over the edge. A bearded fellow, trousers at ankles,
elbows on knees, the classical position. In his hands, the libretto.

The response comes in a voice you know well:

Warm yourself on my mammary glands.

"Ha-ha. Leib Goldkorn translation."

"Ah! Che perversità!" cries the Pavarotti, half rising, then tripping forward.

Already I am clawing at the bolt and dashing through the door. The diva has disappeared into the dewdrops. But not for long.

Lee-ho-lee-hoo! Lee-Leib!

The cry of the huntress. This time I dash into the shop for costumes, pull the first garment I see—it is that of a Carmelite nun—from its hanger, and throw it about me. With pins in my lips I practice the art of Jewish sewing. The Fleming bursts through the door.

"Oh, ho, yo-ho-ho!" she cries. "Maestro! Maestro mio! Where have you gone?"

All within bend over their stitches and their Isaac Singer machines. The soprano turns her eyes, like two Hershey's Kisses, upon truly yours. "Have you seen Maestro Goldkorn?" she asks. "I need him for the love scene."

At the sound of my name, linked with the word *love.* I experience storminess in S. America. Part of me wishes to throw open my garment and wittily cry out, *Miss Fleming! Sweetheart! Get into the habit with me!* Instead, I say not a word, as if I, like the Carmelite, had taken a vow of silence.

She turns. She departs. Yet the same game of hide-and-seek continues—first in the wig-maker's shop, where she mistakes me for Madame Pompadour, or perhaps the curls I have donned belong to M. Antoinette; and then in the carpentry room, which the Valkyrie dares not enter, owing to the sawdust that hangs in the air. Thus she does not see the winged horse—

Up, noble steed, your wings beat, beat, and beat.
Three American inches? Egad! Three American feet!

—under which I am, with averted eyes, hiding.

Once the coast is clear I venture from this workshop and directly into the arms of the general manager.

"Maestro!" he exclaims. "Where have you been? The rehearsal has already started. Come with me."

We once more enter an Otis, and descend to a level marked C. At once I hear music—yes, yes, it is my father's score, the scherzo for the ballet. We advance down a passage. We turn a corner. The intendant opens a door. Suddenly I see before me a replication of the main stage of the opera house, complete with a pit for the orchestra. These musicians are vigorously sawing away under the baton of a squat, bespectacled fellow, through whose skull the springs of a divan seem to have exploded. Behind him, on the stage, ballet dancers are whirling and twirling.

I do what the Zanuck called a take two. Those were my cousins! Hipping and hopping, soaring and skipping, their arms sometimes skyward, sometimes floating like the wings of a swan. A moment, if you please, of nostalgics. I could not help but remember Cousin Kaspar, the son of my Uncle Rufus. It was he who had, at the Wiener Staatsoper, begged me to save his children by allowing them to perform in *The Nutcracker.* Alas, I could not save even myself. Yet here is one of those very same children, Rabbi Yitzhak ben Kaspar, dancing, with his own beloved sons, in the corps de ballet of the Metropolitan Opera.

"Look! Look, Couthin!"

It seems that, despite my disguise, which resembles the Smith Brother on the right-hand side of the cough drops, Abdi has recognized me. Now he stops his gyrations and cups his hands to his mouth:

"I am wearing tighths!"

The man with the baton sets it down and looks up toward the dancer. "Yes. And very well too."

Giuseppe Volpe leans toward me. "That is our principal conductor, James Levine. He has been filling in for you."

Odd, he pronounces the name to rhyme with *wine*; but I suspect it should be spoken to rhyme with the capital of our Austro-Hungarian Empire: *Wien-Wien-Wien*.

The plump principal sees us. "Ladies and gentlemen," he says, addressing the one hundred and forty musicians. "Our maestro has arrived."

With no further ado, this Rhymes-with-Fein beckons me down to the pit and holds out the baton. There is a brief sound of nocturnal crickets: that is, the string section is tapping, with their bow-backs, the tops of the music stands. In a daze, accompanied by the faint tintinnabulation of my watch chain, I approach the podium.

I have played many instruments at both the Wiener Staatsoper and the National Biscuit Company Symphonia. But never before have I been called on to conduct. For a moment I pause, the stick motionless, suspended. I think back one hundred years to the two men who shared simultaneously the directorship of this ensemble. A. Toscanini, with his finger to his lips, his arm in unwavering motion; and, with expressive gesticulations, his features reflecting both agony and joy, my undisputed dad. Who, at such thoughts, would not be inspired?

"A one-ah," I declare. "A two-ah. A one-two-three-four!"

Downbeat.

But before the first note can sound, there is a cry from off-stage left.

Oh, hoo! Ho-hee! Oh, Lee-hee-eeb!

The jig, friends, is up. It is the Fleming! Dressed like a princess in tassels and tiara, she rushes onto the stage. Rouged cheeks. Painted eyes. Hair: bouffant. Bosom: and how.

What to do? Where to hide? I thrust the baton into the hands of Rhymes-with-Stein and dash deep into the pit, where, hump-backed and hunched, I shoulder my way into the percussion section.

Ho-hoo! Hoo-la! La-leeeb!

Pulling my felt low over my forehead, I secret myself behind the lyre-shaped glockenspiel, by coincidence the very instrument I was playing on the night that Herr Göring expelled me from the Staatsoper.

"Leib Goldkorn!" cries the soprano, shielding her eyes and peering out over the rehearsal room. "Where are you?"

"Renée! Darling!" says Rhymes-with-Klein. "Thank goodness you've come. Where is Luciano? We have to start your scene."

"I'mma here!" It's the Pavarotti, now in costume, but still holding a rolled-up copy of the libretto. "Princessa Emma," he says to the Fleming. "We gonna make-a da love!"

At that, Rhymes-with-Schlein raises the baton and, glasses flashing, gives the downbeat. There is a tremolando on the drums. Enter the woodwinds and now the brass. All about me soars the music of Mahler.

Above my burrow, I see a truly terrible sight. The Fleming is running on toes across the stage from the left. The Pavarotti stomps toward her from the right. They meet in the middle!

What's this? What's this? The Prince is taking the Princess in his arms—the fat, swarthy arms of an Italian! An Untermensch! Renée! So delicate! So pale! Encircled in darkness! Horrors! He is kissing her! The Fleming! And she is kissing him back. Now—oh, bitter irony!—my very own words rise to torment me:

PRINCESS EMMA:
  Oh, breast-to-breast and cheek-to-chin!

PRINCE RATIBOR:
  At last you're mine, my dear half-Finn!

Gracious! Have you ever seen such a thing? He is bending her backward!

Without thinking, in a reflex, I seize from the hands of the member of the American Federation of Musicians the twin mallets of my old instrument and with abandonment strike out the silvery chords:

BOING! BONK! BWAK!

Everything stops. The musicians put down their instruments, the conductor his baton. The two lovers, like guilty things, break apart.

The Pavarotti: "What's-a dat? Che fracasso!" He writhes about, holding his ears.

The Fleming: "What a horrible noise!"

Rhymes-not-with-Queen manages to raise his baton. "We are artists. We must go on. Listen, the noise has stopped. Please, we'll take it from where we left off."

Downbeat.

Once again the soaring strings, the call of the clarinets,

the playful trill of the piccolo. Onstage, the Prince takes the Princess once more in his sable arms. Only this time he bends her even farther backward, and yet farther, so that—oh, the shame of it!—all the men and women in the orchestra, including the two gentlemen on the bassoons, can see, rising and falling beneath her dickey, the twin hemispheres of the mams. Not only that: as a cloud will ofttimes blot the silver surface of the moon, so a dark, Italianate hand spreads like a fudge over the mounds of pure vanilla. She resists. Yes, she resists, beating her fists against the torso of the impassioned Prince. To no avail! Out of his mouth uncurls the long red ribbon of a Tuscan tongue. Heavens! He's a-licking! A-licking!

And the band plays on.

PRINCESS EMMA:
Oh, Prince! Desist! Oh, God! Cease!

PRINCE RATIBOR:
But first you must feel what's in my codpiece.

BWANG! BWONK! BAWANK!

A wailing rises through the room. The Pavarotti, hands to his ears, runs from the stage. All of my cousins, similarly holding theirs, dash into the wings. In the orchestra pit there is a tremendous commotion as, with sheet music flying, all of the musicians scramble to get out of what has become this grotto of doom.

In the midst of it all, Wine-not-*Wien* holds up his chubby hands. "Stop! Don't go! We'll get to the bottom of this."

Renée: "I've never heard such a horrible sound. Who is making this caterwauling?"

Futz! Fitz! Footz!

On the lip of the stage, tail out, all hairs outstanding, stands the heartless Hymena. The traitorous tabby is pointing directly at the *cat*erwauler-in-chief.

All the musicians halt in place. They turned to stare at truly yours. I meet their glares with insouciance. "Ha! Ha! This vibraphone is not in tune."

"Oh, there you are," says the principal conductor. "Come back to the podium. I want you to lead the overture."

A female voice. "Maestro?" It is the Fleming.

Mr. Le-wine answers for me. "Yes, this is Leib Goldkorns."

Onstage, the soprano takes a step backward. Her mouth drops open, as if she were hitting a high C.

I hurriedly seize the baton and rap it smartly on the podium. I address my colleagues thus:

"Fellow members of the American Federation of Musicians. We are about to play the overture to the only opera written by G. Mahler, who, with Mendelssohn and Meyerbeer, was one of the three musical *M*'s. We must not approach it as if it were a bagatelle by Pisk or any of the Second Viennese School. I ask you to remember this: In every piece of music, as in every work of art, we shall find the reflection of its creator's life. In the opening bars of this opera the composer returns us to his youth in Iglau. Those horns and brasses? The bugle call of the military barracks. Yon silvery strings? The splash of the shining Iglawa. Mister clarinet and answering contra-bassoon? In you we hear the cry of the geese and the storks above the Bohemian-Moravian Heights. Our steady, four-by-four beat: that is the great rectangle of the Stadtplatz. Have I helped you? Do you understand? We are about to play"—*Here is my life*—"the autobiography of Gustav Mahler.

"So, gentlemen—and I see we have with us some musical ladies: Shall we once more begin?

"A one-ah. A two-ah. A eins-zwei-drei-vier!"

Downbeat.

Ach. What cacophony. A hubbub. A hullabaloo. The more I wave my arm, the more the violins screech and the horns bray. Such bellowing, barking, bleating. Yap, yup, yip. Now a wail, a whine, and a whoop.

This time even the principal conductor surrenders. "Run for it, boys!" he cries. "The animals are out of the zoo!"

At once the instrumentalists pour from the pit. The entire brass section runs off in a phalanx. The bell of a tuba knocks me to the floor. The harp of the fleeing harpist strikes the podium, which in turn topples onto my head. Seeing stars? I see them. The sound of fleeing feet fades away. No one is left in the rehearsal room or the stage but the son of Gustav Mahler. Oh. One other person. Princess Emma! In costume. She approaches the lip of the stage and leans closer. There is, I note, stardust in her hair and on her lashes. I manage to draw myself up on an elbow. Here, verbatim, are the first words I address to my beloved:

THE GRADUATE:
Greetings, Miss Fleming you are looking fine.

THE FLEMING:
Could this be you? Am I dreaming? Or am I in heaven?

THE GRADUATE:
Especially for someone born in 1959.
I believe that makes you, hmmm, forty-seven.

THE FLEMING:
And you, no white in your hair, no bend in your knee.

THE GRADUATE:
Correct, madam. I am a lad of just forty-three.

[TOGETHER]:
  Are we both dreaming? Are we in heaven?

THE FLEMING:
  He's forty-three—

THE GRADUATE:
  She's forty-seven.

THE FLEMING:
  Wait. The man I seek hasn't a hair on his head.

THE GRADUATE:
  Nor is there one on his chinny chin-chin.

THE FLEMING:
  Are you the maestro himself? Or one in his stead?

THE GRADUATE:
  Maestro? Me? You could say I'm sort of kin.

THE FLEMING:
  I admit: I expected someone quite a bit taller.

THE GRADUATE:
  We're all a bit short, we descendants of Mahler.

THE FLEMING:
  Hold on! Those ears! And that nose of a Heeb—

THE GRADUATE:
  This nose? Does it belong to your lover, Leib?

THE FLEMING:
  And that suit. Haven't I seen it before in a photo?

THE GRADUATE:
  Yes, yes. It's in the style of Mr. Moto.

THE FLEMING:
> *And your feet, so delicate, dainty. What size are they, pray?*

THE GRADUATE:
> *Why do you ask? McAns: Size five triple-A.*

THE FLEMING:
> *I'm perplexed. I'm confused.*

THE GRADUATE:
> *Fear not. It's Leib Goldkorn in his very own shoes.*

THE FLEMING:
> *Can it be? Is this the man to whom I have given my heart?*

THE GRADUATE:
> *None other. The Graduate. I play no other part.*

THE FLEMING:
> *My one! My only! Come closer, come near!*

THE GRADUATE:
> *You won't laugh? Won't mock? Not a single jeer?*

THE FLEMING:
> *Never! Look. For you I'll open the whole of my blouse.*

THE GRADUATE:
> *Miss Fleming! Can I be dreaming? My dear Zaubermaus!*

THE FLEMING:
> *I adore you. I love you. Kiss you I must!*

THE GRADUATE:
> *My Liebchen! My darling! Fitz! Footz! Futz!*

Fitz? Footz? Futz? It isn't a kiss. Hymena is licking my lips! And my cheeks! And my forehead! Could I have been dreaming? I blink my eyes wide. Yes, there is Renée, alone on the stage. Her mouth is still open, though not a single note comes out. I open my mouth as well:

THE GRADUATE:
My Schneckchengehäuse, the prettiest sight I ever saw.

No response. Except, with her teeth, the soprano begins to bite on her knuckles.

THE GRADUATE:
What is the matter? Do you have lockjaw?

Now she moves forward, to the edge of the stage. She finds at long last her voice. "Excuse me. Is it true? Are you Leib Goldkorn?"

I do not answer at once. Instead, I get with some pain to my feet and, one by one, climb up the steps of the orchestra pit and onto the stage. We are now no more than five feet apart. I make an Old World bow. I remove my feathered fedora. "Madam, I am."

"The great-grandson of Gustav Mahler?"

"Not exactly." And now I take a bite from the bullet. Off goes my wig.

There is an audible gasp.

"That is not all, madam." So saying, I pull off my black bushy beard. "Ha, ha. Did you think I was Rutherford B. Hayes? Nineteenth pres—"

The soprano holds up her hand. "May I ask, Mr. Goldkorn: How old are you?"

"I will answer, madam. Have you perchance ridden on the Mombasa–Lake Victoria railway?"

"I see. I have made a mistake."

To this there can be no reply. With a slight clink of my key chain, I turn to walk away.

"Wait."

The voice of the soprano. "I have something to show you."

With both hands she takes off her tiara. That is no surprise. But then with a tug she removes the hairpiece of Princess Emma. Her own hair, a reddish dun, lies matted against her skull. "There's more," she says. And there is—the whole of young Emma's face: eyebrows and eyelashes, the stardust, the glitter. Mascara—Avon, "SuperShock"—and kohl. Also, powder, blush, rouge. Finally, with a quick motion, all the paint from her lips. I see her plain.

No spring chicken.

"Well," says the soprano. "Do I look like her?"

"Who?"

"The woman in the other half of the photo."

"You mean Miss Litwack?"

"Yes. Your Clara. Was she not your wife?"

"Ha! Ha! A definite penet—"

"The way you spoke of her. *Gone! Gone!* I was jealous. How you must have loved her!"

"She sat by the window, Miss Fleming. Drying, in the summer breeze, her nails. *Maybe it's Maybelline.* On occasion, she would permit me blow on them myself. And once—"

An astounding thing now occurs. The Fleming, with her hand, takes hold of mine. "*Every work of art is an autobiography,*" she whispers. "Soon, on this stage, we shall tell our stories. Yours and mine. Together."

Then, softly—and this is the sound neither of geese nor of storks above the Bohemian-Moravian Heights—she begins to sing:

O Komm! Willst du dich neben mich nicht betten?

The song of the Princess to the Prince. But she is singing it to me. Which is the dream? Was it the duet—

Are we both dreaming? Are we in heaven?

Or this dalliance?

O come! Lie with me in this bed of petals.

A last confession. Down Argentine Way, at Tierra del Fuego, Cape Horn, The Straits of Magellan:

CURTAIN GOING UP!

INTERMEZZO

BILLBOARD

*The crowd, streaming into the opera house,
sees a billboard.*

THE UNITED STATES DEPARTMENT OF STATE
—Condoleezza Rice, Secretary

and the

UNITED STATES HOLOCAUST MEMORIAL MUSEUM
—Elie Wiesel, Honorary Chairman

in association with

THE METROPOLITAN OPERA

present

THE WORLD PREMIERE OF

RÜBEZAHL
An Opera of the Jewish People
In Three Acts
by
GUSTAV MAHLER

Translated, Directed, and Conducted by
Leib Goldkorns, Graduate, and
THE WORLD'S OLDEST LIVING HOLOCAUST SURVIVOR

With RÉNEE FLEMING as Princess Emma

and

LUCIANO PAVAROTTI as Prince Ratibor

and

PLACIDO DOMINGO in the title role

IN ATTENDANCE AT THE GALA:

President and Mrs. George W. Bush

The Vice President, "Dick" Cheney, and his wife, Lynne Cheney

Mr. Wiesel

Ms. Rice

Mr. Henry Kissinger

His Honor Kofi Annan, Secretary General of the United Nations

Mr. Kōichirō Matsuura, director General, UNESCO

Václav Havel, former President of the Czech Republic

Eva Nowotny, Ambassador Extraordinary and Plenipotentiary,

Republic of Austria

Daniel Ayalon, Ambassador of Israel to the United States

Frantisek Kunc, Lord Mayor, Jihlava, formerly Iglau

Governor and Mrs. George E. Pataki

Arnold Schwarzenegger, Governor, State of California,

with Ms. Shriver

Guest of Honor, His Excellency Reb Moshe Teitelbaum

CURTAIN AT 8 PM

Sunday, April 9th, 2006 [5766]

No latecomers

SCENE TWO

WORLD PREMIERE!

Curtain up! But the turnips contain a surprise.

A REPORTER'S ORDEAL
The Calamity at the Metropolitan Opera
By A Special Correspondent—April 17, 2006

New York—

I am writing from my bed on the seventh floor of Columbia-Presbyterian Hospital. My left arm is in a cast. My left leg is suspended by a system of trolleys. One eye, even five days after the calamitous events at Lincoln Center, remains swollen shut. Still, with my notepad propped on my right knee, I will do my best to prepare this account of what began on the evening of April 9 and ended so tragically on the night of April 12.

[*Brava, Inatukak! Coraggio!*]

Let me say at once that when, early in March, I received a joint invitation from the Secretary of State and the general manager of the Metropolitan Opera to review the world premiere of Gustav Mahler's newly discovered opera, I declined. I do not like public events, nor did I feel that I could fulfill this assignment as well as the paper's regular music critics. Within the hour I received a visit from my editor and the publisher of the *Times*. What they told me was that my presence at the gala had been specifically requested by a direct descendant of the composer, the man who had discovered the score, translated the libretto, and who would be conducting the premiere. I cannot adequately describe the chill that rose through me at that moment. My lips were so numbed I could barely utter the words:

"Who is this person?"

"His name is Leib Goldkorns."

I sank into my chair. *Leib Goldkorn!* In the interest of full disclosure I must admit that I have known of this man for quite some time. I have gone on the public record by describing his autobiographical persona as a "truly enchanting character." A decade ago he invited me to the Palm Court of the Plaza Hotel for what he called cuplets of tea. August 31, 1997. Even that, our first and only meeting, never quite took place. Nonetheless he has energetically continued to seek me out, in spite of my clearly declared wishes.

[*Enchanting, Miss? Enchanting?*]

ON THE NIGHT of April 9th I arrived at Lincoln Center a half hour early, protected, I hoped, by the broad brim of my gray felt hat and the crowd that had already gathered. The plaza looked like the set of a Hollywood premiere. The beams from searchlights moved across the cloud-free sky. Two red carpets led from the street to the five great arches. The jets from the fountain were lit in the orange-red half of the spectrum, spraying upward like lava. Women, many in white sheath dresses, stood about like unlit candles. The buildings to either side gleamed in travertine, as if in a dream of Mussolini.

Most of the audience, delayed by extraordinary security measures, milled in front of Chagall's musical murals. It was already past eight o'clock by the time I reached the X-ray device. I had, in addition to this notepad, only a clutch that I had half emptied out to make room for a pair of opera glasses. Now I had to empty it again. Unasked, I removed my shoes and then my hat. My press pass went through a small whirring machine, and so did my ticket, twice.

Most of the honored guests listed on the billboard must have gone in earlier, through another entrance. There was a burst of applause as Mr. Wiesel was led past the security apparatus to take his seat. *No latecomers.* We were *all* latecomers. Yet no one seemed to mind. In my head, as in everyone else's, the same thought had lodged: What would happen to the world if, on this night, and in this building, someone were able to set off a bomb?

My box was number 1 on the Parterre, directly above the right-hand side of the stage. At first glance I thought it was empty. Then I notice a small, dark-skinned boy, aged perhaps eight, dressed in a suit jacket and a clean cotton shirt. He sat at the front, leaning over the plush with his chin on his hands.

"Hello!" I said. "What is your name?"

[*And what is* yours? *Ha! Ha! Ha!*]

He did not reply, though he did lift his head, with its helmet of hair, and smile—a smile as broad and white as the starched lapels of his shirt.

Mee-who?

I turned. There was another spectator in our box. In a cage sat a cat with three paws. And a red and a blue eye. I leaned toward the metal mesh. "And what is your name, little kitten?"

Futz!

This time the boy spoke. "Ella está Hymena."

I sat next to him and looked down to the Orchestra section. President and Mrs. Bush sat below me in the second row. Much of the first was taken up by what was all too obviously the Secret Service. The two governors, Schwarzenneger and

Pataki, had seats near the aisle. They were leaning across their wives to chat with each other. The Vice President and his wife sat quietly amidst their own Secret Service contingent. Down the right-hand aisle, pushed by an attendant, came a gentleman in a wheelchair. It had to be—with his beaver-trimmed hat and the caftan over his knees—the guest of honor, Rebbe Moshe Teitelbaum. He came to a halt a few inches from the edge of the orchestra pit.

I imagined my box would soon be filled with others, but as time went by and the auditorium gradually filled, we three remained alone. On the opposite side of the Parterre, in the box that mirrored mine, I saw a black man with graying hair and a graying goatee. Of course: Kofi Annan, and with him the rest of the foreign delegation. There, with his tired eyes and full moustache, was Václav Havel. I glanced at my program. The others in box number 2 must have been the Israeli ambassador, the Austrian ambassador, the mayor of Jihlava, and—yes, with his wire-rimmed spectacles, the director of UNESCO. As I focused on these famed figures, I felt another pair of eyes fix themselves on me: those of Condoleezza Rice, who stood obscure in the darkness, staring as if I were the celebrity.

Without fanfare, the starburst chandelier dimmed and with its satellites rose toward the heavens. Simultaneously the audience began to applaud the appearance of a little man in an old-fashioned purple jacket and mustard-colored trousers who seemed to have flown off the canvas of one of the Chagall murals—the Jew with the bass viol, perhaps, or the Jew with the mandolin—only to land in the orchestra pit.

Now the crowd was standing, even the hunch-shouldered President Bush.

Mee-hoo-ay! That from the tortoiseshell cat.

I found myself echoing the call: "Hooray!"

It was, of course, Mr. Goldkorn. He moved through the string section and then the woodwinds, toward the podium, where he stopped and turned toward the audience.

Mee-bow! went the half-whiskered Hymena.

He did so, from the waist, where his key chain glittered in what was left of the light.

"Hooray!" I shouted again, but the conductor, all business, lifted his baton.

"A one-ah. A two-ah. A eins-zwei-drei-vier!"

The music of Mahler filled the vast hall.

After some minutes I became aware of a strange phenomenon. Mr. Goldkorn was raising his arms from both sides, in the manner of a man lifting weights; the musicians played on, drawing near to what must have been the climax of the overture. But there seemed to be no connection between the conductor's gestures and the pace of the music. When in a fury he slashed about with his baton, the orchestra remained in a placid adagio; and when he extended his arms, as though executing a dead man's float, the same players seemed to be reading a score that was marked presto or agitato.

Not only that, all the string section on the left had their heads turned, staring offstage to the right; and the brass and woodwinds on the right were twisting their heads so as to look not at Mr. Goldkorn, who now dipped his knees in a form of calisthenics, but off to the left. I strained forward as far as I dared. Something was glowing there in the wings. A television set, or at any rate a television monitor. And on its screen, in his shirtsleeves, and with a towel over one shoulder, was the unmistakable figure of the musical director of the Metropolitan Opera, James Levine.

[*Rhymes with: Nein! Nein! Nein!*]

Now the baton of the bushy-haired maestro came sweeping down; that of the bald-headed maestro went flying up. The orchestra sounded the last note and fell silent. Amidst the dying reverberations of the overture the great gold curtain rose upon the throne room of His Majesty and the royal court.

> *Mister King! O Mister King*
> *Humble greetings we bring!*

At the sight of the beautiful palace, in ivory and gold, and the shining jeweled costumes, the audience broke into applause. Through it the courtiers and ministers and assistants delivered their next lines:

> *A long life to you if it God please*
> *And Gesundheit! at your every sneeze.*

After a few exchanges between the King and his ministers, three suitors arrived, each attempting to win the hand of Princess Emma. Each, in typical fairy-tale fashion, was soon dismissed. But then, accompanied by the bellowing of trombones and grunts from the tubas, a fourth appeared: Rübezahl, played by the tenor Placido Domingo, hideous in his rags, and leering.

At once the ministers and marshals rushed forward to attack him, but the creature beat them back with his club. Then—in a spine-tingling moment, with a shriek from the violins—he spied Princess Emma:

> *Ah, there she is, the fawn, the deer.*
> *Will you come with me and have a beer?*

The girl shrank back, but the tympanist pounded on the kettledrum, each beat of which accompanied a footfall of the misshapen beast as he drew closer and closer to the Princess.

Ahhh! Ahhh!

Thus did the poor girl scream, holding out her arms not to her father, the King, or to anyone else onstage, but to the large-eared conductor, as if he and he alone could save her. For his part, Mr. Goldkorn threw down his baton and, clambering over the music stands of the string section, tried to reach her. Too late! Emma took a single step toward him, cried out once more, and then, in her velvet slippers, her silver tiara, and her low-cut gown, fell forward—

[*Glimpse of the mams.*]

—and fainted.

Rübezahl uttered a laugh so hideous that it seemed to freeze everyone onstage, and surely many in the audience as well:

Let us leave them behind to mutter and muddle.
Fly off with me. Ho! Ho! We'll kiss and cuddle.

With that the underground spirit swept up the Princess in his arms and in a flash of fire and smoke dropped through a hole in the stage to a land unknown.

The curtain came down on Act One.

THERE WERE NO curtain calls, though there was much applause. It still sounded as the houselights came on.

"¿Cómo te llamas?" I said to the boy.

This time, with another bright smile, he answered: "Jaime."

"Would you like something to drink? ¿Una bebida fresca?"

He nodded.

"And an ice cream? ¿Una galleta de chocolate?"

He nodded again.

I extended my hand and together we began to move to the

back of the box. But something made me turn at the exit. Lightly I addressed the caged cat. "What about you? Poor thing, would you like some milk?"

Futz! The animal's tail slashed and the half-whiskered lip rose on a single sharp fang.

"What, then?"

Fizz!

I retained just enough of my sophomore Spanish to ascertain during the course of the intermission that Jaime's mother had been killed on the streets of Harlem the year before and that for the last few months an unknown benefactor had started to deliver parcels of toys and clothing and even an old Toscanini recording by way of a driver and a Lincoln limousine. Then a stranger appeared, walking back and forth on the street where his grandmother lived. One day he handed Jaime, of all things, a little wooden panpipe. On another day he set up glasses on the stoop of his building and by wetting his fingers managed to play "La Cucaracha" and "Old Black Joe."

"¡Mira!" said the boy, pushing up the sleeve of what was clearly a new brown jacket. There, halfway up his arm, and stretched over the sleeve of his shirt, was a gold watch. He slipped it off and handed it to me. On the back it said:

In Time with your Music

The inscription was signed with a D and an F and a Z.

"Jaime. The conductor tonight. El director. Señor Gold-korn. Did he give this to you?"

The smile like a flash lamp broke out again. "¡Sí! Bulova-brand! From shop of prawns."

Just then I heard a soft gong and the lights dimmed twice. The intermission was—

––––––––

I HAVE BEEN FORCED to stop writing for most of the afternoon. The doctors came in. The staff changed my bandages. Two friends were allowed to stay half an hour. Then I am afraid that I dozed for the rest of the day. The curtains were drawn across the windows when I woke, but the sun, sinking over the Palisades, and over the Hudson, shone through them brightly enough to make me turn away my eyes. Now, in this dusk, I shall resume.

WHERE WAS I? The end of intermission. We made our way back to box 1. There, I opened the top of the closed cage and poured what was left of my Manhattan into the cat's porcelain bowl. Jaime leaned over the edge of the box and pointed downward. "¡Mira! ¡Mira!" Below us, I saw the Rebbe, Teitelbaum, being pushed down the aisle toward his spot at the pit. The boy was pointing at his dark-skinned attendant. "¡El chofer! De la Lincoln limusina!"

Before I could respond, the curtain rose on Act Two. Who among the thousands of souls in their red velvet seats could have imagined what was to occur before that act could be concluded?

This was the scene before us: a fantastical underground kingdom, filled with grottoes and arbors and winding paths. The musicians played an interlude, soft and sylvan and vaguely reminiscent of Mendelssohn, whom Mr. Goldkorn always called one of the great three *M*'s.

Rübezahl stood staring in enchantment at his sleeping captive, whose bosom rose and fell with every unconscious breath and whose legs were exposed by the way her gown had caught on the brambles.

[*Flanken.*]

Suddenly the music changed key, becoming more and more agitated. To these rhythms the famed Spanish tenor did a comical turn worthy of Bert Lahr in his prime. To our delight he continually approached the girl, creeping closer and closer, only on every occasion to dart farther away. Sometimes he hooked his fingers in his mouth, like an awestruck boy. At other times he extended those same fingers to touch the Princess's hair, only to jerk them back, as if her curls had been made from fire.

But the great joke was his club, which seemed to grow larger and larger in both his hands, like a phallus—

[*What? Will this "family"-style journal print such a word? Best merely to refer to the male membership.*]

—that was swelling out of control. It was this part of himself that, with a pitiful groan, he now addressed:

> *You! Begone! Go burn in someone else's lap.*
> *These bumps. These boils. You've caught the clap.*

> (Hurls club behind him)

The weapon hit the ground with a thump loud enough to waken Emma. She sat up and rubbed her eyes.

> *Where am I? Where? It's all so queer.*

> (spies Rübezahl)

> *Ach! It's no dream! Oy veh ist mir!*

What happened next was a complete reversal of our expectations. Rübezahl, so defiant on earth, became timid beneath it:

> *What, dear one, do you wish? What do you crave?*
> *I'll do anything. You are the master. I am the slave.*

Indeed, like an imperious mistress Emma berated him and ordered him about, eventually demanding that he restore to her the most precious things in her life:

> *You bum! Watch out! I'll kick you in the keister.*
> *Bring them here. My friends and my sisters.*

And off the love-struck gnome went on his mission.

THE LAST LIGHT has faded over the city. The first stars have wriggled their way into the sky. Now I must write by the glow of my lamp. If only the bulb would burn out! Or that the doctors would give me some medicine to force me to sleep. Because now I have no choice but to describe how that other evening moved ineluctably toward its terrible denouement.

OFF WENT RÜBEZAHL to fetch Emma's sisters. Emma, weeping, dropped once more into a troubled sleep. In her dreams she saw her Prince, hands behind his head, staring up through the leaves of a tree. Ms. Fleming held out her arms and began to sing the loveliest and most sensuous of solo arias:

> *Oh, come! Lie with me on this bed of petals.*

Unfortunately, before this dream embrace could be consummated—
   [*Eine Nachtemission, eh?*]
—Rübezahl suddenly reappeared to announce that he had brought back both of the royal sisters.

RÜBEZAHL:

You loathe me, abhor me, think I'm a lout.
But look what I give you: Edelgard and Irmentraut!

EMMA:

Is this some kind of joke? For your efforts I don't give two
hoots
There's nothing in this basket but a bunch of roots.

That was true. Even those in the far-off Family Circle could see that the underground spirit had hauled in a load of bedraggled turnips. But to Emma's rebuke he only laughed:

Do not be deceived. These are the sisters and playmates of
whom you are fond.
Just touch each with my phall—I mean, with this magic
wand.

Here the gnome once more produced his weapon, which now protruded from his body at a suggestive angle:

Take it. Touch it. Give it a stroke.
Ah! Ah! That's it! One more and I'll croak.

It is harder and harder for me to write these next words. Princess Emma took the wand, walked to the basket, and touched one of the turnips. There was a puff of smoke, a flash of fire, accompanied by a shimmering in the violins. Before our eyes the turnip swelled, grew rubicund, and swelled some more—
[*Ha! Ha! Ein türkische Schwanz!*]
—until it was at least six feet tall. The princess touched the next turnip, and the same thing happened, and then the next.

Each time there was smoke and fire, a spine-tingling trill in the violins, and a man-sized turnip would so skillfully appear that the audience, unable to see the wires by which it was lowered or the trapdoor through which it rose, broke into applause. By the end there were some eight or ten of the vegetables lined up across the stage.

Emma stamped her foot and turned on the misshapen creature:

> You're a fraud! A rogue! A monster! A meanie!
> How dare you give me such an overgrown zucchini?

To which Rübezahl replied:

> The wand. Touch it. Chaff it. Give it a blister.
> In the blink of an eye you'll see your sister.

Emma, as instructed, touched the wand to the first turnip. Instantly a pair of arms and hands sprang out of the skin, and the plant began to stagger and spin across the stage like a top, all the while singing:

> Hello! Howdy! Put her there, pard!
> Don't you know me? It's your very own Edelgard.

Here the soprano uttered a little scream and stepped back. Who could blame her? For that warbling voice sounded more like that of a brother than a sister. The same thing happened when the wand touched the second turnip:

> Hello! Howdy! I ain't thauerkraut
> Come give a kith to your darling Irmentraut.

The third and fourth and fifth came to life in the same way. They too tottered about, bumping into tree trunks and each other:

> *Hello! Howdy! Please don't take fright.*
> *It's your playmates, Kunigund, Brinild, and Adelheit.*

Soon the entire stage was filled with dancing turnips. They whirled and whizzed this way and that, like planets in a solar system that had lost its sun. At this sight, the Princess turned in fury on her captor:

EMMA:
> *You liar! Look at these things dancing among us.*
> *Roots! Rutabagas! Rhubarb and fungus!*

> *Hurry up. Use your wand. Say shazams and holy molies.*
> *Get rid of these spuds, squashes, and refried frijoles.*

RÜBEZAHL:
> *Yes! Oh, yes! Rub! Rub-a-dub-dub. We'll find the*
> *solution.*

> *Don't stop, you sweetheart. Keep going. Let's make a*
> *pollution.*

Then, as Emma continued to massage the wand, all the vegetables came forward and aligned themselves along the lip of the stage. Rübezahl, panting with pleasure, began to count—though whether he meant the strokes on the wand or the row of turnips was difficult to determine:

> *One-two-three-four—*
> *Oh, oh, just a little more.*

Five-six, and now seven—
  Ah, my Princess, this is heaven.
Eight—
  Don't wait!
Nine—
  What pleasure is mine!
Ten—
  Keep going! Keep going! I'll tell you when!

At the edge of the stage the turnips linked arms and began to kick their legs in unison:

Here we are, friends! Ready to sing our ditty.
Just like the girls at Radio City!

For a moment they all did a kind of raucous cancan. Suddenly a terrible sound, half a scream, half a groan, rang out—
[*Einen Orgasmus haben*]
—with such force that it seemed it might, like a soprano's high C, shatter the starburst chandeliers. Rübezahl, the turnip counter, stood on his toes, with his hands thrown into the air. At that instant the front of each plaster vegetable flew open and a bearded man stepped out.

Chorus of bearded men:

Don't be fooled by these beards. We don't eat bread
  without leaven.
We don't bring blessings. We each have an—

  (The men turn back to their turnips,
  stoop, and turn back, now carrying an)

—*AK-47!*

[*These words: they were not part of the authorized translation.*]

The next thing that happened was that directly below me the man with the caftan over his knees stood up from his wheelchair. The conductor, Mr. Goldkorn, whirled in astonishment and cried out, "Rebbe! Reb Teitelbaum!"

The former paraplegic reached upward and pushed aside his beaver-trimmed hat. Then he shouted orders through his cupped hands:

> *Nobody move! Shut all the exits! Close down the snack bar!*

The men on stage yanked away their beards and began to shout as well:

> *We'll shoot to kill. This is no joke. Allahu akbar!*

For perhaps five seconds, the whole audience sat frozen. The same thought was in every mind, including my own: Was this part of the opera? Was everything we were seeing written down in Mahler's libretto or in its rather free translation?

[*Madam, I have just told you. Pas du tout.*]

Down in the orchestra pit Mr. Goldkorn raised his hands toward the audience.

"Ha! Ha! Don't worry, friends. These are my cousins. From Kopitshinets. Reb Yitzhak, greetings! Abdi, what an excellent demi-plié. And there is the rebbetzin. Yes, yes. All in the family."

Just then there was a convulsive movement along the first row of the Orchestra section. Four or five men, surely Secret Service agents, threw themselves on the President, forcing him to the carpet. Another agent stood with two hands pointing a revolver at the dancer whom Mr. Goldkorn had addressed as Abdi.

"Don't thoot!" the latter implored.

But a shot rang out nonetheless—not from the stage but from near the orchestra pit. The Secret Service agent dropped to the floor.

"¡El chofer!" Jaime cried.

Now a distinguished-looking man, tall and silver-haired, stood up from his seat. "Look here," he shouted, in a Southern accent, even as he reached inside his jacket. "You can't do this kind—"

The chauffeur, clearly a marksman, fired again and the patron whirled, throwing up his arms; the small silver object he had pulled from his inner pocket flew off, making a small singsong sound:

> *Look away! Look away Look away!*
> *Dixie Land!*

"The ambassador!" exclaimed Mr. Goldkorn. "A Vanderbilt man!"

Already two more agents had risen from their seats. But before they could aim their guns a fusillade rang out from the wings and both men fell back on top of their comrade. A dark-haired woman stepped onto the stage and stood squinting down the barrel of her smoking weapon. Mr. Goldkorn gestured toward her with his baton.

"The Bombshell!" he exclaimed.

Up went the cry: "A bomb! There's a bomb!"

Then came pandemonium. It seemed as if all four thousand people in the Metropolitan Opera auditorium were streaming into the aisles and clawing at each other in an attempt to push through an exit. Men and women were screaming, weeping, and collapsing in their seats. Here and there you could actually hear isolated voices shouting into their cell phones. Amidst these moans, this wailing, the chandeliers descended, paused as if in horror at the maelstrom below them, and then rose again.

On the stage Mr. Domingo ripped off his wart-covered mask and the rags of his costume, and stood upright. "Señoras y señores. Be calm. Please be calm."

If anything, the situation grew more chaotic. At the sound of the Spaniard's voice, all of the cast and most of the crew rushed onto the stage. They began to run back and forth, colliding and recolliding, the way we are told molecules do in a gas.

Now came a humming and a buzzing; the stagehands and the cast halted in their tracks and stared upward. An enormous insect, in yellow and brown stripes, flew down from the right-hand wings and began to dart first toward one person, then another. The King and two of his ministers threw themselves flat. Ms. Fleming, though under attack herself, began to sing the following lines:

> *Fly, fly swiftly, little honeybee*
> *To the Prince who—*

But before she could finish the rhyme there was a tremendous rustling from stage left, and a bird as large as an albatross—
[*Nein. Das ist eine Schwalbe. A swallow.*]
—came swooping in from the left-hand wings and, with its beak of steel shears, began to chase the poor insect through the air.

As if that were not enough there was, with a flash and fumes, a terrific report; out of the explosion of yet another turnip, a huge cricket, the size of an ostrich or a kangaroo, began to hop across the stage, making a deafening whirring sound. Flat on the stage went all the humans as, with the *snap-snap-snap* of its mandibles, this creature jumped over this victim or that one and then veered toward the lip of the stage.

A heartrending scream rose from the opera patrons, who clearly were more horrified by this insect than by the terrorists— for such we knew they must be—and their guns. Nor was their dread assuaged when a stork with legs as long as a giraffe's and a beak like a scimitar came striding onto the stage, or when another turnip detonated, releasing a falcon with the wingspan of a Piper Cub into the air.

What turmoil then. What terror. The swallow stalked the bee, and the stork stabbed at the cricket, and the falcon soared into the auditorium as high as the Dress Circle and the Balcony, causing everyone to duck and dodge; then it dove down toward Parterre box number 1.

Futz! Footz went Hymena, raising what were left of her claws.

"¡Hurra!" cried Jaime, leaning precariously outward over the ivory front of our box.

"Achtung! Take cover!" Those words, in guttural English, came from the adjoining box 3. It was Henry Kissinger, ducking out of the way.

Minute after minute this wild helter-skelter continued, with the five animals—

[*Eine Honigbiene. Eine Schwalbe. Eine Grille. Ein Storch. Und ein Falke. Gigantische Menagerie!*]

—swooping and hopping through the air, screeching and buzzing, until there was a tremendous volley of gunfire, and the birds and the insects, which after all had been made from nothing more than plaster and wire and papier-mâché, fell in some cases still and in other cases writhing to the ground.

The terrorists lowered the muzzles of their weapons. Now

all was silent, motionless, hushed, until the conductor, Mr. Goldkorn, turned toward and audience and raised, in their purple sleeves, his arms.

"Will the audience take their seats, bitte? And turn off all Funktelefone. We soon shall begin Act Three!"

SCENE THREE

GÖTTERDÄMMERUNG

Deadlines are set. Deadlines are missed.
Then, on the eye of Passover, the Metropolitan Opera is
blown sky-high. Leib Goldkorn: Auf Wiedersehen!

LATE. LATE IN the night. Impossible to sleep. Doctors. Nurses. Tests. And many tears. A normal reaction, everyone tells me, to the events that began that Sunday. And now the reign of terror begins.

WITHIN AN HOUR of taking command, the dark-skinned terrorists had established a degree of order. The first thing they did was block all the exits with armed guards. Then the man who had impersonated Reb Teitelbaum announced that women and children were free to leave. There was not a mad dash. There was not an exodus. In fact a score of women elected to remain—some with their loved ones, some from orneriness perhaps, and a few, like myself, for professional reasons.

There were only a handful of children at the premiere; they all departed quietly. Jaime, after a hug, left too—though to my dismay he soon returned, pointing to his half-eaten biscuit. "Yo quiero terminar la galleta." Nor, for all my urging, would he budge.

Across the auditorium, in box 3, I saw that Condoleezza Rice had remained as well. Had she refused to abandon her President? Or had our captors restrained her since she was—what? My mind for brief seconds froze: third in line for Commander-in-Chief? No, fifth. But the first two were now hostages. That meant that the country was now being run by another woman, the Honorable Ms. Pelosi. Indeed, the same monitors on which Mr. Levine—

[*Non-rhyming with Ochsenschwanz; non-rhyming with Plotkin*]

—had been conducting were in time wheeled before us, so that we regularly saw the face of the Speaker of the House.

Not long after the women and children had left and all the men had been herded down to the orchestra level, the false paraplegic climbed with alacrity to the stage and raised a megaphone to his lips.

"You. American men. Listen. We are going to separate the Jews. All Jews raise hands."

The woman with the gun, the Bombshell as Mr. Goldkorn had called her, had a megaphone as well. "You heard!" she shouted. "Jews to the center section. All others move left and move right."

At this the conductor cried out. "Ha! Ha! Reb Teitelbaum. My senhorita. Why such favoritism? There is no need to reserve for those of Hebraic persuasion these excellent seats."

"Calar a boca!" the woman shouted in her unknown tongue.

I turned to Jaime, who shrugged. "Portugués."

"But are you not my Grossnichte? Is this not rudeness? To speak in such a manner to a member of the family?" Mr. Goldkorn then turned to the man he had called Reb Yitzhak. "Cousin, are you not family too? The grandson of Uncle Rufus?"

"Ablah! How easy you were to fool."

"Wait. One moment. Do you mean you, all of you, my cousins: you are not Satmarians?"

Here the gunmen broke into high-pitched laughter and the

women into ululations. In their merriment they slapped each other on the back.

"Not even Jews?"

"Yahùd! Ha! Ha! Ha! Yahudi!"

"You are not alone, Leib Goldkorner. They tricked us too."

The conductor and translator shielded his eyes and peered up toward box number 2. "Is that you, Your Serenity? The State Secretary? Mit freckles?"

Ms. Rice started to reply, "You must be——" when almost instantly someone seized her from behind and drew her into the shadows at the back of the box, where all the other dignitaries were standing with their hands tied behind them and white rags in their mouths.

Now from the stage came a sharp rapping, a kind of *Knock! Knock!*

Mr. Goldkorn, with his key chain clanking at his hip, whirled about:

"Who's there?"

No one answered. Our captors had lined up on the front of the stage facing Broadway, that is, to the east, and from their kneeling positions were touching their heads to the floor:

Ash-hadu an la illaha
illa Allah

"Is it possible," asked Mr. Goldkorn, "that I have made an error?"

Just then an aged man, perhaps as old as ninety, came tottering down the left-hand aisle. Everything stopped, even the Arabic prayers. The hall was so silent that for all its soundproofing, its insulation, we could hear the faint wail of a hundred sirens drawing near. On came the gentleman, a half step at a time. He was hairless and his skin was ruddy. He seemed to take forever to reach the first row of the auditorium.

"Is there need," the nonagenarian asked, "for a doctor in the house?"

"Goloshes! M.D.!" exclaimed Mr. Goldkorn.

As if in response, one of the wounded agents sent up a pitiable groan.

The conductor turned toward the terrorists. "First name Milton. Family physician."

Dr. Goloshes bent over the wounded man. "He has been shot in the lung. He must go to the hospital."

In the blink of an eye Abdoul struck the side of the doctor's head with the butt of his rifle—and did so with such force that he tumbled into the orchestra pit in a spray of his own blood.

The middle-aged woman—Mr. Goldkorn had called her the rebbetzin—gestured down toward the dumbstruck musicians. "Take the Jew to the ghetto." Here she pointed toward the center section of seats. "That's where he belongs."

No one moved. Sobs sprang up from everywhere, sounding, in the wonderfully engineered acoustics of the auditorium, like hot springs, or geysers.

Mr. Goldkorn was the first to speak. "Was this Goloshes not offering his assistance? Yet you struck him on the head. The head! Is this not where musical notes are first formed?"

"Muthical noths!" Abdi, one of the gunmen, had a lisp, a surprise in such a muscular type. "Here. Look. Now you know what we think of your muthical noths."

A gasp rose from the hostages as he opened his trousers and, onto the scattering musicians in the pit, began an act of micturation.

One of his companions, thin as a blade of grass, barked out a laugh and walked to the lip of the stage. He likewise micturated onto the abandoned bass viols and instruments of percussion.

[*Micturation. Micturated. An example of* New York Times *straitlaces. We are speaking, friends, of number one.*]

Nor was that the end of this horror. The others lined up and performed with glee the same act. Poor Dr. Goloshes remained alone in the steaming pit until they were done. Only then was his limp, soaked body—luckily with life still within it—taken out to what soon became a makeshift hospital in the carpeted aisle. I must now report that over the course of our ordeal the orchestra pit served the same function for us all, whether infidel or Mohammedan; amazing how quickly our notions of modesty were cast to the winds.

THIS ARTICLE IS growing both long and late. My editors would like it by noon tomorrow. Is this possible? Certainly I can shorten my task by honoring the request of the White House not to discuss, for what they call national security reasons, the actions of the President or the Vice President. I will respect their concerns and say only this: the behavior of George W. Bush was in my opinion exemplary. The Secret Service, though disarmed, continued to keep him isolated and in a sense untouchable in their midst. But we could hear him. He instructed his wife and the wives and children of any government officials, as well as all female government employees themselves, to leave the building. Only Ms. Rice refused.

[*Because of infatuations? With the President? Such are the rumors. Or was there another chap—we need not mention appelations—who had caught her eye?*]

He also made it clear from within his phalanx of bodyguards that there were to be no negotiations of any sort with the terrorists—and that this directive applied to all those in the opera house as well as to his cabinet and to anyone else who could hear his words in Washington, D.C.

Alas, quite soon, no one, whether in the Metropolitan Opera or in the nation's capital, could hear him at all. That was because in the course of that night his protectors were beaten down and the President led away. As for the Vice President, he was found after a lengthy search hiding beneath a row of seats. While shouting out to all who could hear that he was wearing a pacemaker, he too was led out of our hearing and out of our sight.

No need to dwell here on the despair we felt the next morning when our captors announced that both men had been shot. That was, as it happened, the first message that went out over our primitive system of communication. Ms. Pelosi's image was almost constantly on the screen of our monitors. Mr. Goldkorn, perhaps because he was the director of the premiere, or because he was the only one whom the terrorists were familiar with, would talk to her over the cell phone that had been confiscated from the ambassador to the Czech Republic. Imagine our horror when we heard him speak the terrible words, "The excellent President Busch and the Vice President are dead."

The face of the representative from California was instantly drained of all color. Her jaw went slack. "I don't understand. Are you telling me that both of them have been killed?"

Mr. Goldkorn looked toward the young woman with the Portuguese accent. She nodded.

The conductor shouted into the instrument he held at arm's length. "That's right. It's a shame. I always vote a straight Republican ticket."

Every reader of this paper already knows what the terrorists demanded in return for our freedom. We fell into despair as Mr. Goldkorn read the list to the world. First, the release of Sheikh Omar Abdel-Rahman, convicted of seditious conspiracy for his role in the 1993 World Trade Center bombing. Second, even more impossible, the transfer to neutral countries of all those being held at the Guantánamo Bay detention camp. Then the most difficult of all: the suspension of diplomatic ties between the United States and Israel. Last—and this by com-

parison seemed a mere afterthought—the delivery of two million dollars in ransom and a guarantee for the terrorists of safe
conduct to a land of their choosing.

What else could we think but that we were doomed? Our
captors declared that they had traveled thousands of miles and
trained for many years to arrive at this moment—a moment
that for them was a paradise on earth. With their deaths, and
the deaths of the infidels, they would achieve the other paradise
that awaited them in heaven. If the American government did
not meet each of these demands before forty-eight hours had
elapsed, the Metropolitan Opera and all those within it would
be blown to smithereens.

This was no idle threat. At the start of the siege the terrorists
had admitted perhaps a score of their confederates through the
arched doors, which these same men then blockaded with trip
lines, booby traps, and mines. Then they worked ceaselessly
to attach their wires and fuses to the support structures in the
hall. At one point they even lowered the chandeliers, only to
raise them again with enough plastic explosives aboard to crack
the great ornate roof and bring it down upon us.

From the outside world we entertained no hope. Indeed we
dreaded any attempt at rescue. On our monitors we could see
troops deployed on the plaza, along with the tanks and per-
sonnel carriers that choked the avenues. Helicopters hovered
overhead, while below, in the sewers, the subway tunnels,
the communication tubes, sappers and Special Forces were
undoubtedly at work. But we knew that at the first movement
to save us, all the explosives that had been so painstakingly
planted around the auditorium would detonate together, creating a greater *Götterdämmerung* than had been staged at this or
any other opera house in the world.

The deadline Ms. Pelosi had been given was forty-eight
hours. Mr. Goldkorn read the ultimatum at ten o'clock on the
morning of April 10th. By the next dawn, nearly half the time

allotted to us, we had received no response. The rest of that day went by in silence and so did the better part of the night. No one had had anything to eat. There was little to drink. The stench from the orchestra pit, at which there was a constant queue, was overwhelming. Yet there was no resistance. No one cried out in anger or pain. The hours went speeding by. The hostages resigned themselves to the certainty that on the following morning they were going to die.

Old Missus marry Will-de-weaber

The ringtone on the ambassador's telephone!

Willium was a gay deceaber.

The Speaker of the House was back on the line. Imagine our joy, and our astonishment, when we heard that our captors' demands were about to be met. She told us that the proof of the government's compliance would presently appear on our monitors. Never before had so many people stared so intently at such a small screen. Through my opera glasses I could just make out the words that soon appeared at the bottom: *Butner Federal Correctional Complex*. Then a cheer went up from our foes. They cried out what must have been an Arabic blessing— *Da'awatak, ya sheikh!*—at the sight of a blind, bearded man ducking his head to get into the back of an armored limousine. I must report that many of my fellow hostages, including a good portion of the central section, gave a cheer too. For this was Omar Abdel-Rahman, the blind sheikh, on his way out of prison. One hour later we saw the same man depart from the limousine and fly off in an unmarked Gulfstream jet.

An hour after that the monitors lit up again, this time with the familiar sight of the wire enclosures at Guantánamo Bay. The prisoners were in a long line; clearly they were being pro-

cessed for either transfer or departure. The underground kingdom of the monstrous Rübezahl had been filled with trees,
arbors, and fantastical flowers. The terrorists stooped to gather
the petals; they threw handfuls at the screens, which within a
few seconds faded away and became blank.

This time the pause was lengthier. The mood of jubilation
gradually receded, leaving us stranded once more on the hard
stones of reality. How dared we dream that the most difficult
demand—the betrayal of Israel by its oldest ally—could ever be
met? What fools we had been!

The mood among the jailers had changed as well. The ululations ceased. Grimly they set about stringing the last of their
wires. Now when they prayed toward the east it was with a
note of resignation and lament. The sun, we knew, was well
up in the sky. The midmorning deadline would soon be upon
us. At one corner of the stage was an almost comical device: a
black box with a silvery aluminum plunger. It looked like something out of the silent movies or the sort of cartoon in which
the infernal machine would be marked with the letters TNT.
But no one laughed when the cold-blooded Portuguese woman
looked at her watch—my own read nine thirty-two—and sat
down beside it.

[*Correction to* The New York Times: *Brazilian, not Portuguese. The granddaughter of my sister Minchke, for whom
in my present abode I have diligently searched. Sans success.
Ditto sister Yakhne. Ditto Falma, my mother, and the putative père. Over and over I have called out their names. Pas de
response. Is it possible that all those who were on the barge*
Kaliope, *daughter of Zeus and Mnemosyne, are sequestered
together? No sign of Herr Mahler, my non-putative père. Nor,
by the by, of Professor Pergam.*]

The real power, I believe, resided in the false rabbi, Yitzhak,
who had long since strapped a vest of explosives to his torso and

now walked one by one to each of his accomplices, embracing them and saying unintelligible words. Those men shed as many tears as we did in our velour-covered seats. Perhaps I should describe the events of the next half hour as they might have appeared in one of those nickelodeon serials:

9:40
9:50
9:52
9:55

A crescendo of groans rose from the orchestra. There was shouting and cursing. In the left-hand section I noted a ripple, a small movement, and then a group of some twenty to twenty-five men rushed toward the stage. But the moment the terrorists lowered the muzzles of their weapons, the wave broke and soon dispersed.

9:57
9:58

I drew Jaime to me and shut my eyes. But not my ears:

> *Dar's buck-what cakes and Ingen batter.*
> *Makes you fat or a little fatter.*

Again the ringtone! Was it a reprieve? Literally at the last moment? What we saw on the screen was the image of a stylish man with a part in his hair. He too was being moved to a black limousine.

"It's Richard! Ambassador Richard Henry Jones!"

That cry came from across the Parterre, where Mr. Ayalon, the Israeli ambassador, had managed to slip his gag.

Now Representative Pelosi appeared on the monitor to interpret what we had seen. The American ambassador to Israel had been called home. The Israeli ambassador to America was in the control of the terrorists. Diplomatic relations between the two countries were thus at an end.

We were saved! All the demands had been met. Well, not quite all. But the last two—the payment of two million dollars, the arrangements for the escape of the terrorists: What could be easier? Not only that, every one of the hostages had been buoyed by the fact that their captors had asked for such things in the first place. They were not fanatics. They did not seek suicide or any other form of death. To demand money, to think of flying off in an airplane so they could spend it—that meant they wanted to live. And so would we.

"Hurrah!" we shouted.

"¡Hurra!"

Meee-yay!

"Hello? Operator? Hello?"

Mr. Goldkorn shouted repeatedly into the mouthpiece of the cell phone. The face of the Speaker of the House had once more disappeared from the screen. Still, no one was unduly alarmed. The amount required was, relatively speaking, so small. And the terrorists—how strange it was that we all applauded their reasonableness—extended the deadline for its delivery another six hours, to four o'clock that afternoon.

That time sped quickly by. I should say that a certain portion of the Metropolitan audience no longer cared whether the ransom would be paid or not. Scores had fainted or had collapsed from dehydration. The bottled drinks brought in from the snack bars soon ran out. The doctors declared that some under their care were in diabetic hypoglycemia and others in cardiogenic shock.

"Hello? Hello?" cried the conductor into the cell telephone. "Sprechen Sie Deutsch?"

Still no one replied. Inconceivable that the United States government, having given so much, could not or would not raise such a paltry sum. Was there some law, some code, that forbade ransom in cash? To deny us our lives now was madness, though admittedly no more insane than the actions of the terrorists, who, upon completing their midday prayers, once more took up their positions at the detonators. This time, however, we did not go down to—oh, I` do not mean this cruel pun—the wire.

> But when he put his arm aound'er
> He smiled as fierce as a forty pounder.

Breathlessly the conductor picked up the phone.

"Hello? Here is Leib Goldkorn, Graduate of the Akad—"

Yitzhak ripped the phone from his hands. "We are at the deadline. Where is—"

He too stopped in midsentence and turned in a kind of wonderment to his accomplices. "She cannot give the money. Only the President can make that decision."

"The President? What is the matter with you?" cried Mr. Goldkorn, leaning toward the mouthpiece. "Do you not understand plain English? Er ist tot!"

Then the erstwhile rabbi nodded toward his confederate with the lisp, who walked at once from our sight.

Three precious moments went by. Then a fourth. Imagine our astonishment when George W. Bush was led past the drooping props and onto the stage. He had been beaten, it seemed, and his hands were tied behind him. But he was very much alive.

"Greetings, Majesty. I—"

Two of the younger terrorists stepped between the conductor and the President. They held the cell phone to the latter's swollen lips.

"I gave my orders," the President said. "No ransom. No deals. No negotiations."

Those words were our death sentence. The young Portuguese—

[*Brazilian!*]

—woman rushed back to the plunger. Yitzhak and the others took out their electronic detonators. The strapping young Abdi began to count.

"One-two-three—"

Again I shut my eyes.

"Four. Five. Thixth—"

"Wait! Is stopping, gentlemens. Mister! For a moment you wait!"

I opened my eyes. Down the aisle, indeed taking up the greater part of it, was a woman built roughly on the proportions of Grant's Tomb in Riverside Park. Down she came, and down, ineluctably, forcing herself ahead until she had reached the edge of what was now our latrine.

On the other side of that barrier, the conductor squinted, the better to see.

"Heavens! Hildegard! Madam Stutchkoff! You have put on some avoirdupois."

The monument of a woman looked upward. "Is who? From Steinway Restaurant?"

"*Ja!* Musical type. Do you remember? Our moment on the Sealy? When we—"

Here Mr. Goldkorn made a certain vulgar gesture—

[*To wit, a finger of one hand thrusts through the circle made by the other hand's pointer and thumb. Oh, she bit me*

with rows of her little teeth. As folks do on All Saints' Day. I
bobbed at her apples. In short, folks, we made merry.]
—that I am not certain the woman even noticed. She continued
to stare upward.

"Mister? Mister . . . ? Mister . . . ?"

"Goldkorn. Graduate."

At the sound of the name, Madam Stutchkoff reached
upward and removed both of her earrings.

[*Oh, ho! Did she wish once more to retreat to the Sealy?*]

This jewelry she handed to Abdoul, who stood armed
beside her.

"Here. Is gold. Karat twenty-two."

Next she fumbled at the brooch on her breast. She removed
that as well.

[*In Hades, a rum toddy sensation.*]

"Is also gold. And more . . ."

Next she thrust out a plump wrist and unstrapped what
even from my distant location I recognized to be a man's gold
wristwatch.

"I am giving. Not plate. Not filled. Is from husband, Vivian
Stutchkoff."

Abdoul took these treasures into his cupped hands. I believe
he actually licked his lips.

"This is the solution!" That cry came from Dr. Kissinger,
who was leaning over the edge of the box adjoining mine. "Take
meine watch. Take mein bracelet. Both solid gold!"

He threw the objects down to where Abdoul was standing—
no, stooping, because others had begun to toss their rings and
watches and cuff links about him.

"Of course!"

"We can do it ourselves!"

"We'll pay our own ransom!"

Could our possessions save us? I only knew that everyone

became swept up in that hopeful tide. From the two side sections the Christians were tossing their crucifixes and chains, while the Jews in the middle seats were passing forward their six-pointed stars. Jaime started to pull off his Bulova, but I stopped him and threw down my gold ring instead. Now people came pushing forward, clutching handfuls of bills. Others were waving their checkbooks.

"I'll give a thousand!"

"Fifty thousand!"

"Six figures! Whatever you want."

At these offers the terrorists shook their heads. They would not take checks. They would not even take cash. After conferring, they announced they would accept only contributions of gold—and those must come exclusively from the central section or from what other Jews might wish to contribute from the outside world.

Would that be necessary? Already a glittering pyramid of metal had risen on the stage. From somewhere, perhaps from one of the dressing rooms, our foes had dragged out a scale. They heaped the treasure upon it. Yitzhak, peering at the dial, shook his head. The total was not enough.

"How much *is* enough?" someone cried.

The rebbetzin, so-called, replied. "The value of gold is now six hundred dollars an ounce. There are in a pound sixteen such ounces. Each pound of gold, then, is worth almost ten thousand dollars. To reach two million dollars we will require . . ." Here the woman paused for an instant, casting up her eyes.

"May I be of assistance?" It was Mr. Goldkorn. "Lightning calculation. One pound is ten thousand. Ergo, ten pounds equals—ha, ha! Moment! Hmmm. Hmmm. Carry the one—"

To my amazement it was I who shouted out the final sum. "Two hundred pounds. You are asking for two hundred pounds of gold."

Yitzhak pointed at the scale. "Here is only eighty-five."

A convulsive movement of anguish moved through the crowd; they had already stripped themselves bare.

Now, during these renewed moanings and wailings, another woman moved down the right-hand aisle, though this one was in a wheelchair.

"Madam Schnabel!" exclaimed our conductor. "Contralto!"

The woman forced her shaking head upward. "I don't need you, Leib Goldkorns. I need a dentist. I have a gold molar, two gold molars. Take them. Take them from all the Jews."

"Yes, yes!"

"A dentist!"

"Take my teeth!"

"Take mine!"

Alas, even if a dentist had been in the room, the deadline was upon us. Four p.m. Doomed, with our teeth intact, to die. Then, just as our jailers were resuming their places at the bombs and the detonators, a scuffle broke out at the rear of the hall. Somebody was shouting in Arabic. Somebody else shouted back.

"Let us in, for Pete's sake. We've got the gold."

Two men, one plump, one thin, were admitted to the back of the auditorium. There they were searched so thoroughly that each was required to remove his trousers. Bare-legged, they trudged down the aisle, pulling a rubber-wheeled wagon heaped with bowls, bracelets, bagatelles, and bric-a-brac—all made from the glittering metal. As they approached the front of the hall, Mr. Goldkorn called out to them: "Greetings, Ernie! Greetings, Randy! Here are the brothers Glickman."

Up in box number 1 Jaime extended the arm to which his wristwatch was attached. "Shop of prawns!"

Like stevedores, the brothers were handing their treasure to Abdoul, who in turn tossed the loot to his confederates onstage.

"Boy, oh, boy! You never saw so many Jews. As soon as the word got out they lined up around the block." That was the thin brother.

"And nobody asked for a ticket. Can you believe it? These are gifts from our people."

Looking through my opera glasses, I calculated that this haul must weigh over a hundred pounds. Indeed, the so-called rebbetzin soon announced the total: "One hundred forty-seven."

A cheer went up. With the eighty-five pounds already collected, the ransom had been paid.

"Hurrah!" That was the cry. "Hurrah for the brothers Glickman!"

Ernie, the plump one, held up his hands. "It was nothing. Glad to help. Now, if you will just return my seersucker pants, we'll take our leave."

Abdi laughed. "Leave? You cannot leave. Not yet."

Madam Schnabel called out from her wheelchair: "They still are waiting. They want an airplane."

Abdoul pointed to the cell phone in the conductor's hand. "No one leaves until we get the call. Either we fly away or everyone dies with us on the ground."

Randy said, "Did you say *die*?"

Ernie said, "But we are only messengers. The deliverymen. Never mind the trousers. We'll go just the way we are."

"Sit down," said the impersonator of Reb Teitelbaum. "In the middle. With the Jews."

"Say," said Randy. "How much do you want for that hat?"

"We offer a thousand cash for real beaver."

The Bombshell lowered the tip of her assault rifle. "You heard what he said. Judeus! Assentem-se!"

The brothers stepped back, raising their hands. Randy said, "How long will we be here?"

The man named Yitzhak gave a cruel laugh. "For eternity!"
His supposed son said, "Or until eight o'clock. We'll make
that the latht deadline."

"Eight o'clock!" Randy exclaimed. "That's past sundown!"

"Tho what?"

"But it's Passover! The Seder starts at seven!"

Just then a moan went from the first seat to the last of the
central section. It was unlike the sounds of suffering we had
heard before. Half the men were beating their breasts. The
other half were clutching their stomachs. It dawned on me
that in all the terror of the last days every single one of them
had forgotten two things: that this was the first night of their
holy day and that they were hungry to the point of starvation. You could hear both concerns in the chant that rose from
them now:

"Seder! Seder! Give us our Seder!"

The Jews were standing. They raised their fists in the air.
This was the first serious sign of defiance. The terrorists lifted
their weapons; they pointed them at the crowd. But the chant
of *Seder! Seder!* only grew louder. The men at the front began
to push forward. Those behind pressed against them. Out of
this mass of people a tall, thin man seemed to be extruded. As
the crowd recognized him their shouts abated, and when he had
gained the edge of the stage and held up his hands, they entirely
faded away. Here was the Nobel Prize winner, Elie Wiesel. This
was how he addressed us:

"No one here knows what is going to happen. Perhaps in
the next hours our government will relent. I do not understand
their position—or that of my friend President Bush."

[*Poor fellow! I only wish there would be a miracle and the
Constitution, John Hancock author, could be changed to permit him to run again. In my opinion, he'd win in a landslide.*]

Mr. Wiesel continued: "The first principle, the only principle, should be the saving of human life. The lives of the Jewish people and also the lives of our tormentors in this beautiful opera house—heaven forbid it should be destroyed."

Here the laureate paused, pushing a shock of falling hair from his forehead. "So let us pray that in the hours that remain before eight o'clock, God will whisper to our leaders: *Be merciful and spare these many lives.* But if that should not happen—should that telephone not ring—then we must prepare to die. But not before enjoying our last Seder here, among our new friends, our new family. And when these few shall say, *Next year in Jerusalem,* it will be with the voice of all."

Amazingly enough, this Seder occurred. The hours went by. The cell phone remained mute, the screens of our monitors blank. Outside, the sun was setting. We deduced this not by our watches but because the terrorists performed, with their heads knocking the floorboards, the same prayer they did each day as the last light disappeared from the sky.

Then all those onstage, the chorus and crew, the King and his court, Princess and Prince, stepped toward the wings as a small group of Jews set up a long table and chairs. From the prop department they had no trouble finding tablecloths, cutlery, soup bowls, dinner plates, and goblets for wine. Even a candelabrum. One by one the celebrants took their places at the table. Mr. Wiesel sat at one end, the Glickmans took seats in the middle. Madam Schnabel and Stutchkoff were there as well. Mr. Goldkorn squinted up toward the Parterre. "May I invite my former inamorata to join us?"

Did he mean me? I rose a bit from my seat. Then, overcome by a fit of shyness, I sat again.

"You won't come?" called the conductor. "A pity. At such a time a man wishes to have about him all the women in his life."

"What about me, maestro? Am I not your Buttercup? Do I not count?"

The speaker was Emma, the Princess. She had plucked up one of the plants from Rübezahl's grotto and, holding it aloft, approached Mr. Goldkorn.

"The Fleming!" the latter declared. "What's that in your hand? Maror?"

"Mistletoe." The soprano raised the greenery above the conductor. Then she bent low toward him, and lower still. "It is our last chance."

"You mean für einen Kuss? But think about the bowels."

The soprano's face was inches away. But just before her lips met his, someone in the audience started to sing:

> *I'd love to get you on a slow boat to China*
> *All to myself alone—*

The conductor turned from Miss Fleming and peered into the orchestra, where a woman stood, isolated and alone. "What? Could it be? Is this Neptune's Daughter?" Then he broke into song himself:

> *Out on the briny with the moon big and shiny*
> *Melting your heart of stone—*

Futz! Fitz howled Hymena.

The humans, including the Arabians, put their hands to their ears.

The woman said, "I rarely travel. I do not attend the opera. But, dear Leibie, how could I miss your world premiere?"

With the aid of a cane she began to make her way to the stage.

Mr. Goldkorn introduced her to us. "Ladies and gentlemen, the Million-Dollar Mermaid. Miss E. Williams!"

[*I experienced then what I had back in December of 1941, when this very woman had awakened me with her magical prestidigits. In short, a bubbling in the depths and a gathering warmth, which is what it must feel like to be a fondue.*]

I looked down. Yes, beneath what are so often called the ravages of time, I saw the indelible spirit of the swimmer, the actress, the beauty queen.

"Look, Jaime," I said. "Do you see? That is a famous—"

But the boy's seat was empty. He was not in the box. Before I could call out his name I saw him running onto the stage. He went directly to Mr. Goldkorn, who put his hand on his pomaded head.

"I am now the proud papa of this handsome Junge. Reminiscent of myself as a lad. Ha, ha. Without the ears."

Slowly the table filled. One type of doctor, Goloshes, with his wounded head wrapped up like a Sikh's, leaned against the shoulder of another, Kissinger. A man with a freckled face climbed onto the stage.

"It's all a mistake," he announced. "I thought this was supposed to be *La Bohème*."

Mr. Goldkorn beckoned him to one of the few remaining chairs. "May I introduce my landlord and King of the Casa Blanca, Mr. Frank Fingerhut, fils."

"We have less than an hour," Madam Schnabel declared. "We should begin."

The Jews, together with Miss Williams and Miss Fleming, looked dispiritedly at their unfilled glasses, their empty plates.

"Is not even matzoh?" asked Hildegard Stutchkoff.

"Attention, gentlemen. And ladies." Mr. Wiesel held his wineglass aloft.

Blessed are you, Lord, our God, King of the
universe, who created the fruit of the vine.

Mr. Goldkorn held up his glass as well. "Ha! Ha! There's nothing in it." Then he put it to his lips.

"Wait! Wait! Don't drink! It's too soon."

The speaker was an aged man, though he seemed spry enough as he hurried down the aisle. It was difficult to make out the meaning of his words, perhaps because his nose was buried in a thick moustache. "You have to wait until the end of the Kiddush. Greetings, Leib Goldkorn. How is your lovely bride?"

Mr. Goldkorn stood stunned.

[*Yes, stunned. For without a doubt, though his hair tufts were now entirely gray, this was the man who had performed the spousals between myself and Miss Litwack in the year of our Lord, so to speak, 1942.*]

"Rabbi Rymer!" he eventually exclaimed. "Clara? Kaputt."

Instead of replying, the short, stout clergyman took up a glass of his own and began to chant words in Hebrew that I knew from the Seders I had attended were in praise of the Lord for having chosen the Jews from among all the peoples of the earth, and for having—and here Mr. Wiesel and several others joined him in English:

> *granted us life, sustained us, and enabled*
> *us to reach this occasion.*

Madam Stutchkoff looked down to where her husband's watch had once been. "Is what time?"

"Seven-thirty," answered Mr. Fingerhut.

Said Dr. Kissinger, in his rumbling voice, "We have to hurry."

Even Goloshes murmured, "Only a half hour left."

All too true. Over their shoulders those at the table could not help but see how their modern oppressors were moving once more toward their deadly machines. There would be no miracle here: the sea would not part. Instead the sky, that is, the ceiling above us with its gold-plated clouds, would crack and fall, burying Israel and Egypt alike.

"Mah nishtanah?" piped little Jaime, prompted by the Nobel Laureate at his ear:

What makes this night different from all other nights?

Then, at breakneck speed, came the answer, along with the questions of the other children, simple, wicked, and wise. Rabbi Rymer never stopped chanting and swaying, holding up glasses filled with nothing and uncovering plates that were bare. Yet no matter how quick his words, how swift his gestures, the hands of a thousand different clocks moved ever faster: twelve minutes to the hour, ten minutes to the hour. Eight, seven, six.

Now those at the table dipped their fingertips into the optical illusion of the wine and shook the drops onto empty dishes:

Blood
Lice
Wild beasts
Pestilence
Boils
Hail
Locusts
Darkness
The slaying of the firstborn

[*You have forgotten, my half-Finn, frogs.*]

Four minutes. Three. The terrorists unbuttoned their jackets, revealing once more the dynamite strapped to their chests. The young, curly-haired woman gripped the metal plunger with both hands.

Rabbi Rymer was chanting faster than a tobacco auctioneer. But all the minute hands now trembled at the top. The rabbi stopped. He looked about. Then, with the stiff cloth of a napkin, he covered the immaterial matzoh and began slowly, and in English, to say the following words:

> *Thus it is our duty to thank, to laud, to praise, to glorify,*
> *to exalt, to adore, to bless, to elevate, and to honor the*
> *One who did all these miracles for our fathers and for us.*
> *He took us from slavery to freedom, from sorrow to joy,*
> *and from mourning to festivity, and from deep darkness*
> *to great light, and from bondage to redemption. Let us*
> *therefore recite before him, Halleluya, praise God!*

God did not answer. The cell phone remained mute. No one appeared on the screens of the monitors. Instead, the woman who had posed as the wife of a rabbi announced, "It is eight o'clock. The government of America has chosen not to reply. We shall now carry out our task."

"Allahu akbar!" Thus cried out the Mohammedans.

"Sh'ma!" answered the Jews. "Sh'ma Yisroel!"

There was a loud noise. Not an explosion. A knock. A knocking. As if someone were at the door.

"Heavens!" cried Elie Wiesel. "It is Elijah!"

Everyone strained to see what was happening at the rear of the auditorium. Two of the guards stood aside, and into the open space stepped an old and stooped gentleman. Both his feet were splayed outward and so were his arms, on which were balanced plate after plate of steaming delicatessen.

"Barney Greengrass!" he announced. "Home delivery!"

"Ha! Ha!" laughed Leib Goldkorn. "212-724-9927. Weep, Uncle Al! I remember the number!"

Forward came the waiter, skillfully balancing his burden, until he reached the ramp to the stage. Nor did he hesitate then, but without spilling a morsel walked directly up to the table.

"Okay," he said. "Who gets the scrambled with horseradish cheddar?"

Deftly he set down the platters of food.

"Excuse me, Mr. Mosk," Mr. Goldkorn said. "I'm partial to the sable and whitefish."

Mr. Mosk took out a pad. "That'll be nine hundred and fifty-seven dollars. Not counting the tip."

All around him people were grabbing for knives and forks. One or two had started to shovel the food off the platters with their hands.

"Wait, gentlemen. Be patient, ladies." That was Rabbi Rymer. "We have to assume a reclining position."

The man called Yitzhak strode forward. "Fools! Do you think the condemned man receives a last meal?"

So saying, he swept all the plates and dishes off the table to the floor of the stage.

Mr. Mosk: "Visa, MasterCard, American Express. No Diners Club."

"Jews! The time is up! It is we, not you, who shall dwell in Jerusalem. Look: I raise my arm."

The terrorist did indeed lift his arm, like the blade of a guillotine, into the air.

"Allahu akbar!"

"Allahu akbar!"

"Tawakalt ala Allah!"

Down came the arm. Simultaneously, there came a faint, muffled sound:

Den hoe it down an scratch your grabble

It was the cell phone! It was Speaker Pelosi! Everyone gasped. But where was the song coming from? You could barely hear the ringtone:

To Dixie land I'm bound to trabble.

Then the head of Mr. Goldkorn appeared above the table-top. He had the ringing instrument in his hand.

"Sorry. I was unter der Tafel. Ha. Ha. I found a schmaltz herring."

"Give me that!" Dr. Kissinger swiped the cell phone from the conductor's hand and put it to his ear.

"Hello? Nancy? Hello. What? *What?* Now? Gott sei Dank!"

He addressed the assemblage. "The government has relented. It has made all the arrangements."

Then he turned to the terrorists. "You will be able to fly away."

No sooner had these last words left the diplomat's mouth than from out of the false blue of the sky a great winged horse descended. For an instant everyone, including the oppressors, stood in awe at the beauty of the animal and the enormity of its endowment. Down and down it came, until it stood quivering and hovering a few inches from the floor of the stage.

Suddenly Ms. Fleming, in her famous clear tones, sang the notes from the Mahler score:

Come, noble steed. O'er field, forest, and huts.
My goodness! My gracious! Just look at that putz!

[*What? Ribaldry? In this Familienzeitung?*]
Then, gripping the animal's mane, she attempted to pull

herself onto the broad expanse of its back. Before she could do so, two overweight men came running from the wings. One was the musical director of the Metropolitan Opera, James Levine.

[*J. Levine, huh? Rhymes with H. Heine.*]

He pushed Ms. Fleming aside and tried to climb onto the beast himself.

The second man was our Prince, the tenor Luciano Pavarotti. He dashed ahead, waving a white handkerchief.

"I'm-a surrender! I'm-a give up! I got-a una indisposizione!"

He barreled straight into Mr. Levine, knocking him backward, then tried to haul himself aboard. For the next seconds all three figures hopped up and down in the vain attempt to mount the colossal stallion.

Then, in unison, they stopped. They stepped back in wonder. Those three saw what we thousands did too: From the great flaring nostrils of the beast came a kind of spray, a cloud, a coil of fumes.

"Khatar!" shouted Abdoul.

"We have been tricked!"

"Hazir! It is a gas!"

"Haziru!"

Immediately the terrorists rushed for their weapons. All at once there was a loud sound, a *crack!*, and the entire flank of the horse sprang open and at least a score of armed men, all with black hoods, sprang out.

"Ein Trojanisches Pferd!"

There was a fusillade. Everyone, on the stage, in the Orchestra seats, flung himself down. A crossfire of bullets was clanging, zipping, thudding. Two of the terrorists fell. Then a third. In the thick roiling cloud I could see flashes and hear cries of pain and shouts of exultation. The smokescreen spread, filling the whole of the auditorium. People were coughing, choking, gasping. Was this a poison? A narcotic? Would it kill us? Or just put us to sleep?

I strained to see through the bank of vapor. Amidst all the sounds of warfare I could make out the voice of Rabbi Rymer, who had not budged from his spot at the table, and who was still chanting over an empty glass of wine. Sprawled about him on the floor, Mr. Fingerhut, the Glickman brothers, and the others were simultaneously covering their heads and reaching for crumbs of spilled food. My heart leaped to my mouth when I saw Jaime rushing through the fumes and the bullets and the puddles of gore.

"Dónde está el Afikomen?" he was shouting. "¿Dónde está el Afikomen?"

The battle was already drawing to a close. Through the back door, through all the exits, more troops were pouring. They wore packs on their backs and their faces were covered with rubber masks. The remaining terrorists turned their fire on the invaders, but they were quickly overwhelmed—either by firepower or the anesthetic that was now affecting us all. I saw Yitzhak fall. And Abdi. And both of the females. Abdoul clutched at his chest and dropped to his knees. So did the false Reb Teitelbaum. By now there were only scattered shots. Rabbi Rymer had stopped praying. He lay slumped at the table. Dead? Or merely asleep? His congregation lay on the floor. Their meal was done. There was a last salvo. Then a single shot. Then silence.

Was the siege over? I fought to keep my eyelids open, though they seemed to weigh as much as the iron shutters on a merchant's shop. On the stage I could see only shadows, some moving, some still. The great horse was entirely obscured, yet the fumes of steam or smoke or gas kept pouring from its nostrils. Not only had they blanketed the whole auditorium but they now billowed upward, hovering over the stage in a thick, dark, menacing cloud.

One person stood standing below it. It was Mr. Goldkorn. I could tell by the chain that glittered and gleamed as it dangled to his knees. He was pointing at the towering mound of vapor, which had gathered its coils into the shape of a gigantic figure, brown as blown dust, with a black cap like a thunderhead at its top. There was even a kind of rumble within it, like thunder itself.

Was I asleep? Was I dreaming? I watched as the aged musician pointed to the apparition that hovered above him.

"I know him! The Golem! The Furor!"

I leaned over the side of box number 1. I tried to see what he saw in the cloud. A human figure. Blurred. Overcast. But with a black shock of hair. A smudge of a black moustache.

"No, no!" I cried. "It is only a dream. A figure of imagination."

Mr. Goldkorn was groping this way and that, stumbling about the stage. "I know what to do. I know what I need. Where is my Rudall & Rose?"

Then he stopped in his tracks. He leaned forward, squinting. Something was shining in the dark. A line, a bar, of silver light. He staggered toward it, reaching out.

"My flute!" he cried. "A gift from the Emperor! Meine Zauberflöte!"

He took three steps toward where his shining instrument floated horizontally amidst the vapors. Then he paused. Behind him, above him, a flash of light shot through the cloud. Thunder rumbled within it.

"Stop!" I cried. "Oh, my dear Leib! Do not move!"

I had suddenly realized that this was no flute, no instrument, no Rudall & Rose. It was the plunger of the infernal machine.

"Musik! Ah, Musik!"

These, as it happened, were, on this earth, Mr. Goldkorn's last words.

I leaned out even farther, as if I could stop him. I slipped. I lost my balance. Reaching back, I caught only the cage of the cat.

Footz? Flutz? Fwist?

Down we tumbled together. We were in midair as Mr. Goldkorn, in his ultimate act, reached for the shining, silvery bar.

I heard the explosion. It was not a large one. Not much more than a firecracker's pop. But it was enough to bring all the world's curtains down.

CODA

OBITUARY

LEIB GOLDKORN, 103, WEST SIDE CHARACTER

By Susan Dominus—October 24, 2005

M R. LEIB GOLDKORN, a familiar figure on the Upper West Side, died some two weeks ago, though his body was discovered only last Friday in his apartment on West 80th Street. The apparent cause was suicide, since he was found with his head thrust inside his kitchen oven.

Mr. Goldkorn was born in 1901 in the Austro-Hungarian town of Iglau, now Jihlava in the Czech Republic. His father, Gaston Goldkorn, was a well-known grower of hops. Mr. Goldkorn's nature was musical. To all who would listen he claimed to be a graduate of the esteemed Akademie für Musik, Philosophie, und darstellende Kunst and a former student of Julius J. Epstein, the instructor of Mahler and friend of Brahms.

Mr. Goldkorn was a bit of a jack-of-all-trades on the orchestral scene, playing glockenspiel at the Vienna State Opera; the piano at the Steinway Restaurant, now defunct, on Rivington Street; and flute during a brief stint with the NBC Symphony Orchestra under Arturo Toscanini. He often boasted that his artistry could be heard during that orchestra's recording of Wolf-Ferrari's *Il Segreto di Susanna*, though no copies of that disc have been found. He was best known perhaps for two things: his street concerts on musical glasses—old-timers fondly recall his rendition of "The Bells of St. Mary's"—and the highly fanciful accounts of his life in two autobiographical though little-read novels, *Goldkorn Tales* and *Ice Fire Water: A Leib Goldkorn Cocktail.*

Mr. Goldkorn came to America in 1938, narrowly escaping the fate of his family, all of whom died in Auschwitz. It seemed he worked for a time in Hollywood as a composer for films. He enjoyed regaling passersby with tales of his intrigues with some of the most glamorous stars of that era, including Sonja Henie, Carmen Miranda and Esther Williams. "Who?" said Ms. Williams, when contacted by a reporter at her home in Beverly Hills. With his passing we can close the book on a colorful part of a musical Vienna that no longer exists, and on a familiar figure on the Upper West Side of Manhattan, which is also changing into something new.

Mr. Goldkorn leaves no relations. He was married to the former Clara Litwack and had a daughter, Martha, who is thought to have died in childbirth. A private service will be held at the cemetery of Hachilah Hill.

FINALE

PARADISO

HA! HA! HA! And they claim to be the "Newspaper of Record"! Not a word about Gustav Mahler. No mention of the favorable reviews of my books by You Know Who. What about Emperor Franz Josef and my first-prize flute? Most surprising of all, not a single line dedicated to the events at the Metropolitan Opera or my world premiere. Do they think it was all a fantasia?

Should I write a letter of protest to the editors? But how to mail it to their offices? We have here no stamps mit volleyball athletes. I have, alas, discovered what so many others have before me: that wall between us and those we love. Miss Esther! The half-Finn! The Fleming! We may shout. We pound with what are now metaphorical fists. We might even gather our thoughts and attempt to penetrate our darlings' dreams. There is no availing.

What does it matter? Let those below live their lives and think what they think. All here is sympathisch. True, it is not the existence that people imagine. No milk and no honey. No grapes. Nor do we meet the great or the near-great. Forget about dalliances. Forget about having, with B. Spinoza or Émile Waldteufel, a tête-à-tête. Though once, at a distance, off on a cloud of their own, I believe I glimpsed Bloch, Bruch, and Blanter, the three great musical *B*'s. Now and then there drifts toward me the sound of laughter, a thumping, and beer hall melodies: Can there be non-Jews on the premises?

Humans! Men and women, children and babes! If only you knew. What we are allowed is the one person most precious to us, the one material object that has the most meaning, and even one wee little pet. Hence, Hymena.

Mee-how?

"I do not know, my kitten. There are more things in heaven and earth, Horatio, than—"

"Mr. Goldkorn! If you please . . . ?"

Ah, that is the former Miss Litwack. She wishes me to assist with her fingernails. Also, should fortune smile, the nails of her toes.

"Coming! Coming, you Turkish delight!"

Do you see her there, with legs crossed, en dishabille?

"Make it snappy."

Look. Look again. That flash of light. Gott im Himmel! A garter trolley.

Thus, my dears, heavenly bliss. To pass the time we may look down on the blue and white earth. The to and fro of all its busy people. Then angels float by with their songs. We hear the music of the spheres.

"Are you going, Mr. Goldkorn, to take all day?"

"Coming, you gummy bear! You little sweetmeat!"

For the nonce I shall blow on the nails of this lovely. To help dry the paint. Later, at my repose, I shall blow over the embouchure of my Rudall & Rose. What shall it be today? Perhaps Köchel number 299, the concerto for harp and flute.

TUWATT! TWIRPFF! TOODLEDEDOO!

This for amusement is a game that we play. First I make the musical notes; then the heavenly host cover, with their wingtips, their ears.

"Yoo-hoo! I'm waiting! Yoo-hoo! My fingers are wet!"

"Coming, Miss Litwack. Coming, my Clara. Ach! How pretty you are. What a beauty. Here is Leib Goldkorn. Your husband. With all privileges. So give me your hand. There. Is that how you like it? And there. Is it good? I am on my knees before you. A paroxysm? Shush. Shush. Strictly forbidden. But, oh, my Liebchen, you have instead the whole of my heart."

DA ULTIMO

CORRECTION

AN OBITUARY THAT appeared in some Monday editions
misstated the name of its subject. It is not Leib Goldkorn
but Leib Goldkorns. The *Times* very much regrets the error.

A WORD ABOUT *RÜBEZAHL*

RÜBEZAHL, ONE OF THE BEST-KNOWN Silesian folk tales, has been retold in countless variations, most famously in the work of E. T. A. Hoffmann and the Brothers Grimm. Long before Gustav Mahler hoped to turn the story of the turnip counter into an opera, other composers—what Leib Goldkorn might call the non-Jews Flotow, Würfel, and Schuster—had already completed the task. Mahler began his own version in either 1879 or 1880, when he was twenty years old. According to his wife, the notoriously unreliable Alma, Mahler and his friend Hugo Wolf together came up with the idea of writing a fairy-opera based on the Rübezahl legend. She claims that Mahler ran off and wrote the libretto in a single night and a day, an act of preemption that led to the end of what might have been, between these two young composers, one of the greatest of musical friendships. Be that as it may, every line of the German opera that you have read in this novel comes from the libretto that Mahler wrote in his own hand, a libretto that now rests secure in the Osborn Collection of the Beinecke Rare Book and Manuscript Library at Yale.

But what of the score? We know that Mahler worked on it in the winter of 1882 and had abandoned what he came to call his "youthful fantasy" by the fall of 1883. We can only speculate about what the music might have been like. Does the first movement of the First Symphony, and the funeral march from the Third, incorporate the "bright humor and the dark, biting, perverse" motives that Paul Stefan, the composer's first biographer, believed to be part of the texture of *Rübezahl*? Is that same biographer correct when he argues that the theme from an early song of 1880, "Mai[en] tanz im Grunen," was used as a chorus in the opera a year or two later? To these and many other tantalizing questions there can be no answers.

How is it, then, that Leib Goldkorn, the translator of the libretto, can state with such assurance that the horns and brasses of the overture replicate the bugle calls of the military barracks in Iglau? Or that the strings are meant to sound like the silvery splash of the Iglawa itself? Or that in the woodwind section we hear "the cry of the geese and the storks above the Bohemian-Moravian Heights"? Are such things simply a fantasia? Spun from the last thoughts of an aging, even expiring mind? Perhaps.

And yet . . . and yet: think of how many incontestable facts our hero does tell us about his famous father. Mahler really did return to Iglau to give Red Cross concerts. He was indeed in Abbazia during the fateful spring of 1901. He actually did own—and how could our centurian know such a thing?—a Vopaterny grand piano. Moreover, he did study with the great Julius Epstein, the same Julius Epstein—not to be confused with this author's uncle—whom little Leib entranced with his panpipe at the age of five. Most astonishing, not so long ago, perhaps even within the last decade, there were almost certainly people still alive who had either seen or heard of the celebrated 1907 *Tristan* at the kaiserlich-königliche Hof-Operntheater: G. Mahler, conductor; L. Lehmann, the Isolde; and, who knows?, a young gentleman in the Promenade with a weak moustache and a salt-and-pepper suit.

[Those wishing to learn more about Mahler and *Rübezahl* may consult, as I have, *Gustav Mahler: The Early Years*, by the estimable Donald Mitchell.]

—LESLIE EPSTEIN

ACKNOWLEDGMENTS

I WOULD LIKE to thank the friends who read the manuscript of *Liebestod* in various stages: Gene Goodheart, Joe Kanon, Bernard Katz, David Kleinbard, Harry Thomas, and Jim Thomson.

Thank you, too, Iveta Nechvátalová in far-off Jihlava for your many favors.

Stephen Lefkowitz once told me about some faux cousins; that led to things.

I owe Jenny Schlossberg a great deal for her industry, dedication, and unwavering devotion to the hero of this book. *Leib Conquers All* was her title—and with her help he did.

Hurrah for Hadassah Felderbaum (who knows who she is), and much love for demanding that I ignore the advice of all those listed above and forcing me to remember that whatever imagination I am blessed or cursed with cannot be tamed.

Thank you, Saskya Jain, for your help with the German language and for advising me to stay away from italics.

Thanks to Laura Gross, my agent, who, luckily enough for both of us, has a stalwart heart.

Gratitude, admiration, and a bit of awe for Dave Cole, who climbed the jagged peak of copyediting this impossibly difficult book and waved the flag of victory at the top.

And all hail Robert Weil, once again, and happily, my editor.

ABOUT THE AUTHOR

LESLIE EPSTEIN was born in Los Angeles. His father and uncle were, respectively, Philip G. and Julius J. Epstein, legendary wits and writers of dozens of films, including *Casablanca*, for which they received an Academy Award. Leslie studied at Yale University and then at the University of Oxford on a Rhodes Scholarship. He has published ten previous books of fiction, including *Pinto and Sons*, *Pandaemonium*, two volumes on the adventures of Leib Goldkorn, and, most notably, *King of the Jews*, which has become a classic of Holocaust literature. For many years he has been the director of the Creative Writing Program at Boston University. He lives with his wife, Ilene, in Brookline, Massachusetts. They are the parents of three children—Anya, Paul, and Theo.